FIRECRACKER

G. P. PUTNAM'S SONS / NEW YORK

FIRECRACKER

RAY SHANNON

G. P. Putnam's Sons
Publishers Since 1838
a member of
Penguin Group (USA) Inc.
375 Hudson Street
New York, NY 10014

Library of Congress Cataloging-in-Publication Data

Shannon, Ray.
Firecracker / Ray Shannon.
p.   cm.
ISBN 0-399-15146-X (alk. paper)
I. Title.
PS3558.A885F57   2004   2003058427
813'.6—dc22

Printed in the United States of America
1   3   5   7   9   10   8   6   4   2

This book is printed on acid-free paper. ∞

Book design by Lovedog Studio

For being the first to know this was possible:
Mrs. Willena Butler, the Teacher
My Noni, Hazel Bordenave, the Reader

WHILE THE AUTHOR is more than happy to take credit for all things lacking in this volume, the following people must be held accountable for its merits, and properly thanked for their time, wisdom, and generosity:

DOMINICK ABEL, my veddy British agent
CHRISTINE PEPE, my very American
    (and very spectacular) editor
GINGER CAMPBELL, Ginger Snaps Promotions
BRUCE FELPS, editor, www.sportspagedallas.com
PAULA FELPS, editor, *Where Dallas*
ADAM ALEX and CALVIN HIRAHARA, masters of
    the three-way parlay ticket
BETSY WITTEN, the New Yorker's New Yorker
JODY BALSAM, the National Football League
D. P. LYLE, M.D., the man with all the answers
BARRY A. J. FISHER, Crime Laboratory Director,
    Los Angeles County Sheriff's Department

LANCE O. KEEBLE, Firefighter, LAFD

R/KAINEBLAZE, freestylemega

JOE TARTARO and PEGGY TARTARO

REVS. YAHYA BAYYAN and DICKER TUCKER, Prison
  Fellowship Ministries

DAVID PEPE, sports agent

BILL CRISWELL, former bartender and present Good Guy

KEVIN SHELBY and DYLAN WILEY,
  masters of all good 411

JAMES M. DEEM, who loves mummies

The gang at Silver Lake Coffee:

  SOO

  SUNNY

  MIRIAM

  JEROME

  MYLENE

  MICHELLE

And my Brothers-in-Arms:

  JOHN RIDLEY

  GDOGG PHILLIPS

  HARLAN COBEN

THE PASS WAS PERFECT. A spiraling blur of brown leather slicing through the air without the slightest tremor or wobble, moving in a gentle arc like an arrow fired from a crossbow . . .

. . . and the guy dropped it.

Number 84, whatever the hell his name was. The ball hit him right in the white-gloved hands. All he had to do was draw it to his chest, saunter *backward* ten yards into the end zone if he wanted to—and he flubbed it. Bobbled the ball like a juggler who'd lost his rhythm, watched it tumble around benignly on the grass even as he slowed to a stop and threw his hands up to his head in exaggerated disbelief. Henderson, the announcer said his name was. Gene Henderson.

Sandy watched Reece jump up from their table and cry, "Yes!," joining about a third of the hundred or so people in the Santa Monica sports bar exalting in Henderson's ineptitude, as everyone else groaned expansively. Reece sat back down, eyes on the big-screen TV nearest them, and Sandy said, "I don't believe what I'm seeing."

"That was fourth down. Wasn't that fourth down?"

Sandy had no clue and zero interest, but a guy at the next table, an accountant type wearing a white Arizona Cardinals jersey like three other fanatics here, looked over and said, "Yeah, fourth down. A minute-four left, they gotta give it up. It's over, we're goin' to The Dance!" The poor little man using the communal "we" like he was a Cardinal himself, and not just some pink-faced wannabe who'd bought his jersey on sale at JCPenney for $29.99.

"Reece, what's up with this? What are we doing here?"

"Shhhhh!" Reece said, turning away from the tube just long enough to snatch some fries off her plate and toss them into her mouth. "Game's almost over."

It was the third time Sandy had asked the question, and the third time Reece had evaded it. Whatever the big secret was, it had to be good. The two women had known each other for three years now, and in all that time, Sandy had never seen Reece show more than a passing interest in any sport other than basketball. She could discuss football intelligently, perhaps, but only when conversation demanded it. Otherwise, she couldn't be bothered. Why that had changed today, on this particular Sunday in January, Sandy couldn't imagine, except that it most likely had something to do with a man.

Not that either of them ever had to resort to trolling for fish in a place like this. Both were beautiful, intelligent young women in their mid-thirties who drew quality male attention wherever they went. Sandy was a blonde with crystal blue eyes and an athlete's lithe body; Reece was a caramel-skinned Cajun brunette who, even in her present "condition," could stop traffic on the last lap of a NASCAR race. Doing the sports bar scene was neither new to nor beneath either of them, but only if there was a purpose to the exercise. Business or romance, something. Yet, as near as Sandy could tell, Reece had dragged her here today in pursuit of only fattening food and the game. Twice she had sent back a round of drinks without even measuring up the men behind them, just shook her head apologetically in their general direction when the waitress pointed them out and returned her attention to the TV.

Sandy squinted up at the little graphic in the upper-right-hand corner of the TV screen and saw that the score was Arizona 23, San Francisco 19, late in the fourth quarter. Gene Henderson played for San Francisco, the accountant (at least in his dreams) for Arizona. The little clock beneath the score was running, :51, :50, :49, and the white-clad Cardinals were now engaged in the bizarre practice of doing absolutely nothing. Their quarterback just kept taking the exchange from center and dropping to a knee, nobody but his own teammates within five yards of him. This was football?

Two minutes later, the game and Sandy's suffering ended simultaneously, and the Arizona segment of the house exploded in wild celebration, a virtual orgy of high fives and chest bumps erupting everywhere. Even Reece participated, preempting the accountant/Cardinal's attempt to embrace her with a fist pound instead, that over-under-forward handshake thing men did with such alacrity these days.

"You gonna tell me what this is all about now?" Sandy asked when Reece settled onto her stool again, grinning and out of breath.

"I want a beer," Reece said.

"You can't have a beer. Answer the question, Reece, or I'm gonna strangle you, I swear to God."

"The Cardinals won."

"I saw that. So what?"

"So next stop, the Super Bowl. Next Sunday, in Miami."

"Wonderful. You wanna tell me why I'm supposed to care? Or, more to the point, why you do?"

Reece bounced off her stool and threw some bills atop the check, preparing to leave. "Come on, Sandy, let's go."

"Reece . . ."

But she was already gone. They were halfway to the parking garage where they'd left Reece's car by the time Sandy caught up to her. As she shuffled along at Reece's side, like a breathless terrier dragged on a leash, Sandy asked her question again: "Why the hell do you care about the Super Bowl?"

"Because if the Cardinals win it," Reece finally said without slowing, "maybe I don't care anymore whether Raygene comes through with my money or not."

"What? What the hell do you mean, that asshole—"

"Please. The baby can hear you." Reece rubbed a hand across her inflated belly as she continued to move.

"Jesus, Reece, you aren't telling me you're gonna bet on the Super Bowl just to try and get Raygene off the hook?"

"Actually, girlfriend, I already have. Eight months ago, in Vegas. Twenty-five thousand on Arizona at fifty-to-one."

Sandy could feel all the blood in her face draining to her feet. "Oh, my God . . ."

"That's one-point-two-five million if Arizona comes through, in case you were wondering," Reece added as they started up the parking garage stairs. "But that's not even the best part."

"It's not?"

"No. The best part—"

"We should take the elevator."

"The elevator? Don't be silly. I've got a few weeks to go yet, the stairs aren't gonna kill me."

"I wasn't thinking about you, I was thinking about me," Sandy said. "I think you're giving me a heart attack."

They reached the garage's fourth level and found Reece's car where it sat right off the staircase landing, a pristine, candy-apple-red Plymouth Barracuda, circa 1972, resting in the parking structure's cool, dark shadows. Reece was fishing in the depths of her purse for the keys when somebody behind them caused both of their heads to spin:

"You must really think you're hot shit."

It was one of the male patrons from the sports bar. A neckless, barrel-chested white man in a triple-extra-large 49ers jersey who was almost too drunk to stand vertical against the incline of the garage floor beneath his feet.

"What's that?" Reece asked him, as Sandy glanced around to confirm what she feared to be true: They were the only three people on this level. At this very moment, maybe even in the whole garage.

"I said, you must think you're hot shit. Man tries to be nice and buy you bitches a drink, you throw it back in his face. What kinda bullshit is that?"

Sandy still didn't remember him, but Reece did. Like she had when a pair of other guys had tried it earlier, she'd declined the fresh round of drinks he'd sent their waitress around to offer them, shook her head and smiled in his direction to say thanks anyway. For all the good this courtesy had done, apparently.

The big man was three sheets to the wind, feeling sexually humiliated, and his favorite football team had just been knocked out of the playoffs by a ten-point underdog. At home. Sandy was ready to scream *now*.

But she didn't. She didn't dare. She was way over on the passenger side of the car, and Reece was standing right there in front of the guy on the driver's side, where he could do anything he pleased to her before running off if either woman did something, anything to spook him.

"Look . . ." Sandy started to say.

"No, *you* look!" the drunk said. He had a set of keys in his right hand, and was holding a large one out between forefinger and thumb like a tiny dagger. Sandy thought he meant to use it on Reece somehow, but Reece understood what his real intent was immediately.

"Nice car," the guy said, smiling.

He was referring to the Barracuda. Reece had bought the restored coupe three years before from a mechanic she knew for $14,000, and today, as then, there wasn't a blemish on it, inside or out. The car was Reece's pride and joy.

"Don't do it," she said, as the drunk eased the point of his key toward the gleaming skin of the Barracuda's left flank.

"We'll scream," Sandy said.

"No. We won't," Reece corrected her. Their voices seemed to boom throughout the garage, further evidence that they remained alone on this level.

The guy grinned in Reece's face as his key made contact with the car's fender.

"I'll let you cop a feel," Reece said suddenly, just before the drunk could set the key in motion.

He blinked at her, mind too thick with haze to accurately assess what he was hearing. "What?"

"Leave the car alone, and I'll let you cop a feel. Tits, ass, whatever you want. Five seconds, one hand only."

"*Reece!*" Sandy snapped.

"Come on," Reece told the guy, ignoring the other woman completely. "I know I'm not as svelte as girlfriend over there, but there are parts of me that still feel damn good." She cupped her left breast with one hand, hefted its considerable weight for his inspection. "Put the key away and let's go, before I change my mind."

"Reece, for God's sake . . ."

The drunken 49er fan was overcome with astonishment. He'd come here for revenge, but now was on the verge of receiving something far better, and more unexpected: the realization of every sex offender's dream. A free ticket to heaven. Reece's round, full bosom called out to him. With child or otherwise, this lady was still spectacular.

Mouth hanging open despite his best efforts to close it, left hand extended toward the object of his desire, he took a step forward to accept Reece's offer and caught an earful of brain-jarring, high-decibel sound instead.

She had used the magician's most basic trick on him, misdirection, and removed the little alarm canister from her purse while his attention had been drawn to her upper body. As he screamed and fell away, clutching at his left ear with both hands, Reece hit him on the jaw with an overhand right, exactly the way her grandfather had taught her to more than twenty years before, and the guy in the big red jersey dropped to the garage floor, out cold. A meteor could not have fallen to earth any harder.

"Fucking moron," Reece said, returning the roll of quarters

in her fist back to the purse from which she'd withdrawn it. Something else her Grandpa Troy had taught her to do a long, long time ago.

She unlocked the car and got in, then gestured for Sandy to do the same. The interior of the Barracuda was silent for a long while as Reece paid the attendant and pulled slowly out of the garage, and Sandy sat beside her decompressing, seeking a sense of normalcy after yet another Reece Germaine misadventure. As soon as the guy had put his key to Reece's car, Sandy had known he was doomed. Nobody ever threatened anything Reece had worked hard for without paying the price. And she could do things in their defense that would occasionally scare the living hell out of you.

"So what's the best part?" Sandy asked eventually, still in a daze. She was staring straight out the Barracuda's windshield, like a cardboard cutout Reece had placed in the seat just to use the carpool lane on the freeways.

"Excuse me?"

"You said if the Cardinals win, you'll win a million dollars, but that's not the best part. So what is?"

"Oh." Reece turned in her direction as they waited for a signal to change, a broad grin spreading across her face. "The best part is, it was Raygene who bought me the ticket."

1

SHIRELLE MILBOURNE was not a business manager by trade. She was just a fifty-one-year-old black woman with a master's degree in business from Fisk University, class of '98, who knew the difference between a slick con and a genuine investment opportunity. But that was all the help the one client she'd just taken on really needed.

Almost three years earlier, at the tender age of twenty-one, Raygene Price had signed a three-year contract with the Dallas Cowboys of the National Football League for $2.65 million, plus a $1.25 million signing bonus. Gene the Dream was a tight end out of Florida State who was blessed with soft hands, 4.9 speed, and the body of a Greek god, and the Cowboys had made him the eleventh overall pick in that year's collegiate draft. In the thirty months since, he had caught twenty-nine touchdown passes, made All Pro twice, broken the Cowboys' single-season receiving record for tight ends, and lost exactly $1.25 million in a series of real estate deals that fell through the roof like a 747 with its wings clipped.

Although "lost" was a woefully inappropriate term for what had happened to the money, in truth, because Raygene knew exactly where it all had gone: into the pockets of one Cecil Jerome Blumenthal, aka Cecil Bloome, his former financial advisor. Cecil, as the FBI and several other law enforcement agencies only recently made Raygene aware, had advised Raygene and the three other pro athletes on his client list right into bankruptcy court, all his many highly touted investment schemes having been specifically designed to enrich Cecil himself before anyone else. In the wake of Cecil's arrest on federal racketeering charges, Raygene was left with the remnants of a personal fortune that was now equivalent to, his agent and lawyers said, a quarter of a million dollars.

Which didn't seem possible to Raygene because, well, he was Raygene Price. Gene the Dream. Pro athlete, Nike pitchman, *Sports Illustrated* cover boy, and sex machine to *Playboy* playmates, movie starlets, and Victoria's Secret lingerie models everywhere. How the hell could he not be a millionaire? If the Ferrari and Rolls were still in his three-car garage, wasn't that evidence enough that his wealth remained as inextinguishable as ever?

Prone to such backward thinking as he was, it was easy to dismiss Raygene as an idiot. Just another poor black man from the projects who could turn a lob pass into a reverse slam dunk, or a four-yard loss into a ten-yard gain, but could not add two and two without the aid of a calculator. And yes, a lack of smarts was indeed one of Raygene's most glaring deficiencies. But what hobbled him far more than his underdeveloped intellect was his readiness to give love to those around him indiscriminately. Raygene, Shirelle had observed, dispensed trust and compassion like a drunken fireman wielding a full-on water cannon. No smile was too artificial, no plea for help too hollow or contrived for him to question their authenticity. He was soft in the head, but softer in the heart, and the combination of the two made him the most vulnerable rich man a thief like Cecil Bloome, or a gold digger like this Clarice Germaine woman, could ever hope to encounter.

Clarice—or "Reece," as Shirelle understood her friends liked to call her—was the third woman Raygene had unwittingly impregnated in less than thirty-three months, and the only one who'd refused to go away. The first, a Florida State junior Raygene had been dating off and on while in school, had stupidly taken $20,000 just weeks before the NFL draft and agreed to have an abortion. The second, a legal secretary Raygene had met in a Dallas nightclub three months into his rookie season, had given birth to their son, Princeton, demanded $7,000 a month in child support, then settled for a meager $1,500 a month when Raygene's lawyers promised to make her penchant for getting knocked up by fat-cat pro athletes like Raygene—who was, apparently, the fourth in a series—a cornerstone of any defense they would bring to bear against her if she forced them into court.

A similar arrangement had been offered to Reece Germaine, but she'd declined. Flatly. She wasn't asking for seven grand a month in child support, which was excessive, but she did want three, which was merely fair, and she was showing no signs of ever caring to negotiate for less. Prior to Shirelle taking charge of Raygene's money, his lawyers had been pushing him toward a settlement with Reece, whom they'd determined was a major player in the field of entertainment public relations, and could therefore, at least in theory, afford to fight for what she was seeking indefinitely. But Shirelle had said no, to hell with that. Fair or not, she didn't want her new client setting any precedents by paying somebody in excess of $24,000 annually simply to feed and clothe one of his illegitimate children. She had an idea that Reece Germaine wouldn't be the last pregnant lady to come knocking at Raygene's door, and those to follow would probably prove easier to deal with if they could be shown a consistent pattern of previously negotiated support settlements.

Raygene himself, of course, disagreed. He wanted to give Reece what she was asking for, and more. Raygene was not at all insulted by the indifference she had openly shown toward his ever participating in the raising of their as-yet-unborn child. Reece, he told Shirelle, was by far the most together woman he had ever been with, even if it had only been for three crazy days in Las Vegas last May, and he didn't want to treat her in any way that might cause her to think badly of him. He wasn't in love with her or anyone else, but Reece's opinion mattered to him. She was unique. She was special.

"She gets eighteen hundred a month," Shirelle said, "and not a penny more."

Sitting in Shirelle's office now, long legs splayed outward from the leather chair his giant form was sinking into, Raygene shook his head at the woman's resolve, almost beginning to regret having hired such a hard-ass to save him from himself.

"Aw, damn, Momma," he said.

2

"HIS MOTHER?" Aeneas Charles asked.

"Yeah. Can you believe that?"

Only barely, Aeneas thought. He had seen a lot of momma's boys in his time, but he couldn't recall ever hearing of one worth millions who'd put his mother in charge of every dime. Usually, homeboy would buy his Number One Girl a new car or build her a home somewhere, and leave her and the old man, if he was still around, to live the rest of their days in relative leisure. See the world, play golf. If he hired his mother to do anything at all, it was to open his mail, or head his fan club, something entirely innocuous like that.

"Does she know what she's doing?"

Stanley Winston shrugged, a gesture almost completely lost behind his giant maple desk. "Who knows? She's got a business degree from someplace back east, if that means anything."

"So did Cecil Bloome, as I recall."

"Yeah. From Syracuse, yet. When the hell did Syracuse start turning out confidence men?"

Stanley sounded hurt because he was. Like everyone else, he'd been fond of Cecil. As Raygene Price's beleaguered agent, he had advised his client against trusting the self-proclaimed president of Blumenthal Enterprises, Incorporated, with any substantial cash, but only because Stanley was incurably paranoid, not because he really thought Cecil would rip Raygene off. When the Feds first came to him with all their allegations about the "investment advisor," Stanley had damn near cried a river.

"Well," Aeneas said, "look at it this way. At least anything Raygene loses now will be more the result of incompetence than greed. Assuming his mother's not a thief too, that is."

Stanley smiled forlornly and nodded, using the tip of one finger to slide the thick black frames of his eyeglasses back up the lengthy slope of his nose. Aeneas couldn't remember the last time he'd seen somebody actually wearing such old-school, Buddy Holly–ish spectacles for something other than effect on Halloween. But Stanley Winston was an original. Short, pale, and as soft around the middle as a jelly roll, he was a man so busy making millionaires out of high school 'ballers he couldn't be bothered with the trifling variances of fashion. Stanley was the sports agent of sports agents, and his thinning brown hair and weak chin didn't mean a damn thing when he entered an NFL owner's office to negotiate a client's contract. In there, from everything Aeneas had heard, Stanley looked and behaved like Rambo in search-and-destroy mode.

"So how can I help you, Mr. Winston?" Aeneas finally asked, deciding not to wait until nightfall for Stanley to broach the actual purpose of this alleged job interview himself.

Stanley paused, choosing the most precise route for his answer. "Raygene's in a pretty deep hole, as I've already explained, Mr. Charles. Cecil Blumenth—Cecil *Bloome*"—the agent corrected himself painfully—"didn't break him, by any means, but he set him back financially a good five years. So we can't afford any more financial indiscretions. Raygene needs to get his house in order, and keep it in order, and it all starts with getting a new contract out of the Cowboys this spring. His present deal expired this past season, as you probably know, and we're looking to get him re-signed for somewhere in the neighborhood of seven-point-five over four years."

Aeneas didn't whistle, but the numbers in millions Stanley had just dropped impressed him nonetheless. Full-service private investigators, even high-end operators like himself, only saw money like that in the movies.

"Needless to say," Stanley went on, "the Cowboys will only ante up if the market demands they do so. And right now, thankfully, it does. But should anything happen to Raygene's value between now and then . . ."

"They'll offer you substantially less."

"Yes. The Cowboys, and any other franchise that might choose to bid for his services. At the moment, Raygene's the best tight end in football, bar none, and he deserves to be paid accordingly. But nothing is forever. Things change. Until a new deal can be reached with somebody, he has to take care of himself. Watch his weight, lay off the pickup basketball . . ."

"And stay out of trouble."

"You read my mind."

"Only up to the point of what kind of trouble, in particular, you think he might get into. Drugs, women . . . ?"

"Raygene doesn't use drugs, as far as I know. They're against his religion."

"His religion?"

" 'The Church of the Immaculate Raygene.' His mind is the deity, his body the temple. I think he'd chug a can of acetone before he'd smoke a joint. And as for women . . . If making babies with strangers still offended people the way it used to, Raygene would be burned at the stake. The man just doesn't take the necessary steps to protect himself. It's not so much irresponsibility as it is a Pollyanna complex. Raygene's a good guy, and he expects the gods to protect good guys from all misfortune, even when they're behaving somewhat recklessly." He shrugged. "He sounds like a dummy, I know. But he's really just an overgrown kid who's yet to learn you've got to look for water in the pool before diving in headfirst."

Aeneas was tempted to say that Raygene was a big boy, and only looking for good things to happen, rather than the bad, was no excuse for not slapping a condom on when circumstances demanded it. But such observations would only have digressed from the real subject at hand.

"Okay. So he doesn't do drugs, and he doesn't abuse women. So what *is* his problem?"

Stanley's office window afforded him a decent view of Central Park, and he studied it now for several seconds before acknowledging Aeneas's question. Though the tall, strikingly handsome black man had come highly recommended, and seemed physically fit enough to tackle any endeavor—Aeneas was damn near as big and buff as Raygene himself—Stanley was still not convinced the investigator was the right man for the job the sports agent had in mind. The assignment was that delicate.

"His problem—or more accurately, mine—is a man named Thomas Stiles," Stanley said at last, finding just the utterance of the name distasteful. "People call him 'Trip.' Maybe you've heard of him."

Aeneas shook his head.

"He's a thug. A deeply disturbed white man who suffers the delusion he's black. He wears big gold chains and fist rings, tattoos on his throat, even a black leather duster with a matching porkpie hat. None of which would bother me, particularly, except that he didn't come by any of it making bad rap records. He's a drug dealer, if my information is correct, and not a very nice one."

"And he's a friend of Raygene's?"

"They grew up together back in Florida. Raygene says Trip used to eat half his meals at Shirelle's table, right up to their freshman year in high school, when Trip went into lockdown on an assault charge of some kind. That was the last Raygene saw of him, until one day last fall. Trip showed up at a personal appearance Raygene was doing down in Dallas, the grand opening of a sporting goods store, I think it was, and they've been fucking inseparable ever since. If you'll excuse my French."

Aeneas allowed himself a feather-light smile, amused as always by the endearing delicacy of gentlemen like Stanley who could never utter a genuine curse word without begging the indulgence of anyone who might choose to be offended by it.

"So far, I have no reason to believe Trip has involved Raygene in anything illegal," Stanley said. "But I know it's just a matter of time before he does. Raygene's an easy mark, as Cecil so ably demonstrated, and sooner or later a player like Trip Stiles is going to take advantage of that. Correct me if I'm wrong."

"If Stiles is the man you say he is? You can pretty much count on it."

"Then you understand why you're here."

"Well, I get that you're afraid of this Trip's influence on your client. But I'm not sure I know what you think I can do about it."

"*Do* about it? You don't have to do anything about it. All I want you to do is monitor the situation for me. Keep an eye on Raygene and let me know the minute you think he's about to engage in something stupid or dangerous. Or both. At least, until we can get a new contract for him out of the Cowboys, or whomever. After that, he can become an axe murderer, for all I care."

Aeneas knew Stanley didn't really mean this last, of course. Anything Raygene did to seriously tarnish his image would void any future contract he were to sign with the Cowboys or anyone else, personal conduct clauses being as commonplace in such contracts as they were these days. But Stanley no doubt figured it would be better to fight for the enforcement of a pact already in hand than to try to negotiate one in a diminished marketplace, which was precisely what he'd be forced to do if Raygene created any scandals now.

"How close can I get to him?" Aeneas asked.

"As close as you want. He already has a bodyguard, so that cover's out. But my intent is to tell him you're a writer doing research on a book about him who needs total, twenty-four-hour access, and the man's just egomaniacal enough to give it to you. He'll probably let you in the shower stall with him if he thinks there's a best-seller with his face on the cover in it for him."

Aeneas endorsed Stanley's plan with a small nod and asked when the agent wanted him to start.

"The sooner the better. We'll give him a couple of days to think about it, get used to the idea of having you around, then fly down to Dallas together so I can introduce you."

"Okay."

"I understand your regular rate for this kind of work is three hundred a day, plus expenses. Is that right?"

Aeneas nodded his smooth, clean-shaven head again, the tiny gold hoop fastened to his right earlobe swaying faintly to and fro.

"Well, I'm prepared to double that. I need this job done right, Mr. Charles, and I don't mind paying a little extra to get it. Do we have a deal?"

"I think so."

"Good." Stanley stood up, Aeneas followed suit, and the two men shook hands. "There's just one more thing."

Aeneas waited for Stanley to explain himself, doing nothing to ease the man's sudden, somewhat comical discomfort.

"As you might imagine, I've put a great deal of time and effort into researching candidates for this assignment. Doing background checks and such. So I knew quite a bit about you before you ever came in to see me today." Stanley cleared his throat. "For the most part, what people have to say about you is extraordinarily positive. But . . ." Now the sports agent actually squirmed on his feet. "Several did mention something to me they thought I might find worthy of note."

Aeneas smiled, trying to disguise his weariness with an all-too-familiar subject. "My methods can sometimes be viewed as a little extreme?"

"Well . . . This incident with Lloyd Coen's nephew in D.C., in particular."

"Dr. Coen's nephew tried to impress a lady in a Georgetown dance club by bouncing a barstool off my skull. Getting it bounced off his own skull instead was the chance he took, wouldn't you say?"

"They say the kid may never walk again."

"Actually, only his lawyers say that. His doctors are somewhat more optimistic."

"Yes, but—"

"Come now, Mr. Winston. You can't ask me to mix with undesirables like Trip Stiles and not expect a little drama to occur, can you?"

Stanley wanted to ask him what he meant by "drama," and then he wanted to say it didn't matter, because there wasn't going to be any. Stanley wanted Charles's word in *writing* that he wouldn't cripple anybody else with a bar stool while under Stanley's employ, or the deal was off.

But after a lengthy pause, this was all Stanley Winston, master sports-contract negotiator, said instead: "No. No, I don't suppose I could, at that."

3

TRY AS HE MIGHT, Raygene couldn't recall where he and his boy Trip Stiles had hooked up again, after eight years of being apart. Had it been Michael Irvin's regular season kickoff party in September? Up in the private room of the Hot Wire club in Houston in August? That circuslike grand opening for Power Sporting Goods Stanley had booked for him down in Dallas last October? Raygene had no clue. His memory was just too overrun with snippets of such indistinguishable events and their respective attendees to catalog them in any useful way.

In any case, he and Trip *had* found each other again, one way or another, and that was the problem.

Because Trip was no longer as fun to have around as he used to be. From the very first moment of their reunion, Raygene had embraced him as if they'd last run together only yesterday, thinking they could pick up their friendship right where Trip's incarceration had left it, nearly a decade ago. But no. Once again, Raygene's blinders to the bad in people had set him up for a fall. Eight years of hard time had changed Trip for the worse.

Up until recently, the wannabe-black white boy in all the black-on-black gear seemed content just hanging with Gene the Dream, filling the role of upper-echelon *entouragee* with aplomb and good humor. But now Trip was asserting himself in ways that made Raygene more and more uncomfortable. Not only was he openly affecting the vulgar mannerisms of a gangster and drug dealer, Trip had begun to aggressively solicit Raygene as a financier of his activities. Raygene didn't mind kicking it with criminals as a rule, especially if they were homies from the old neighborhood. But if they were going to both rub his nose in the sleaziness of their business *and* ride Raygene's ass to help bankroll it . . .

Well, Raygene wasn't going to have that shit. And tonight, he was going to let his boy Trip know about it.

They were going out to Club Life. It had been Raygene's intention to ride out alone in his Viper, needing his fears of impending financial collapse assuaged as only a ride in a $60,000 sports car could assuage them, but Trip had insisted they go together in his Benz instead. Any other time, the big, gold-trimmed luxury sedan would have been fine, but tonight, it wasn't the ideal setting for the conversation Raygene was hoping to have with the vehicle's owner. When you were jumping in a man's shit, running down the law for him, you had to be in control of the entire situation; the passive role of a passenger in the other man's car was not conducive to your purposes.

But it was either the Benz, or an argument with Trip that would only exacerbate the one Raygene was already prepared to have with him, so Raygene had let it go. Now he found himself immersed alongside his boyhood friend in the Mercedes's plush leather backseat, watching the lights of downtown Dallas rush by outside the car's windows as Trip's boy E.Y. drove them west on the 35E toward the club. Raygene's plan was to hold his tongue until they were there, surrounded by gorgeous women and becalmed by liquor, both of them feeling too good to start anything crazy should Trip not want to hear what Raygene had to tell him. But Trip had a plan of his own, and Raygene realized this the minute he saw the white man's driver/bodyguard deliberately miss the Dallas Parkway turnoff.

"Hey, what's up?" Raygene asked. "We just—"

"I forgot to tell you," Trip said casually. "We gotta make a stop first. Only take a minute."

"Now?"

"I just gotta see this associate of mine a second. Then we out. Chill, homie."

Raygene didn't want to chill. This was precisely the kind of shit from Trip he had no more patience for. Where the hell were they going and what "associate" were they going to see at nine-fucking-thirty on a Tuesday night that didn't spell trouble for a man with a reputation to protect like Raygene Price? He'd been playing with fire as it was just hanging with Trip, but this could be The End, the ultimate public relations fiasco no amount of legal wrangling or spin doctoring could keep from destroying Raygene's career if something went wrong now and Five-Oh became involved. The league office was growing more and more intolerant of players bringing shame upon themselves and the game via criminal associations and/or behavior, and somebody soon was going to be made an example of. Raygene would be damned if it was going to be him.

"You should'a told me 'bout this earlier, Trip," he said angrily. "So I could'a gone on ahead to the club with Brew if I'd'a wanted to."

"Brew" was Michael Brewster, Raygene's own bodyguard, whom he hoped was still following behind them now in his own car, rather than sitting at a table at Club Life wondering why they'd missed the turnoff.

"Hey, I told you: We only gonna be a minute. Stop cryin' like a bitch, man, damn."

Trip was smiling good-naturedly, but Raygene took full offense all the same. He had a thing for being called a "bitch" no matter what the context, and Trip knew it. Raygene couldn't see the purpose behind it, but Trip had to be testing him, looking to see how far he could push before Raygene set their friendship aside and started treating him just like anyone else who was openly stepping to him.

Raygene wasn't going to take the bait. Trip would get his fight, if that was what he was after, but not now. Not here. Raygene wasn't that stupid, despite the evidence to the contrary his troubles with money and pregnant women might have seemed to offer. When Raygene finally put his foot in Trip's white ass to revoke his membership in the Dream's inner circle, he would do it on his own turf, with Brew and plenty of other friends and witnesses around to watch his back. Because, while there were a lot of things about Thomas "Trip" Stiles that were as counterfeit as his blackness, one aspect of his persona Raygene knew for a fact was legit.

He really was fucking insane.

. . .

TRIP WATCHED his old friend Raygene wriggle around on the car seat beside him, wanting to get in Trip's face about their unscheduled detour but too concerned about the consequences to open his mouth, and wondered how in the hell anybody was paying this punk a million dollars–plus a year to do a goddamn thing.

He could run past people and catch a thrown ball, that was what Raygene could do. That was all he could do. The size and the muscles and the occasional run-through-a-tackle Sportcenter highlight gave those too ignorant to know better the idea Raygene held great potential for violence, but Trip knew size and muscles didn't mean shit. He had seen dozens of bigger and harder men than Raygene back at Florida State Prison who'd been even more gutless than he, and Trip had punked them the same way he was about to punk Raygene now.

The nigger's blackness was just totally wasted on him.

And a man's blackness, make no mistake, was a valuable commodity on the street. It wasn't right, but it was real. Americans were conditioned by all facets of the media to look upon crime as the Angry Black Man's game, he of the twenty-four-hour crack-induced high and seething hatred for all things good and decent, so that's who got the lion's share of respect. Niggers were feared on sight, no questions asked, while white thugs like Trip were treated as an aberration, just quirks in the societal magma who could safely be gauged for volatility on a case-by-case basis, no automatic presumption of same necessary.

It was a double standard that drove Trip to the edge of madness.

Because it made everything he did harder than it had to be. Being a white boy, he had to prove himself to people over and over again, and this took time and energy he didn't have to waste. The cool blue menace in his glare, and the crooked, yellow-toothed grin that usually accompanied it, should have been all the evidence needed of the mayhem he was capable of. Constantly having to make someone bleed in order to get their full attention was both unjust and dangerous, and Trip was sick of it.

But such was the fate of a man born in the wrong skin, as Trip had understood he had been since he was six years old. Growing up in the slums of Riviera Beach, Florida, where white people were mere speckles on an all-black cat, Trip had taken on the mannerisms and speech patterns of the black people around him naturally, without conscious thought or intent. Getting his ass kicked daily just for *being* a white boy, at least until he was able to kick some ass of his own, was merely an added incentive to adopt a nigger's street persona.

He could have easily gone the opposite way, as he knew other white men with similar backgrounds had, and learned to despise all things black with a passion. He had in fact had to pretend to be just such a white man for eight years back at FSP, to stay in the good graces of the Aryan Brotherhood, the only gang in the joint that would have him. It had been an unbearable masquerade. But now it was over, and Trip was once again free to be the walking contradiction he truly was: a twenty-five-year-old nigger in a white boy's body.

If that made him a joke at first glance to some people, so be it. They wouldn't laugh long. Sooner or later, Trip would show them how genuine the player within really was, and all the snickering would stop.

Raygene had seen this for himself many times, back in Riviera Beach. They'd been best 'boys back then, two halves of a whole that was rarely if ever found incomplete. Trip's white trash mother and Raygene's alcoholic one—prior to the clean-up act Shirelle had done on herself since—had proven themselves equally incapable of sparing their sons a childhood in the ghetto, so the two boys had been left to form a partnership of convenience just to survive. Raygene was the physical intimidator, while Trip was the grunt who did all the bloodwork when physical intimidation failed to suffice. Raygene could throw down with proficiency, but Trip had a talent for it, finding in the act of breaking bones and splitting skin an outlet for his hatred of being poor. By the time Trip's conviction on an assault-and-battery beef brought their days in Florida together to a close, even Raygene had learned to treat Trip with the care of a pinless grenade.

And yet, here he was tonight, copping attitude with Trip like he held some kind of immunity from the white man's outrage. His memory had to be awfully short, Trip thought. He'd made the mistake of angering Trip more than once in the past, and gotten his ass royally kicked each time. What made him think things were any different now? His money? His fame? The few extra pounds of muscle he'd packed on in the weight room since the two men had associated last?

He was delusional. As far as Trip was concerned, it was Trip who had grown bigger and badder over the last eight years, not Raygene. While "Gene the Dream" had been catching touchdown passes and posing for magazine covers, Trip had been fighting for his life, 24/7, 365 days a year, at FSP. No demonstration of his superiority to Raygene should have been necessary at this point.

However, if a demonstration was what it was going to take

to straighten Raygene out, fix it in his mind once and for all that he was and always would be Trip's flunky, Trip would give it to him. Some people, you just had to hold their hands over the fire to get them to respect the heat.

Trip figured putting on one more show for a fool who wouldn't take him seriously any other way wasn't going to kill him.

BREW WAS just about to walk through Club Life's front door when he finally realized Raygene and Trip weren't already here. Trip's Mercedes had missed the turnoff back at the freeway almost ten minutes earlier. Raygene's bodyguard had *seen* the big white sedan continue on ahead of his Acura as he pulled onto the Dallas Parkway off-ramp, but the sight was only now rising to his level of consciousness. That's how messed up Brew's head was these days, contemplating Jesus and salvation and what part either one could possibly play in the life of a professional hit man.

Or, to be more precise, a hit-man-to-be. Michael Brewster hadn't actually killed anyone yet, for professional or personal reasons. He'd simply maimed and terrorized hundreds, leaving more than a few right at death's door. Murder-for-hire wasn't as much an ambition for Brew as it was a seemingly inevitable destination, the trade a behemoth's body and a mannequin's even temperament had been preparing him for for practically all his twenty-two years.

He'd done a little of everything to get to this point. Nightclub bouncing, event security, even arm breaking for a couple of Houston-area drug dealers with music business connections. Now he was a self-employed "personal security consultant," which was all of the above, only in more expensive and legitimate clothing. The next step up the career ladder was where the real money was: murder. And why shouldn't he go there eventually? Conscience? His could barely be heard above a whisper. Fear of incarceration? Brew had been in the joint twice already, and the place didn't faze him.

But religion . . .

Religion had been a big zero to Brew up to now. His grandmother Osbie down in Sweetwater had tried to make a Southern Baptist out of him from the day he was born right up until his fourteenth birthday, and it didn't stick. Daily Bible study, nine-hour Sunday services, one-on-one "consultations" with Reverend Cooper—nothing she tried could make her beloved Jesus more than a fairy tale to Brew. It all sounded a bit too much like an elaborate scam to him, a self-induced form of mind control people leaned on like a crutch just to feel better about the unredeemable world in which they lived. And Brew didn't need such a crutch. Even as a boy, he had known the world was fucked up, and had learned to live with the fact. The only savior Michael Brewster needed was Michael Brewster.

Realist that he was, however, Brew was not an entirely immoral man. Despite his abiding agnosticism, the six-foot-two-inch, 250-pound former outside linebacker for the Sweetwater High School Mustangs was at heart a more decent human being than most. He had never harmed anyone he hadn't been paid to harm, and he never took pleasure in it. But Brew had the physical resources and emotional detachment to do almost anything to anyone for a price, and that was a skill set that more often defined a killer than a saint.

Which was why his sudden fascination with matters related to the Lord Jesus and his love of sinners like Brew was so confounding to him. What the hell was happening to him? For the crime of turning the dial on his car radio to a religious station one day last week, KPCE in Fort Worth, in search of nothing more than a lively Gospel number, he had fallen victim to the draw of a celebrity preacher named Galvin Morrison. Morrison was a white ex-con who claimed to have been saved, both physically and spiritually, three years prior in the infirmary at Darrington State Prison, where he'd been miraculously healed from a shanking that should have been fatal. Now he was a radio sermonizer with a growing ministry whose only interest in the material world was saving the souls of others like him, or so he claimed. Brew had heard similar stories of rebirth, of course; no preacher ever claimed to have found God without first lying down with the Devil, because where was the drama in that? But Morrison, by some sleight of tongue Brew could not quite ascertain, was able to make it all sound new and believable. His passion and earnestness seemed to come from someplace deep within, not put on like a work coat he only wore for show.

That first day, Brew had changed the station halfway through Morrison's sermon, pretending to be bored, but the reality was, he'd taken the hook and swallowed it. Morrison's preaching was tailor-made for people like Brew, men and women with criminal histories and no interest in God, and parts of what he'd said on the radio that day had stayed with Brew for days. In fact, nearly a full week later, they were still with him, as were snippets of two additional Morrison programs Brew had felt the need to tune in to.

It was crazy.

Crazy, and destined to be a short-lived phenomenon. Because Brew wasn't about to be "saved" without a fight. Finding Jesus now would complicate his life beyond any possible point of repair. Raygene Price had no use for a cheek-turning bodyguard, and neither would anyone else. If God and Galvin Morrison wanted to bestow the gift of faith on Michael Brewster, they were going to have to wait until he'd reached retirement age, when having a heart brimming with love for his fellow man might not be so contrary to everything he was now, and expected to become later.

Club Life was a zoo, as usual, and Brew hadn't even gone inside yet. He stood out in the parking lot, surrounded by swarms of achingly beautiful young people rushing headlong toward their latest evening of wicked excess, and thought back, decided Raygene hadn't mentioned anything to him about a pre-club detour. Which meant this one must have been unscheduled, and since Raygene had been riding in Trip's car . . .

Brew didn't care for his boss's crazy white homie, and sensed that the feeling was mutual. Trip had plans for Raygene, Brew was sure of it, and having the football player's security man constantly underfoot was no doubt something of an annoyance for Trip. Which was just how Brew liked it, because that was his job, standing between Raygene and all those who would do him ill. Aside from his professional obligation to do so, Brew looked out for Raygene because he genuinely liked the man. Raygene might be a little short on smarts—even Brew could see that—but he was kindhearted and generous, and he handled his fame with more good humor than vanity.

Brew got out his cell phone and dialed Raygene's number, deciding against just hanging at the club until his client and Trip showed up, if in fact they ever intended to. With thugs like Stiles, Brew knew, a wait-and-see approach could get your ass burned to the ground.

And Trip wasn't going to burn Raygene, in whatever man-

ner it was he had in mind, without going through Michael
Brewster first.

THE CELL phone in Raygene's coat pocket began to ring as
Trip's Mercedes eventually stopped somewhere in the Oak
Cliff area of Dallas, absolutely the last place in the entire state
of Texas Raygene wanted to find himself. Oak Cliff was to the
Dallas drug trade what Atlantic City was to New Jersey
tourism, and Raygene would have hell getting anyone to believe he hadn't come here to make a buy if his presence became
known. There was no other reason to even drive through the
neighborhood, let alone stop at a little clapboard house sand-
wiched between two dilapidated apartment buildings that,
like the house itself, each looked like something you might see
in a photo of Berlin at the end of World War Two.

Trip had his door open before the car even came to a full
stop at the curb, said to Raygene, "Tell Brew we'll be with his
ass in a minute and come on, I want you to meet somebody."

"I ain't goin' in there," Raygene said, smirking at the very
idea. He slipped the ringing phone from his pocket and started
to flip it open, but Trip yanked it out of his hand without
warning and did it for him.

"Yo, Brew, check it out, man, this is Trip. Raygene says to
tell you we had a little stop to make, he 'pologizes for forget-
tin' to mention it to you." He paused a moment, listening,
then said, "Yeah, well, soon as we get through here, we'll be
down there, a'right? Peace out."

Standing outside the car, Trip slapped the phone closed
again and peered down at Raygene through the open door
with grave impatience. "Now, nigga. You wanna do this and

go on to the club, or fuck around out here bitchin' about it? I thought you was in a hurry."

Fuck, Raygene thought, *I knew this shit was gonna happen!* He held his ground for a long beat, listening to a woman across the street somewhere yell her fool, drunken head off at someone named "Cee-Cee," but his hesitancy was only a weak attempt to save face. He was going to have to go inside the goddamn house with Trip or have the drama he had planned to have with the white boy later in the evening here in the car, right now. In the Oak Cliff middle of nowhere with Trip's sumo-sized bitch E.Y. standing at the ready to do what? Sit there quietly behind the Mercedes's wheel while Raygene kicked his employer's ass? Sheeeit . . .

Raygene flung his door open and stepped out onto the sidewalk, slammed the sedan's door closed behind him with the full intent of shattering its raised window into a million pieces.

Trip just laughed and shook his head, led both Raygene and E.Y. up the weed-choked walk to the door of the little single-story house. Three different shades of paint spotted the home's ravaged exterior, and a dim light behind one of the two front windows suggested life within, but Trip had to knock several times before someone inside finally opened the door for him. The wait worked on Raygene's nerves like the howl of a colicky baby: Standing there on the open porch, he felt as conspicuous as an elephant in an empty swimming pool.

The man who Trip had apparently come here to see was a young, bushy-headed Hispanic with a dark, unshaven face and a beer gut big enough for two. He'd yanked the door open without first asking who was calling, and the instant he saw it was Trip, his lidded eyes grew wide with regret over this decision. He could have found a dead man standing there on the porch and not have been struck with greater dread.

"That's right, Louie, it's me," Trip said, grinning. "Get the fuck out the way and let us in."

He put a hand in the Hispanic's chest to shove him back into the house, then stepped inside himself as his bodyguard, taking up the rear, forced Raygene to follow directly behind. Raygene turned to object, drawing the line at being pushed around by the hired help, and saw E.Y. enter the room next before easing the door closed again. Something in the cool, deliberate way Trip's man had performed the function caused Raygene's mouth to suddenly go dry, and he looked back at Trip just in time to see him point a chrome-plated revolver point-blank at their host's head and pull the trigger.

A brief light flashed across the living room walls, a familiar bang filled Raygene's ears, and a red cloud of brain matter blew out the back of the fat Hispanic's skull, only seconds before his lifeless form crumpled slowly to the floor.

"What the fuck!" Raygene cried, backpedaling so fast he damn near fell to the floor himself.

Trip studied the dead man's body for a moment, appraising his work, then showed his bodyguard a tiny nod. As E.Y. went off to check the house for other occupants, a gun in his own hand suddenly visible, Trip finally looked at Raygene and said, "Yeah, I know. That was fucked up, right? Walkin' in a man's house and cappin' his ass without any kinda conversation beforehand."

"Jesus Christ, Trip, what the hell you got me into?"

"Nigga, you got yourself into this shit. Only reason we here is 'cause you wouldn't do bus'ness with me 'less I showed you you ain't got no fuckin' choice in the matter."

"What the fuck you mean, I ain't got no choice in the matter? The hell I don't!"

"You stupid-ass bitch!" Trip stepped forward to reduce the distance between himself and Raygene by half, used the nose of the gun he was still wielding to point at the corpse on the floor. "That's what this fool here thought too, and you see what he knew about it, don't you?"

"You ain't gonna shoot me, Trip. You're crazy, all right, but you ain't *that* crazy."

"You're missin' the point here, Raygene. I ain't *got* to shoot you. You just whacked a motherfuckin' crackhead named Luis Ortiz, and me and my boy E.Y. both seen you do it. Ain't that right, E.Y.?"

"Uh-huh. Sho did," Trip's man said, stepping back into the room. There was a slight smile on his wide face, the first Raygene could ever remember seeing on it.

"Hey, *I* didn't whack *nobody*," Raygene said, fear rising up in him now faster than even his huge ego could contain.

"That's what you gonna say, sure," Trip said. "But the Man gonna have two witnesses tellin' 'em otherwise, and the gun homeboy was shot with's gonna have your fingerprints all over its ass. Or don't you remember this bad boy?"

He was talking about the chrome revolver, holding it out now toward Raygene so as to give him a closer look at it. The stamping along the barrel was too small for Raygene to read, but it was superfluous in any case. The gun was a .38-caliber Charter Arms "Off Duty" Special, and Raygene had seen it before, the last time almost a decade ago.

Tickled by the black man's mute astonishment, Trip laughed and said, "Yeah, that's right. My moms put this up for me. You believe that? Everything I had 'fore I got locked up, I go back home to see her a week after I get out and it's all in boxes in a closet. Clothes, shoes, comic books . . . and this. Had it in a goddamn Ziploc bag, just like a cop collectin' evidence or somethin'."

"Bullshit. That ain't—"

"What you want me to do, Raygene? Show you the scratches on the cylinder? From that time you dropped it in the street after we jacked up Dale's? Here, nigga, look! *Now* what you got to say?"

Trip turned the gun over in his hand, and sure enough, there they were for Raygene to clearly see: the old, familiar scuff marks in the silver metal. Raygene had also torn an inch-wide patch of skin from his left palm in the post-burglary pratfall Trip was referring to, and the memory of this now almost moved the black man to finger the scar his hand still bore as a result.

"So it's my old piece. What the fuck of it? Eight years later, ain't no way my fingerprints are still on that shit. No goddamn way."

"You ain't listenin' to me, nigga. I said it was in a *bag*. Sealed up, airtight. This piece ain't been touched since I got locked up."

"Still—"

"Fingerprints're like diamonds, Raygene. They fuckin' forever. 'Less you wipe 'em off, they stay on shit for a hundred years."

Raygene's mind was racing like a brakeless 16-wheeler careening downhill, thoroughly overwhelmed by the task of assimilating the threat his old homie was breaking down for him. Could that shit be real? Fingerprints stayed on a gun forever? It sounded like bullshit, but Raygene couldn't be sure. The science of modern forensics was constantly evolving, growing more and more capable of the improbable. If they could lock a man up now based solely on the DNA evidence left behind on a single goddamn carpet fiber . . .

"Trip. Come on, man," Raygene said, outrage giving way to quiet desperation. "Why you doin' this? What the fuck I ever do to you?"

"It ain't about what you done *to* me. It's about what you gonna do *for* me. I told you, Raygene, I need a little chedda', and you the man can give it to me. I can't take no for an answer, you understand?"

"Trip, you the one don't understand. I ain't got two hundred G's to give you, my lawyer says—"

"You gonna hand me that shit about bein' broke again? 'Cause if you are . . ."

"Dog, it's the truth! My motherfuckin' financial advisor jacked me up, my lawyer says he cleaned me the fuck out!"

Trip shook his head and smiled. "Naw. That's bullshit. You a superstar, Raygene. Largest livin' motherfucker I know, ain't no way you ain't got my money."

"*Your* money?"

"You heard me! *My* money! As many times as I saved your ass back home, you *owe me,* bitch!" Trip stomped right over to where Raygene was standing, mad eyes climbing the six inches between his line of sight and the larger man's. "So what's it gonna be? I'm all through talkin' here. You gonna help me out, or have I gotta put that dead fool on the floor over there on *you?*"

Raygene glanced over at Luis Ortiz's body again, blood seeping out of its head onto the carpet beneath it like water from a backed-up toilet, and envisioned his own corpse in its place. It didn't take much imagination. He wasn't all that concerned about beating the rap Trip was threatening to pin on him, because the gun and the eyewitness testimony of two felons were all the evidence Trip had against him. But there were things he had done as a boy in Trip's presence that no one else knew, things that were almost certain to leak once the media frenzy around Raygene's alleged "murder" of Ortiz began, and if they did, his football career would be over. The NFL would disown him, the public would crucify him, and being able to catch an under-thrown forward pass with two defenders on his back would no longer buy him a thing.

"I'm gonna need some time," Raygene said. "To figure out how to get it."

He was trying to cut the top of Trip's head off with his gaze, that being the only way he could bitch up to the white boy and still feel like half a man.

"How to get it? What the hell you mean, 'how' to get it?"

"I told you, nigga! My finances're all fucked up, I ain't got that kinda scratch in cash." *And my moms is holdin' what little I do got,* Raygene thought to himself, but didn't dare say aloud.

"How much time you talkin' about?"

"Ten days. Maybe more." Because it was going to take Raygene at least two days to think of a lie to tell Shirelle, and then a few more days after that to find the courage to try it on her.

"You got a week," Trip said.

"Trip, Jesus Christ—"

"Seven days, motherfucker. You a smart, educated young man. You try hard enough, I'm sure you'll find my chedda' somewhere." Trip smiled warmly and moved to the door, his man E.Y. following suit without needing to be told. "Now, come on, dog. We was goin' out to the club, remember?"

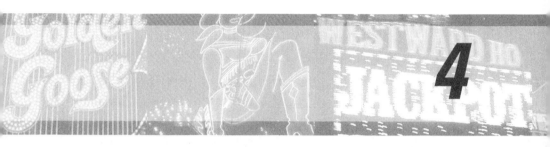

4

"GOD, I LOVE YOU, REECIE," Peter Crockett said, laughing as he watched Reece pack.

"Yeah? Why's that?"

"Because you can do no wrong. You're going to go up to Vegas this weekend and come back a millionaire. It's in the stars."

A white, forty-three-year-old gay man, Peter was Reece's junior partner in her public relations company, 4One-One Promotions. He had the chiseled physique of a Hanes underwear model and the business approach of a pit bull on acid, and the last time Reece had seen him genuinely distressed about anything, it was the fondness his latest lover had for fast food.

"I don't get it," Reece said, navigating around her partner like a tree someone had inconveniently planted in the middle of her bedroom as she continued to toss clothes into a suitcase. "You should be trying to stop me. Why aren't you trying to stop me?"

"Why? Because I can handle things at the office perfectly well without you, you're free to run off and party at any time."

"That's not what I mean and you know it. What I mean is, why are you encouraging me to go, instead of telling me how ridiculous this is? Flying off to Vegas Super Bowl weekend on the faint hope Raygene's bet will pay off . . ."

"It *will* pay off. I'm certain of it."

"Because I can do no wrong?"

"That, and because Raygene deserves nothing less. God, can you imagine the look on that boy's face when you tell him? That the bet you made with his money eight months ago has hit to the tune of one and a quarter million dollars?" Peter threw his head back and howled at the ceiling. "Oh, father, that would be beautiful!"

Oh, father! was the exclamation point Peter always put on things fiendishly ironic, and in this case, Reece had to admit it was appropriate. Turning the $25,000 Raygene had given her at Caesars Palace last May into the equivalent sum of thirty-four times the annual child support payment he was denying her now would be nothing if not the height of poetic justice.

Raygene had thought he was throwing the money away, showing the beautiful stranger he had met only two days before, and with whom he had been tearing Las Vegas down, casino by casino, ever since, just how impervious he was to financial loss. "Here, little girl," he had all but ordered her, "take this twenty-five G's and go bet on the lousiest team in football to win it all next year." No more believing such a ridiculous bet would pay off than that pigs could fly. He *knew* the Arizona Cardinals, he had *played* against the Arizona Cardinals, so if anyone had a right to summarily dismiss the woeful team's chances to win five games during the upcoming season, let alone the Super Bowl, it was Raygene Price.

But here it was eight months later, and like they had all the other "experts" who had called for them to remain a lifeless doormat of the league, the Arizona Cardinals had proven Raygene wrong. A fortuitous confluence of unforeseeable factors had conspired to bring the team immediate success—one key trade for a quality running back, and the spectacular play of two first-round draft picks and an All-Pro veteran signed as a free agent late in the off-season—and to the amazement of the entire sports world, Arizona was today only one win away from the NFL championship. It was a Cinderella story so improbable, even someone as casually acquainted with pro football as Reece had known better than to expect it.

And yet, she had held onto the Caesars Palace betting slip, rather than chuck it and forget about it only minutes after her whirlwind fling with Raygene had come to an end. She had no idea why. When she'd remembered the wager two weeks ago, in the course of fuming over her attorney's latest failed attempt to negotiate a support settlement with Raygene's people, she had known exactly where the slip was: at the bottom of an old jewelry case in her bedroom closet. And that was what Peter meant when he said Reece could do no wrong. Where any other lady would have been lamenting her shortsightedness for having left the betting ticket in a trash can somewhere back in Vegas, Reece had it in hand, crisp and clean and ready to exchange at a Caesars cashier window for a million dollars and change.

"The Cardinals aren't going to win, Peter," Reece said. "The line on the game right now is Oakland minus seventeen. Seventeen!"

"So? What was the line for the Forty-niner game?"

"As I recall, Arizona plus ten. But—"

"The Forty-niners took Arizona too lightly."

"Yes. And that's why they lost. The Raiders won't make that mistake. If they aren't up on the Cardinals by twenty-one at halftime, it'll be a miracle."

"So why are you going to Vegas? If you're that convinced they're going to lose, what's the point?"

"There is no point. That's why you should be trying to stop me. I'm thirty-five weeks pregnant, for God's sake, this is insane!" Reece dropped a short stack of underwear into her suitcase and fell onto the bed beside it, feigning emotional collapse.

Peter moved in to look down upon her, smiling, and said, "Did your doctor tell you not to go?"

"He strongly advised against it, yes."

"Yet you're going anyway."

Reece just looked at him.

"Shall I tell you what the truth is? The truth is, deep down inside, you believe Arizona's going to *win*. You *want* Arizona to win. You want to see that stupid look on Raygene's face just as badly as I do, and you want to do it after you've already cashed the ticket, when there's nothing he can possibly say or do to talk you out of it."

Reece lazily studied the bedroom ceiling over her head, let her body sink deep into the satin embrace of the comforter beneath her. Peter was right: Somewhere beneath all the logic and common sense she was espousing, she *did* believe the Cardinals were going to win Sunday's Super Bowl. Not because this was a supportable belief, because it wasn't, but because such an outcome would be fair and just, and would bring the war she and Raygene Price had been waging for months to a far overdue conclusion. Reece was tired of fighting for something she felt she should have simply had to ask for to receive.

Unwed motherhood had never been in her plans, but she had always known how she would deal with it if the fates ever demanded that she must: with her child's welfare first and foremost in mind. Reece could take care of herself, she was a big and successful girl who had no interest in gold digging. But Daddy—who- or whatever he was—was going to help support their baby to the full extent of his capacity, whether he was inclined to or not.

In her best-case scenario, the child's father would have been someone she could eventually marry, a nuclear family still being the most ideal for childrearing, in her opinion. But Raygene was not that man, and she had known this from the moment he first approached her at the MGM Grand slots that fateful night last May, dressed like a god in Hugo Boss and flashing a smile that could have induced a nun to shuck her habit right there on the gaming floor. Reece hadn't recognized him, but she could sense that he was no stranger to fame, as he appeared somehow larger than life, the way celebrities always did.

"Excuse me, but you're doin' that all wrong," he had said. "May I?"

He held up three dollar coins in his right hand, asking for permission to drop them in the machine she had been feeding without apparent purpose for almost twenty minutes. Reece just raised an eyebrow, not annoyed or suspicious enough yet to send such a stunningly handsome man on his way, and let the stranger make his move. Without ever breaking eye contact with her, Raygene deposited his three dollars, pulled smoothly on the slot machine's lever, and waited for the three cylinders behind its glass facade to stop spinning.

Two gold bars and a wildcard came up on a diagonal, good for a $100 jackpot that began to spill noisily into the machine's payoff chute.

"See? You were only playing two dollars at a time, and you can't win nothin' 'round here like that," Raygene said. "Vegas is like life: You gotta go all the way, or there ain't no point in even playing."

Reece laughed, incredulous. "I don't believe it. This is a setup." She started scanning their surroundings, searching for either accomplices to Raygene's scam, or hidden video cameras recording it all for airing at a later date on cable television.

"A setup? No, no, that money's all yours." He threw his palms up and backed away. "I just saw a lovely lady in trouble, so . . ."

"You're telling me you're just that lucky? You want to put a move on a girl, all you've gotta do is drop three dollars in her slot machine and watch it hit for a hundred?"

"Well, it ain't always for a hundred. Sometimes . . . No, actually, most times . . ." He shrugged. "Hell, you wanna know the truth"—he cut a glance at the two gold bars and single wildcard again, amused—"this is the first time I've ever hit *jack*."

He broke into a wide grin that soon gave way to laughter, and Reece couldn't help but join him. Whoever this player was, his act was fun to watch, and fun was precisely what Reece had come to Las Vegas to find.

So she did what she almost never did and rode the wave, following the lead of a gorgeous man with money to burn to see where it would take her, and how long the thrill of the ride could possibly last. Her last serious relationship had faded to black going on two months ago now, and she hadn't given sex much thought since. She was ready for a brief and thoroughly irresponsible romance.

Discovering early on who Raygene was only encouraged her to take the plunge, as a star professional athlete would almost certainly want their liaison to be as temporary as she did. And Raygene did not disappoint her in that regard, or any other. For over seventy-two hours, he treated Reece to the best of everything Sin City had to offer—food, drink, and oh, God, yes, *sex*—without demanding a single thing in return. His money flowed like rain as he escorted her from casino to casino, playing the tables, taking in the shows, and signing autographs for the hordes of adoring fans who inevitably recognized him wherever they went.

It was not until the pair had shared a final, uncomplicated good-bye kiss, and flown off to their respective homes with the unspoken understanding that their paths would never cross again, that regret began to sink in, at least for Reece. Because three weeks later, she found herself waiting anxiously for an overdue menstrual period that was destined never to come, and soon after that, she had the clinical explanation for why. Somewhere under one set of Vegas hotel sheets or another, a name-brand condom had failed to live up to its promises of unfailing contraception, and Reece was pregnant as a result.

Her initial reaction to the news was shock, then grave concern. She felt as unprepared to be a mother at this time in her life as she knew without question Raygene Price was to be a father. Abortion was an obvious alternative, and she grudgingly gave it consideration, but its moral complications had always left her conflicted, so she quickly ruled out that course of action. She would either have her baby and raise it as her own, alone, or give it up for adoption soon after its birth.

She carried Raygene's child inside her for all of six weeks before she grew irreversibly committed to the former.

By that time, Raygene had been informed of his impending fatherhood via telephone, and gone into full denial-of-responsibility retreat. First, speaking for himself on one of the last occasions Reece would have the honor of conversing with him personally, rather than one of his many representatives, he had categorically denied the very possibility that Reece's child could be his, as if he were a eunuch and had the medical records to prove it. Then he tried the blame game, accusing Reece of getting pregnant on purpose in order to bleed him dry, conveniently forgetting that he had used a condom every time they'd slept together only because she'd insisted upon it. Now, finally, Raygene had taken up penny-pinching as a defense, assigning his attorneys, and lately, a new ball-busting female "financial advisor," the task of buying Reece off as cheaply as possible. Which to Reece was perhaps the most infuriating insult of all, because the support numbers she was offering Raygene had always been more along the lines of what one would ask of an insurance salesman than a professional football player. Here she was bending over backward to be fair to the asshole, and he was treating her like the complainant in a nuisance suit.

So yes, hell yes, Reece was hoping the Arizona Cardinals were going to win this weekend. Because God was good, and God didn't like ugly, and if He had any kind of sense of humor at all, He would goad the Cardinals to victory in the Super Bowl just to show Raygene how upside down the world could be when a man who needed a lesson in humility was begging to be cut down to size.

"Raygene? Reece here. Hey, you remember that twenty-five grand you gave me out in Vegas to bet on Arizona in the Super Bowl last May? Well . . ."

Reece already had her part of the conversation all plotted out. She rehearsed it now in silence, staring up at her bedroom ceiling with Peter patiently hovering over her, and fell out laughing, so hard she had to throw a hand across her mouth to keep from sounding completely insane.

"You see?" Peter said. "You're giddy with anticipation. I couldn't stop you from going up to Vegas this weekend if I wanted to."

"You don't think I'm making a mistake? Holding onto the ticket rather than auctioning it off on Ebay right now for whatever I could get?" Among her many options, Reece had realized shortly before the 49ers game that she could sell the Caesars betting slip either to someone willing to spend a hundred grand for a chance to win over a million, or to Raygene himself, in exchange for the support agreement she hadn't been able to get out of him any other way.

"It's only a mistake if the wrong team wins on Sunday. How many opportunities like this does a person get in life? To win a million dollars?" Peter shook his head. "I wouldn't sell that ticket prior to kickoff for any amount of money, if I were you."

"And if I end up with nothing? Peter, I could pick up that phone right now and *blackmail* Raygene's ass, tell him I'll inform the NFL Security office that he bet twenty-five grand on this year's Super Bowl if he doesn't come correct. He'd have to play ball with me then, wouldn't he?"

"Either that, or dare you to prove it. Can you prove the money for the bet came from him?"

Reece had to admit that she couldn't; Raygene had given her cash for the wager, and she'd brought it up to the bettor's window alone. Only the casino's security videos could possibly connect the money to him, and perhaps not even those would turn the trick.

"No matter," Peter said. "Blackmail wouldn't be anywhere near as much fun as simply winning the million outright, then rubbing his nose in the fact that you have his twenty-five thousand to thank for it. Would it?"

Reece allowed herself a small grin. "No. It wouldn't."

It was impossible to hate any man as innately childlike and good-natured as Raygene, even when he was denying you something as basic as substantive support for your unborn child. But being a boy in a grown-up's body was no excuse for evading one's responsibilities, and hiring a cadre of iron-fisted legal representatives to make sure your evasions stuck. Lovable lug or no, Raygene had been treating Reece like a bill collector undeserving of his respect, and she was tired of it. "Gene the Dream" was overdue a little comeuppance, and Reece was itching to be the lady to show it to him.

" 'Let it ride,' the gamblers like to say," Peter said, taking a seat on the edge of the bed at Reece's side. He patted her affectionately on the thigh. "Which is to say, go for the gold. Leave all your chips on the table, and let whatever's going to happen, happen. Why the hell not?"

He wasn't suggesting Reece do anything she hadn't done before. Aside from Peter's levelheadedness and organizational genius, 4One-One Promotions was the public relations powerhouse it was today because Reece Germaine was a woman completely unafraid to take chances. As far back as she could remember, putting herself at risk for the sake of a given goal had been her instinctive approach to everything, and rarely had it failed her. Maybe it had something to do with both of her parents having died before her ninth birthday, leaving her to be raised by grandparents in Conway, South Carolina, who had nothing more to offer her than love and a warm bed to sleep in at night. As Raygene himself had reminded her that first night in Las Vegas, what was the point of going after something halfway when you had nothing to lose by going all out for it?

"Are you going to be able to deal with Marvin all by yourself?" Reece asked. "You know he's going to have a fit when he learns I'm gone."

Marvin Riggs was the anal-retentive business manager of three of the biggest R & B recording acts 4One-One represented—singer Adryanna Hart, and the vocal groups Jam-Street and Angel's Flight—and he relied on Reece's expertise to protect his clients' pristine images the way a smack addict relied on his needle. Reece had to take calls from the man several times a day, as he was the most obsessive mother hen she had ever met.

"Don't worry about Marvin. I can put out any fire his little monsters care to start, and if he doesn't think so, he can just wait for you to come back on Tuesday to throw his tizzy."

Reece pulled herself up from the bed and resumed packing. "Monday. I'll be back *Monday* morning."

"Nobody goes to Vegas for the weekend and comes back on Monday, Reecie. Especially not after they've won a million dollars."

"God! You really think I'm going to win, don't you?"

Peter turned suddenly serious, his ubiquitous smile dimming to suit a more earnest mood. "Yes. I really do."

Reece snapped her suitcase closed and looked over at her partner, matching his sober expression with one of her own. "Then why haven't I heard from him? If he thought there was one chance in a million the Cardinals might actually win on Sunday . . ."

"What? He'd call and say the money's his if you cash the ticket? Come on. Even if he remembers the bet, and I'd like to go on record right now in guessing that he doesn't, what could he possibly do about collecting on it? Nothing. The ticket has your name on it, Reecie, not his."

"Yes, but . . ."

"The only way he could see any part of that money would be if you decided out of the goodness of your heart to give it to him, under the table, where the NFL couldn't see it. And he knows better than to expect that would happen after all the shit he's put you through, doesn't he?"

Reece didn't answer him.

"Reecie. He knows better than to expect that, right? That you'd just *give* him a piece of one-point-two-five million dollars out of the goodness of your heart?"

"If you mean any piece above and beyond his original twenty-five grand? Of course. I wouldn't give him a dime above that. But—"

"Reecie, Jesus . . ." Peter buried his face in his hands and began to shake his head from side to side.

"—but he gave me the money for the ticket, Peter! Am I supposed to just pretend that he didn't?"

"In one word? Yes!"

"Well, I couldn't do that, I'm sorry. At least, not with a clear conscience."

"I don't believe this. You're telling me that if that asshole called you right now and said—"

The phone rang, cutting Peter off. They stared at the pearl-white instrument on Reece's bedside table for several seconds before she moved to answer it.

"Relax," she said, grinning nervously. "He's forgotten all about the bet, remember? This isn't him." She brought the phone's receiver up to her ear and said hello.

And then a low, mellifluous voice on the other end of the line brought her to the very edge of a dead faint.

5

REECE GERMAINE WAS NOT the only one packing a travel bag that Wednesday night. While she was throwing one together in Los Angeles, Aeneas Charles was assembling a bag of his own in New York. But not for the trip to Dallas Stanley Winston had told him to prepare for. Coincidentally enough, Aeneas was now scheduled to take a red-eye flight with Winston out to L.A., the very same city Reece was planning to leave for Las Vegas on Thursday.

It seemed Winston's client Raygene Price was already en route to the City of Angels from Dallas, having embarked on the sudden journey for reasons he had left disturbingly vague upon informing his agent of his plans by phone, and Winston was too deep in a panic not to pursue him immediately.

"He asked me if I knew what the lifespan of fingerprints were," Winston told Aeneas, having called the investigator within minutes of signing off with Raygene. "Why would he ask me something crazy like that?"

Aeneas said he didn't know, though he could have made a wild guess.

"What *is* the lifespan of fingerprints?"

"That's hard to say. It depends on a number of variables."

"Jesus," Winston said, sounding like a man who was watching his entire life race down the roiling gullet of a flushing toilet. "I knew that psycho Stiles was bad news. I *knew* it!"

"Did Raygene say Stiles was going with him?"

"No. But knowing how I feel about the man, I'd imagine he would have been careful not to."

Aeneas asked if Price had friends or family in Los Angeles, and Winston said no. "There's the usual collection of entertainment people he likes to run with from time to time, but they're all just casual acquaintances."

"What about women?"

"Women? Oh, you mean . . . Well, again, there's the usual bevy of anonymous suspects, probably somewhere in the neighborhood of two or three hundred, and that's only a mild exaggeration. But someone special? I don't think—"

Winston's voice cut off like somebody had stuffed a sock down his throat.

"What?"

"I just realized . . . Clarice Germaine lives in Los Angeles. Raygene's latest paternity victim. She's been playing hardball over a support agreement for months; maybe Raygene finally decided to go out there and try talking to her himself." Winston thought it over, said, "Only . . ."

Aeneas waited him out.

"Only, Shirelle would kill him if he tried a stunt like that. She's got total control of his finances now, like I told you, and she's put a moratorium on support payments to anybody above a certain dollar amount. Raygene wouldn't dare cut a deal with Germaine without talking to Shirelle first."

"So maybe he did."

"Not a chance. Let Raygene negotiate a contract with a beautiful woman? All by himself? That's like trusting your five-year-old to hand out the candy on Halloween."

Raygene always stayed at the same hotel when he was in Los Angeles, Winston said—the Four Seasons in Beverly Hills—so finding him upon their arrival would probably present little difficulty. Winston promised to call Aeneas back later with the details of their flight out and hung up without another word, apparently too frazzled for the thought of a good-bye to occur to him.

An hour later, Aeneas had left the office for his SoHo loft, where he was waiting for Winston's call, when someone else rang his number instead. It was John Ferranza, a private ticket of Aeneas's acquaintance who ran a small practice down in Queens, working mostly missing persons cases.

"I had a meeting this afternoon with a lady wants me to find a guy named Vincent Wong," Ferranza said. "And I seem to recall you wanted to know about it if I ever did."

After a long pause, Aeneas gave up a weary sigh, leaden with dread, and said, "That's right. What have you got?"

ARLENE MCKINNIE had been stalking Vincent Wong for more than three years now. The thirty-six-year-old, sporadically employed beautician and the twenty-two-year-old NYU film student had dated for all of six weeks in the winter of 1999, until Wong had taken all the possessive, clinically depressed behavior from McKinnie he could stand and broke things off, not knowing he might have been better off leaping headfirst into the maw of a running thresher machine. Six weeks had been just enough time for McKinnie to decide that she and Wong were soul mates destined to be together forever, and she had no problem resorting to guerrilla warfare if that was the only way she could help her beloved reach this same conclusion.

In the first twelve months alone following their breakup, McKinnie—whose physical appearance and mode of dress were as consistently black as her mood—had burglarized Wong's apartment, vandalized his car, attacked him in the middle of several NYU classes, and flooded his email in-box with dozens of obscenity-laced threats of mayhem, all while following him about relentlessly. Naturally, he filed numerous police complaints against her, and one court after another slapped her with restraining orders, then put her behind bars when she violated them. But nothing deterred McKinnie with any permanence. Having at some point given up the ghost of ever actually winning Wong back, it seemed she was intent on punishing him indefinitely for having been wise enough to leave her, and it didn't matter how intermittent the occasional arrest and prison term rendered her attacks upon him.

Then Wong hired Aeneas.

Rescuing victims of sexual harassment was not one of the private investigator's routine services, but Wong was the son of an old friend, a surgeon Aeneas played ball with at the McBurney Y, so he took on the kid's case as a favor to his father. By the time Wong came to see him, a little over two years into his Arlene McKinnie nightmare, the NYU film student was a wreck, a once handsome, vibrant young man so worn down by fear and despair, his hands flitted about in his lap like windblown leaves, and his eyes darted from one side of his head to the other without provocation. Aeneas never took cases out of pity alone, but for Wong, he might have made an exception. The kid was that bad off.

For the next two days, Aeneas placed McKinnie under discreet surveillance, taking careful stock of the pest he was now duty bound to eradicate. Then he took the gloves off and went to work.

If there was one dictum experience had taught him never to question, it was the one that said nothing had a greater impact on some bullies than a taste of their own medicine, and Arlene McKinnie turned out to be living proof of this dynamic. She could dish the harassment out, but she couldn't take it. The minute Aeneas dropped any pretense of stealth and began to follow her openly, making every effort to ensure her awareness of his presence everywhere she turned, the pale-skinned, wispy-thin woman started to fall apart. Ordinarily, she moved through the world as if she were the only animate object in it; unless circumstances required her to navigate around you, she didn't even know you were there. But once it became clear to her that Aeneas was tailing her, she was forced to take the blinders off and scan every face in a crowd for his, head snapping left to right, right to left, like that of a mouse on the lookout for a snake lurking in the high grass.

By the afternoon of Aeneas's fifth day of work for Vincent Wong, McKinnie was ready to slit her wrists just to be free of his constant scrutiny. Much to the investigator's relief, she had proven herself to be an abject coward, one so devoid of backbone that she'd yet to make a single attempt to demand that he identify himself. Without any further encouragement, she seemed sufficiently shaken to receive any suggestion Aeneas might care to make to her. But Aeneas was a cautious man, and just to be certain he was reading her malleability correctly, he put the screws to McKinnie one more time. While she was out for the afternoon, he broke into her sixth-floor walk-up on Essex near Broome and swapped the entire contents of two cabinets in her kitchenette before turning her nineteen-inch television upside down on his way out the door.

When McKinnie returned to the apartment hours later, Aeneas could hear her screams of rage and panic from the street below.

The following morning, Vincent Wong's ex-lover walked into the Grand Street bagel shop she routinely stopped at for breakfast to find Aeneas already in attendance, sitting alone at a remote table in the back. He was reading a newspaper as if to pass the time, but with its pages held down low where they wouldn't block her view of his face. She spotted him instantly and, after choking down the instinctive urge to run, finally found the courage to confront him he had been waiting five days now for her to muster. *"Who the fuck are you?"* she screamed as she charged toward his table, petrifying customers and service personnel alike. *"Why the hell are you following me?"*

Aeneas looked up at her with tremendous calm, smiled for the benefit of everyone watching. "Following you? I've been sitting here for almost an hour. Didn't you just walk in?"

McKinnie glanced around, saw more than a few onlookers nod in agreement. When she turned to face him again, Aeneas could see she was already starting to lose her nerve, the adrenaline that had fueled it all too rapidly abandoning her.

"Sit down. We need to talk," Aeneas said softly.

Eventually, he earned her compliance, luring her with the

irresistible promise of full disclosure, which he delivered succinctly, and with painful directness. He told McKinnie she was a lovely girl, but Vincent Wong could never be with her again, and he was all through asking her to accept the fact. Vincent was *telling* her now. *Aeneas* was telling her.

Initially, of course, McKinnie refused to believe what she was hearing. "Vincent put you up to this?" But once her skepticism wore off, she asked Aeneas the obvious question, the bile in her voice daring him to offer her a credible answer for it: "And what if I *don't* leave him alone? What's going to happen?"

"Better that you understand what's *not* going to happen. He's not going to file any more charges with the police. You're not going to be arrested and thrown in jail for a month or so just so you can get out and start in on him all over again. That stage of the game has been played, Arlene, the old rules don't apply anymore."

Starting today, Aeneas said, if McKinnie took one step in Vincent Wong's direction, her world was going to turn to shit in a hurry. And he wasn't talking about upside-down television sets and surprise visits down at her favorite bagel shop. The next time there was a break-in at her apartment, for instance, the only thing she was going to find intact inside was the ceiling.

"I know where you live, where you eat, where you play. Consider the possibilities."

"You can't—"

Aeneas leaned forward so that only McKinnie could hear, said, "Yeah, I can. I can, and I will. Vincent didn't come to me for help in this matter because I'm good at spooking people, Arlene. He did it because the people I *can't* spook get hurt.

That's my reputation. You make me prove myself to you, and who's going to call me off? The police?" He shook his head. "I wouldn't count on it. Your sexual harassment record's a mile long, they'd no more believe you as a victim of that offense than they would a skinhead of a hate crime."

Aeneas paused to see if McKinnie cared to disagree, but all she did was glower at him and nibble on her bottom lip, having done the math and reached the disturbing conclusion that his logic was incontrovertibly sound.

"You're an angry lady, Arlene, and you're more than a little bit imbalanced. So it could be I'm wasting my time here trying to reason with you. But I don't think I am. I think all the shit you've been putting Vincent through is more about you having fun at his expense than your being crazy. So I'm going to ask you one more time, based on the assumption you're sane enough to get off the tracks when somebody tells you a train is coming: Let Vincent go and get on with your life." He got to his feet and peered down at McKinnie with grave intent. "While you've still got a life to get on with."

And with that, he was gone, leaving the black-clad woman behind with such immediate disregard, she had to wonder if he hadn't forgotten she was sitting there before he even hit the door.

That he would eventually have to bolster his threats to her with a demonstration of some sort, in order for all his talk to have any lasting effect on her, was never in doubt. Aeneas had been resigned to this fact going in. But McKinnie surprised him. Over the next several weeks, which would eventually turn into months, he continued to look in on her from time to time, and not once was he given any reason to suspect Vincent Wong remained an object of obsession for her. As near as both he and Wong were able to determine, McKinnie made no attempt to either approach her former lover again, or communicate with him in any way. Despite her history of irrational persistence to the contrary, it appeared Aeneas's hunch about the lady had been correct: However motivated by mental illness she was to make Wong miserable, Arlene McKinnie was not so far gone that she couldn't give up the game if she thought her life depended on it.

A full three months after his bagel shop showdown with her, Aeneas officially terminated his surveillance of McKinnie and turned in his final report to Wong. The ten-page document stated that Wong's ex-lover was no longer an immediate threat to him, but the likelihood existed that she would explore the possibility of harassing him again, at some indeterminate point in the future. There were no guarantees that she wouldn't. If Wong wanted to be rid of McKinnie forever, Aeneas suggested, leaving New York for parts unknown was his best bet.

Shortly thereafter, Wong's father reported that his son had fled to Los Angeles, immediately following his graduation from NYU.

Though his interest in both Vincent Wong and Arlene McKinnie should have come to an end upon receiving this last bit of news, Aeneas did not close the books on Wong's case until he had made a few final phone calls, thinking more of his own peace of mind than that of his ex-client.

One of the people he called was a private investigator he knew out in Queens named John Ferranza.

"WHO'S JOHN FERRANZA?" Arlene McKinnie asked.

"The man who called you out here tonight. The private investigator you met with this afternoon. Come on, Arlene."

"I don't—"

"Look. Let me offer you a little advice here: The pleading-ignorance bit? You don't want to go there. That's only gonna make a rough night for you rougher."

She had shown up at the Blarney Stone restaurant and bar on Eighth Avenue at nine o'clock sharp, just as Ferranza had told her to over the phone an hour before, and followed an overworked hostess back to a dark corner booth close to the kitchen after dropping Ferranza's name. But Ferranza hadn't been there upon her arrival, so she sat down and waited for him, the thought never once occurring to her, even after a full twenty minutes had passed, that Aeneas Charles might appear in Ferranza's stead. By the time she'd recognized the black man heading her way, Aeneas was practically standing over her, making a clean escape impossible. So she did what little she could to mask her mounting terror and asked simply, "What are *you* doing here?"

Same old Arlene.

All done up in her trademark black, from her hair to her lips to her short leather skirt and knee-high boots, she looked as much like a movie assassin today as ever, but the only thing genuinely hard about her remained her head.

"Okay. So I know the man. What's that prove?"

"It proves you don't listen so well. At least, not to me. Or did you simply forget what I told you the last time we met?"

"If I want to know where Vincent lives, I've got a right to find out. The judge said I had to stay away from him, not that I couldn't write him a letter or a card if I wanted to."

Aeneas shook his head, getting visibly pissed now. "Don't quote the judge as an authority, Arlene, because we both know you don't give a shit what he said or didn't say. If you did, we wouldn't be here."

Aeneas had a midnight flight to Los Angeles to catch, and he had neither the time nor the patience to talk in circles with McKinnie. If he could have boarded his plane without worrying about how much she might accomplish toward renewing her campaign of terror against Victor Wong during his brief absence, he would have deferred this conversation until his return. But that was impossible. He knew the thought of her would nag him throughout his stay in California if he didn't deal with her now, inconvenient timing or no.

"I thought you'd wised up. Found an active brain cell still functioning inside that anvil you call a skull and decided to give Victor up for good. But obviously, I was dreaming. Some people just can't do the right thing on their own. You have to give them a little push." He produced a sheet of paper from a jacket pocket, unfolded it with a flourish before sliding it across the table toward her. "Consider yourself pushed."

McKinnie looked at the page like it was a tarantula he was ordering her to pet. When her right hand finally reached out to pick it up, it almost seemed to be acting of its own volition, independent of any directive from her.

"That's a little something I put together back in March, just in case," Aeneas said as McKinnie's eyes darted over his report, the white around her irises flickering with horrified recognition. "Amazing how much of a person's life you can cram into five single-spaced paragraphs, isn't it? The trick is to be selective about what you include. Nobody cares what somebody's favorite color is, or the size of their shoes. But how many illegitimate children they've given up for adoption, or how many times they've been expelled from college for cheating . . ."

"*You asshole!*" McKinnie screamed, leaping to her feet as she flung the dossier at the investigator's face. He thought she might take off running, but then he realized she didn't have it in her. She was crying like a baby, standing on legs as wobbly as those of a newborn foal. He let her glower at him for a full minute, being generous, before telling her forcefully to sit back down.

"I figured you for a trust fund baby from the moment I first saw you," he said. "You didn't have a job, and you only seemed to be looking halfheartedly for one, at best. Which meant you either had a sugar daddy somewhere who almost never comes around, or you had access to money from other sources." A waiter arrived at their table to take their order, but Aeneas did away with him quickly, requesting only a Courvoisier neat for himself and, per a little shake of her head, nothing for McKinnie. "As it turns out, you've got quite a few other sources to choose from, don't you? Assuming you and the CEO of PhotoMagnetics Technologies still get along, that is. What the hell's the old man worth these days, anyway? You have any idea?"

"Leave my father out of this," McKinnie said.

"I'd be glad to. Just as I'll be happy to leave the attorney who drew up your grandmother's trust out of it, as well. Whistle-blowing isn't really my thing, Arlene. If you aren't living up to the conditions the trust places on you to remain eligible for your monthly stipend, that's your business, not mine."

"God*damn* you . . ."

"Yeah. I'm a real piece of shit. And now that we're finally clear on that point, here's the deal: I want this to be the last time you and I have to meet. Ever. If your name so much as crosses my mind again, both your father and his late mother's attorney are going to get a phone call, and you're going to find out how hard it is to keep your refrigerator stocked with Michael Recchiuti chocolates on food stamps. I'm a busy man, Arlene, I'm all through fucking around with you."

He picked up his menu for the first time, and added, "Now. Would you like something to eat before we say good-bye?"

6

"SO JUST WHERE THE fuck d'you think *you're* goin'?" Trip asked.

"I gotta go out to Cali. I'll be back in a couple days," Raygene said. His bags were already sitting in the foyer where Brew had set them down to answer the bell. What else could Raygene say?

"Cali where?"

"L.A., where else?"

"And you was just gonna leave without tellin' me you was goin', that it?" Trip fell into a seat on the living room couch without being invited, signaled his man E.Y. to do likewise on a lounge chair nearby.

"I ain't gotta tell you everything I fuckin' do, Trip," Raygene said angrily, staying on his feet. He didn't want to sit down himself and make his old Riviera Beach homie feel any more at home than he already did.

"The hell you don't, nigga. 'Til I see the money you owe me, I wanna know where your ass is at all times."

Standing off to one side, before the darkened fireplace, Brew steamed in crossed-arm silence, anxiously waiting for Raygene to give him the order to send Trip Stiles and his bitch on their way. He had no love for the crazy white boy in any case, but something about his habit of constantly calling Raygene a "nigga" to his face sincerely rubbed Brew the wrong way.

Equally burning, but constrained by the precarious position Trip still had him in, Raygene said, "If you want me to get your money, I've gotta go to L.A. There's somebody out there I gotta see."

"What, to borrow the shit? You really are that busted?" Trip spread his arms along the back of the couch and crossed his legs, setting down roots like he and E.Y. were going to be here awhile.

"I ain't gonna 'borrow' nothin'. The shit's already mine."

"Okay. So who you goin' out there to see? Gimme a name, Ray."

There was no way in hell Raygene was going to give up Reece's name. His cowardice wasn't that advanced. Because whatever threat to life and limb Trip might pose to Raygene himself was nothing compared to the danger he would represent to Reece, were Trip ever to learn about the Vegas betting slip Raygene was hoping to extract from her in L.A. tomorrow. Raygene had not even the slightest illusions about this point.

"Lady's name ain't none'a your bus'ness, Trip." *Shit.* He hadn't meant to say "lady." "All you got to know is, she's holdin' a few dollars belong to me, and I'm goin' out there to get it, so you an' me can get straight. For *good.*" Telling Trip in no uncertain terms that after this shit was over, they didn't know each other anymore. "Now. Unless you want me to miss my plane . . ." He dipped his head toward the front door.

Trip smiled, glanced briefly over at E.Y. to communicate a message of some kind, then said to Raygene, "And when d'you say you'll be back?"

E.Y. stood up, but didn't move away from his chair. Waiting for further instructions. Brew, on the other hand, eased his way over to his employer's side without being told and trained his eyes on E.Y. exclusively.

"A couple days. Maybe sooner," Raygene said. Biting down on every word as if his jaw were wired shut.

"You'll be back Friday mornin' at the latest. Otherwise, you ain't goin'."

"Say what?"

"You heard me, nigga. You wanna get on that mother-fuckin' plane, you gonna do what I tell you to do. And you gonna start by givin' me the bitch's name you goin' to see. In case you ain't back here on time and I gotta go out there lookin' for your ass."

"I ain't tellin' you her name, Trip," Raygene said. More certain now than ever that both Reece and the unborn child she was carrying were as good as dead if, for any reason whatsoever, he had to come back to Dallas without his Caesars Palace betting slip.

E.Y. finally got the small nod from Trip he'd been looking for, and slowly crossed the thickly carpeted floor to where Raygene stood, only to have Brew step forward to bar his path.

"Brew, hold up," Raygene said, trying to defuse the situation.

But E.Y. looked down on the smaller man and smiled, actually looking forward to things between him and Raygene's boy getting physical. "Naw, naw," he said. "Let's see what the little bitch thinks he's gonna do."

A heavy sigh was called for, but Brew withheld it. Somebody needed to take this fool and his *massa* out in a field somewhere and put a couple of large bullet holes in each.

"How you like that, boss? That tight enough for you?" he asked E.Y. casually.

Though Trip had been sitting in wait for it, concentrating on nothing else, when Brew made his move, the white man never saw it. Had it not been for E.Y.'s face, eyes suddenly threatening to explode from his head, mouth agape, Trip might never have known that something had just gone terribly wrong for them both.

Brew's right hand was clamped on E.Y.'s crotch like a vise, so hard Trip could see Brew's biceps bulging through his shirt sleeve. E.Y. tried to speak, but Brew squeezed harder still, and all Trip's man could do was let out a small grunt, knees almost buckling beneath him.

Raygene suppressed a small, self-satisfied grin and said nothing.

Trip sprang to his feet, hand darting to the waistband of his pants, but Brew said, "That's right, come on. See if I don't rip this man's jimmy clean off," and torqued his right fist again to prove it, eliciting a howl from E.Y. that froze the white man cold.

"He ain't wearin' a cup, Mr. Price," Brew told Raygene, his eyes never leaving E.Y.'s tortured face for a second. "What good's a bodyguard ain't got sense enough to wear a cup?"

Trip came running, just as Brew and Raygene both knew he would eventually, and in yet another blur of barely perceptible motion, Brew reached his free hand inside E.Y.'s jacket, jerked the semiautomatic handgun from the hapless man's shoulder holster, and released him, backing off a few steps so as to give both of Raygene's unwanted guests a good look at the business end of his new toy.

"What the hell is going on in here?" someone standing in the foyer abruptly demanded.

All heads spun at the interruption, but only E.Y. failed to recognize the woman's voice immediately, despite the fact that Trip had last heard it almost a decade ago.

"Momma! What a surprise," Raygene said.

BURBANK'S SOLARIS Studios was a three-unit cluster of gutted warehouses outfitted for the production of porno movies, but today the place had gone marginally legit. Instead of yet another XXX-rated, direct-to-DVD masterpiece entitled *My Big Fat Greek Boning,* or *Red Drag-Queen,* a six-million-dollar music video was being shot on the facility's main sound stage, and while the differences between the two visual art forms were not immediately obvious to Reece, they were real nonetheless. The number of nude and half-nude people on the set, for instance, may have been about the same, but for once, all the sodomy and fellatio was strictly simulated. Impressionable teenagers and little children would be watching this video on all the cable music channels within months, after all, and *real* sex was something nobody associated with the production was irresponsible enough to foist upon them, least of all the video's star, JAXsun.

JAXsun was the twenty-two-year-old hip-hop artist whose song "U Can't Play a Playa" was the inspiration for the video being made, and he was as sensitive to public criticism as any client Reece had ever represented. Self-made hip-hop icon P. Diddy was his role model, so the kid took what people wrote and said about him very seriously, ever wary of the damage bad press could do to a man's record sales. Unfortunately for

Reece, he only seemed to care enough about negative publicity to be stung by it after the fact; his concerns in this area never had any noticeable effect on his actual behavior, which, more and more, best resembled that of a deranged ten-year-old.

The concept he had personally devised for the "U Can't Play a Playa" video served to illustrate this point perfectly. While the song's lyrics were all about a street thug's admonitions to his enemies that he dared not be taken for a fool, the video's storyline, such as it was, seemed to tell a wholly unrelated tale of intergalactic warfare, alien invasion, and zero-gravity fornication between the last living human—JAXsun—and a space station full of understandably sex-starved female honeys. Not that the orgy-as-metaphor theme was a unique one in the music video universe, but this one was so far beyond the pale, only its star seemed oblivious to its excesses.

Still, Reece was only here to argue about one of them.

"She ain't my mother," JAXsun said.

"You emerge from her womb in the previous scene, don't you?" Reece asked. "Didn't she just give birth to you?"

"Yeah, but she's an *alien.*"

"Just the same, you can't turn around and make love to her. That's called incest."

"The shit ain't meant to be taken serious, Clarice. It's symbolic. Ain't you never heard of symbolism?"

"I've heard of it. And I'm sure the good people at MTV have heard of it as well. But they still won't air your video, Jefferson, if you 'symbolically' get busy with your mother in it. You need to trust me on that."

Referring to each other by their proper names—"Clarice" for her, "Jefferson" for him—was something they always did when an argument was starting to turn ugly. He knew "Clarice" took her back to her days of want and need in South Carolina, and she knew "Jefferson," as in "Jefferson Bailey Johnson," started a song playing in his head that had haunted him throughout his childhood: The theme song from the old *Jeffersons* television show. He had to wince at the very thought of it: *Movin' on up* . . . If he had a dollar for every time one of his homeboys had serenaded him with that shit, singing that one line over and over into his ear, he'd never have to cut another CD in his life.

"The bitch is an alien," he said again. The gold-trimmed, pearl-white latex bodysuit he was wearing would have been completely useless in space, but its skintight adherence to his washboard abs would have no doubt made him irresistible to every woman in the galaxy.

Reece turned her head away in frustration, eyes moving across all the grips and extras milling about the set she and JAXsun were standing on the outskirts of, everybody waiting for the pair to reach some kind of agreement so they could either go back to work or call it a day and go home. The video's fresh-out-of-film-school wunderkind director, who had called JAXsun's manager in a panic over the last-minute script change his star was insisting upon, hovered nearby, feigning the artiste's indifference to crisis with only a modicum of success. In five minutes, Raygene would be here for the meeting Reece had agreed to on the phone last night, and two hours after that, her flight for Las Vegas would be in the air. If the former Jefferson Bailey Johnson thought she was going to joust with him all morning over this nonsense, he was crazy.

"Look. Roxanne's your manager; I'm just your P.R. rep. But since she's in New York and can't argue with you about this in person, and I promised her I'd come down to give it a try in her stead, I'm telling you straight: What you want to do here will render this video unairable on every music channel on television, period. Is that what you want?"

JAXsun tilted his head to one side, gangster lean–like. "But the bitch is—"

"Jefferson, if you tell me one more time she's an alien, I'll slap you clear into next week! It doesn't matter that she's an alien! You cannot have sex, simulated or otherwise, with a female organism with breasts who has just given birth to you in the previous scene. Do you understand?"

The kid didn't understand, and he had no desire to, but what he did understand was that Reece would not only quit his employ on the spot if he didn't bitch up, she would also slap him clear into next week, in front of all these people, exactly as promised. So he shrugged after letting a long silence build to convey his undiminished self-determination, lest anyone here think he was relinquishing it, and said, "Awright, fuck it, then, I won't bone 'er. But they ain't 'breasts,' Clarice. How the hell they gonna be 'breasts' when the woman got *four* of 'em?"

Reece wanted to laugh, but she was both too relieved and too exhausted. "Thank you," was all she said.

She went off to find the dining area near the catering truck where she intended to meet with Raygene as JAXsun began barking orders at the director and his crew to get back to work, acting like they and not he had been responsible for the long delay. Her stomach was churning. She hadn't had anything to eat but a bowl of oatmeal and an apple all morning, and she still wasn't sure that seeing Raygene was the right thing to do. He'd refused to offer her anything in the way of motive on the phone with her the night before, deferring all her questions on the subject until today, and both his secrecy and the timing of his call left her with little choice but to fear the worst: He had remembered the Arizona Cardinals Super Bowl bet and wanted in on her possible winnings.

If that was indeed the case, and he had come here to try to bully her out of the betting slip, rather than negotiate a deal for it, her trip to Vegas would go on as planned. An arrogant, impenitent Raygene, demanding she give him something he felt entitled to, was somebody she'd be able to rebuff with ease. But a needy and desperate one, open to discussing a fair and equitable child support agreement . . . Well, that Raygene Price she had yet to meet, and she wasn't sure she ever wanted to. In the flesh, the man was disarming enough as it was.

She wandered through the buffet line on the empty lunch patio and made herself a small plate of greens and mixed vegetables, then sat down to nibble at it aimlessly as she strongly considered standing Raygene up. Running away would definitely have its advantages; war generals of great renown had adopted the tactic throughout history. But Reece just didn't know how.

Courage was both her greatest gift and her most inconvenient curse.

WHEN HIS limo pulled up to the Solaris Studios' main gate, Raygene was deeply disappointed. This was the "movie studio" Reece had moved their meeting to at the last minute this morning? The place looked like an old aircraft factory with a fresh coat of paint, what the hell kind of movies could anybody possibly make here? He was destined to come and go without ever finding out, but had someone given him a list of the classic "films" that had been taped on the makeshift lot in its brief eleven-year history, he would have been duly impressed, as more than a few of them held a place in his own private video collection back home.

But he hadn't come here to stargaze, in any case. He had come to take care of business, find out if Reece still had that Super Bowl betting slip he'd given her the money for out at Caesars last May, and charm her out of it if she did. It was the only way he could think of to get Trip his fucking 200 grand.

He knew better than to ask Shirelle for the money; not only would his mother have flatly denied the request, she would have smelled Trip's scent on it immediately and had a cow. She had always been oddly fond of Trip, despite the unsavory influence he had on her son, but now, especially after that O.K. Corral–like scene in Raygene's living room last night, she had no patience for him. They weren't all still penniless back in Riviera Beach; times had changed. Whereas Raygene's association with the white boy might have once cost him the only thing he had worth fretting over—his freedom—today, he had a great deal more to lose by keeping Trip's company, and there was no way Shirelle was going to let him lose it without a fight. A fight far more substantial than the one she'd put up in throwing Trip and his bodyguard out of her son's home the night before.

His mother in Trip Stiles's face, full force. That was the last fucking thing Raygene needed to have happen right now.

7

SHIT, REECE THOUGHT when Raygene finally appeared, *he looks as fine as ever.*

She'd been hoping the man would look different to her now than he had when last they met, less absurdly irresistible in some way, but no such luck. He walked toward her table grinning, as she knew he would, and his gait had the same smooth, muscular rhythm she remembered from their wild Las Vegas weekend. He was wearing a black cashmere turtleneck and a slate-gray suit, the latter tailored to his frame like a second skin, and if he'd gained an ounce of fat since the last time they'd met, Reece didn't know where in the world he was hiding it.

"Reecie. Damn, girl, you look good," he said.

He bear-hugged her the moment she stood up, giving her no chance to simply stick her hand out for a less intimate handshake, and even in her "delicate" condition, the warmth of his body against her own caused her mind to drift.

This was going to be harder than she needed it to be.

"Don't start, Raygene," she said, smiling despite herself.

She asked him if he wanted something to eat, but he shook his head without even glancing at the buffet table first, intent on getting right down to business. They gave minimal lip service to the obligatory amenities—his flight out, Reece's and the baby's health, yadda-yadda-yadda—and then she said, "Okay. I only have a few minutes here, Raygene. What do you want?" Straight out, no lead-in, the question coming so far out of nowhere, it almost qualified as a non sequitur.

"I've decided I wanna do the right thing," Raygene said. "By you and the baby."

"The right thing," Reece echoed.

"Yeah, you know. I wanna work somethin' out. About the money you been askin' for." He paused. "But first, you gotta do me a favor."

Here it comes, Reece thought to herself. "And what's that?"

He was having trouble saying what came next. "You prob'ly don't even remember. But that weekend we were in Vegas, up at Caesars . . . I gave you some money to place a bet." He chuckled to emphasize the total weightlessness of the matter. "A football bet. Arizona Cardinals to win the Super Bowl at fifty-to-one. As a gag. Remember?"

Reece threw her best poker face up, dying inside, and said, "I remember. What about it? You aren't going to ask for your money back, are you?"

"Huh? Oh, hell no. Fu— I mean, forget about the money, that ain't important. I told you that back then, twenty-five G's to me don't mean nothin'."

"Then?"

"It's just that, see . . . You remember how you asked me if I could get in trouble givin' you that money, and I said no, I couldn't, 'cause I wasn't the one placin' the bet, you were?

Well, that wasn't 'xactly true. Truth is, the league's rules against sports bettin' are strict as hell, 'specially on football. The Security Office finds out you were involved in a football bet, even if all you did was put the money up for it . . ."

"They can fine you."

"Fine and suspend you. Or worse. I only just found this out myself, see, but apparently, you make a bet on a league game big enough, they can ban your ass from the game for life."

"And twenty-five grand—"

"Is big enough. Yeah, exactly. So you understand my problem. Assumin' you still got it, and didn't trash it or anything, I need that bettin' slip back. Like, just to be sure."

"Just to be sure of what, Raygene?" Reece asked, starting to burn. He was coming at this from a direction she hadn't at all anticipated, and if he was leading up to the con she thought he was, he was an even bigger asshole than she'd given him credit for.

"Just to be sure, you know—that the league never finds out about it. Not that I think you'd turn me in, or anything, but . . . Sometimes, things happen, Reecie, that's all. If I could get the ticket back and destroy it myself, I'd feel safer about it. You hear what I'm sayin'?"

"But the Super Bowl hasn't been played yet. Has it?"

"The Super Bowl?" Raygene's face collapsed like a house of cards, then instantly re-formed again, a testament to his alacrity for bullshit. "No. But what—"

"Why would you want to destroy the ticket before the game has been played? Can't the Cardinals still win it?"

"The Cardinals?"

"I'm not sure, but I thought I saw something about them beating San Francisco in the playoffs last weekend. The Forty-niners? Doesn't that mean the Cardinals are in the Super Bowl?"

Fuck, Raygene thought, *she knows.* Reece hadn't demonstrated all that much knowledge of or interest in the game last May—she hadn't even known who he was, for chrissake—so it had seemed safe to assume she hadn't been following the present NFL season very closely, if at all. Granted, the Caesars betting slip had given her at least one good reason to do so, but the woman had acted so unimpressed by his $25,000 gift at the time, he wouldn't have been surprised to learn she'd flushed the ticket down the toilet in their hotel suite that very night. What the hell was he supposed to do now that she was talking like a goddamn Cardinals season ticket holder—tell her the team *wasn't* in the Super Bowl?

"Well, yeah, that's right, they are in the Super Bowl," he said. "But—"

"Then I stand to make a lot of money if they win, don't I?" Reece asked. "Providing I still have the ticket."

He gave up the only answer to her question he could possibly offer like a drowning man relinquishing his hold on a life preserver. "Yes. Technically. But—"

"Technically? My *ass,* Raygene. 'Technically,' I'm going to be one-point-two-five million dollars richer Sunday than I am right now if Arizona beats the Raiders. Isn't that right?"

"Yo, Reecie, hold up a minute now . . ."

"No, *you* hold up a minute. I know I wasn't exactly in my right mind that whole weekend in Vegas, Raygene, but did I really look that stupid to you? So stupid that you could come out here and smooth-talk me out of a ticket that might be worth a million dollars in three days?"

"No. No! If you'd just let me explain—"

"You want to explain? Go ahead, please." She crossed her arms in front of her chest and sat back. "I want to hear this."

She looked like a judge on the bench, his guilt already decided. He had no right to be offended, but her smugness pissed him off all the same. She had him squarely on the defensive, backpedaling on the balls of his feet, and Gene the Dream no more enjoyed that position off the football field than he did on it.

"First of all," he said, "it ain't really your ticket. Since I'm the one who paid for it, it belongs to me if it belongs to anybody."

"Excuse me?"

"It's true, Reecie. If I wanted to be an asshole 'bout this, I could just tell you to give me the damn ticket, instead'a offerin' to trade you for it like I came here to do. But I wanna do the right thing, like I said. And since you were the one actually placed the bet . . ."

"The ticket has my name on it. Not yours."

"Yeah, yeah, but we both know—"

"I'll tell you what I know, Raygene. I know you've got no way of proving to Caesars, or anyone else, that that twenty-five thousand dollars I bet on the Cardinals last May was yours and not mine. Just as I also know that whatever brought you out here today, it wasn't the 'right thing.' Because if you had any interest in doing what's right, you'd have done it seven months ago and given your child—*your child*—the security I've been asking for."

" 'Security'? You ain't been askin' for no damn 'security,' you been askin' for three thousand dollars a month!"

"That's right. I've been asking for three thousand, when I could be asking for five. When I *should* be asking for five!"

The video crew had taken a break in taping, and a few people were starting to wander into the dining area, providing Reece and her guest with an unwelcome audience for their rapidly escalating spat. Raygene was visibly put off by the intrusion, but Reece didn't give a damn, thoroughly unwilling to back down simply to save herself a little embarrassment.

"Reece," Raygene said, lowering his voice like a lawyer discussing tactics with a client, "I didn't come all the way out here to argue with you, all right? I came here to get that bettin' slip back, on account'a one, it's mine, and two, it was a mistake, I should'a never given you the cheddar for it in the first place."

"And if I don't have it?"

Raygene assured himself she was bluffing, just to keep the idea that she wasn't from sending him into a state of unfettered hysteria. "You sayin' you don't?"

"I'm saying I haven't heard anything yet about what's in it for me if I do."

He refused to wince, but Raygene knew his eyes had betrayed his irritation nonetheless. What in the hell had he ever seen in a woman this goddamn hard? "Two grand a month," he said. "That's the best I can do, take it or leave it."

It wasn't a laughing matter, but Reece had to chuckle regardless. "Raygene, we just agreed that the ticket has a potential value of one and a quarter million dollars. I could probably sell it to a speculator right now for almost a tenth of that. Why in the hell—"

"All right, all right. So what do you want? Name your price."

"My price?" Reece was taken aback. Suddenly, Raygene was talking like a man who *needed* the Caesars betting slip returned to him, as opposed to one who simply *wanted* it back.

But why? In Vegas, he had blown off her questions about the possible repercussions of his bankrolling a sports bet like one might deflect a child's fears of the boogeyman. He was Gene the Dream, a star too high in the NFL heavens for the league to ever even *think* about bringing down. What could have changed in eight months to so drastically alter his view of his own professional immortality?

And it couldn't be the ticket's dollar value he was after because, even given his recent money troubles, which his attorneys were constantly propping up as justification for stiffing her, another $1.25 million or so should have been too trifling a sum to hold Raygene's attention. Unless he was in an even bigger hole than she knew. Could his penchant for throwing cash around like a parade watcher tossing confetti have finally brought him to this, flying halfway across the country to beg Reece for a piece of paper he couldn't even be certain she still possessed?

"Raygene, what's going on?" Reece asked.

"What's goin' on? Ain't nothin' goin' on. I'm waitin' for you to tell me what you want, that's all."

"No. There's something else going on here you're not telling me. You weren't worried about getting busted by the league when you gave me that money at Caesars, and you aren't worried about it now. You think you're above the league. So this has to be about the ticket itself. Either what it's worth now, or what it might be after the game on Sunday."

Raygene was starting to feel warm and uncomfortable, like the clothes he had on were too heavy for the weather. It was a combination of rage and abject terror he hadn't experienced since his first days as a rookie with the Cowboys, brought on this time by Reece's apparent determination to see him on his knees before she'd give him what he was asking for.

"I ain't got time for this, Reecie," he said.

"And neither do I. But you're going to be straight with me, Raygene, or you can go back home right now. If you need that betting slip for financial reasons . . ."

"What, you think I'm *broke*? Is that what you're sayin'?"

"No. I was simply wondering—"

"Shit, you must be trippin'! I flew out here last night first class, the goddamn ticket cost me eighteen hundred dollars round-trip. I got a room at the Four Seasons runs seven-seventy a night, and a limo's gonna take me everywhere I wanna go, 'less I decide I wanna drive myself, in which case, I'll go out and rent a Porsche or a Ferrari for six, maybe seven hundred dollars a day. That sound like I'm broke to you?"

"I never said you were broke."

No, but she'd implied it, and that was insulting enough. Raygene's pride was already wounded, what with Trip's threat of blackmail having sent him scurrying out here like an old woman spooked by a barking dog. There was no way he was going to let Reece accuse him of being busted when the only money-related problems he really had were a backstabbing homeboy from the old neighborhood and a mother bent on treating him like an infant who didn't know how handle his own affairs.

"Look here, Reece. I've always liked and admired you. You're a beautiful lady with mad smarts, and you're a helluva lotta fun to party with. But just 'cause you messed up and got yourself pregnant don't give you the right to play me like this. Now, I'm tellin' you I gotta have that ticket, and I'm gonna get it from you, one way or another. My generosity only goes so damn far."

"Just because *I* messed up? Is that what you just said?"

"Well, you did, didn't you? I mean, hell, *I* was careful, right? Didn't I have a hat on that whole weekend?"

Reece had entertained minor concerns about this meeting with Raygene possibly harming the baby, should things get nasty and she was moved to lose her cool, but she hadn't really been afraid for its safety until this moment. The baby was a thumper by nature, but in times of extreme crisis for her, its gymnastics were often equivalent to those of a cat trying to escape a burlap bag. It was behaving like that now, Reece's rising blood pressure alerting it to something it could only perceive to be danger. Reece took a deep breath, trying to calm them both, but Raygene's words kept ringing in her ears: *Just 'cause* you *messed up . . .*

She stood up, rubbing the sides of her distended belly vigorously, and said, "I'm sorry, Raygene, but this meeting is over. I've got a plane to catch, I've got to go." *Before I strangle your pompous ass,* she wanted to add, but somehow managed to withhold.

"Go? Go where?" Raygene demanded, rising to his feet.

"Not that it's any of your business, but I'm going back out to Vegas." Reece flashed a smile intended to maim. "For the game. It should be fun, don't you think?"

"Then you *do* have the ticket."

"Oh, yes. I have it. And I intend to keep it, at least until sometime early Sunday night. Unless, of course, somebody up there makes me an offer for it before kickoff that I can't refuse."

"I already *made* you an offer for it! I told you to name your price!"

"You can't afford my price, Raygene. Not anymore. You think *I* made a mistake last May? Wait until the Cardinals win on Sunday, and see what you think about the one you just made here today. Ciao."

She marched off. Raygene raced after her, snagged her right arm to turn her around. "Reecie, wait. You can't do this to me."

"Or else what? I'll hear from your lawyer? I seriously doubt it, Raygene. Because you can't sue me over that ticket without tipping the league off to where the money for it came from. Can you?" She smiled again. "Besides. Been there, done that. Your lawyer and I are old friends, remember?" She finally glared at the hand on her arm. "Let me go."

He wasn't ready to, but they were making a scene now, performing before a throng of extras and crew members that had grown to a crowd of over two dozen people.

He opened his hand to release her and Reece was gone for good. She went back inside the studio sound stage and disappeared, looking for all the world like a woman he had set eyes upon for the last time in his life.

As Raygene stood there in the embarrassing remains of their public display of disaffection, certain that every witness to it knew who he was and would soon be relating an account of his punking to every sports reporter of their acquaintance, it dawned on him that Reece had at least been wrong about one thing: He wasn't going to have to wait until Sunday to figure out he'd just made a big mistake.

He knew that much right now.

8

FROM AN AISLE SEAT on an American Eagle Airlines SF3, cruising northeast at an altitude of 25,000 feet above the California/Nevada border, Reece gave herself one more stiff, figurative kick in the behind for telling Raygene two things he'd had no earthly need to know: She still had the Caesars Palace betting slip he wanted, and she planned to spend the weekend in Vegas waiting for the slip to pay off.

God, how could she have been so stupid?

Pride, that was how. She had agreed to meet with Raygene hoping for the best, prepared to refund his $25,000 if the subject of the betting slip came up and he insisted on being compensated for it. Like she'd told Peter last night, she wanted to be fair with Raygene. But then he'd tried to sucker her out of the ticket with that bullshit about wanting to destroy it before the league's secret police could find out about it, and insulted her further by accusing her of being solely responsible for her unwanted pregnancy, pushing one of Reece's most touch-sensitive buttons. It had all just been too much for her to take, so she'd fired back, looking to send her unborn child's muscle-headed father back to Dallas with nothing more to show for his journey west than the fear that he'd just thrown away a possible piece of $1.25 million. That was the least the man deserved.

But the shaken expression on his face, gratifying as it had been to see, was not worth the trouble it could cost her if Raygene decided to come out to Vegas after her. She should have simply lied to him, acted like she barely remembered the betting slip he was talking about and told him she'd lost it ages ago. It would have been such an easy lie to tell, and an easy one for him to believe. When he'd given her the money for the bet eight months ago, she had, after all, treated it with the same air of mild amusement he had. Twenty-five thousand dollars on the Arizona Cardinals to win the Super Bowl? Apathetic fan of the game that she was, even Reece had recognized the pure frivolity of such a wager.

Now, thanks to her big mouth, Raygene not only knew that the ticket was still in her possession, but where he could find her for the next several days if he cared to try at least one more time to relieve her of it. Unless—did Reece dare hope?—he hadn't believed her. She could have been bluffing. Telling him she still had the betting slip just to piss him off. He'd offered her the child support agreement she'd been begging him for for months in exchange for a piece of paper that, if it existed, would probably be worthless in three days, and she'd turned him down flat. Wouldn't he wonder about that? On the surface of it, didn't her refusal to cut a deal seem like the kind of thing a woman would do who was only *pretending* she had something to bargain with?

Yes, Reece decided. Raygene could have come away from their meeting today thinking she'd been lying. But it wasn't very likely, and it didn't really matter if he had or not, in any case, because there was nothing he could do to get a piece of Reece's action now. She was adamant about that. He could follow her out to Vegas with an army of lawyers if he wanted to, and all he'd get for his trouble was a bird's-eye view of his $25,000 making somebody else filthy rich. When Reece either auctioned off the betting slip to the highest bidder prior to Sunday's game, or cashed it in after an Arizona victory.

And if the Cardinals ultimately failed her and the ticket turned up a loser? By that time, Reece mused with a smile as the American Eagle SF3 banked into its approach to Las Vegas International Airport, Raygene will have died from sheer aggravation, watching her tear up the Vegas Strip from one end to the other, like she already had his $1.25 million in the bag.

STANLEY WINSTON called Raygene on his cell from the Four Seasons lobby just after 11 A.M. He had somebody with him he wanted Raygene to meet, he said, and they were wondering when Raygene was planning on returning to the hotel.

"You're in Los Angeles?" Raygene asked, stunned. His life seemed to be spinning more and more out of his control by the minute, even as he chilled in the backseat of an aimlessly cruising limousine, trying to stay out of reach of any further trouble.

Stanley said yes, they were in Los Angeles. When could they expect him back at the hotel?

Raygene thought about saying "never," that his business in

L.A. was over and he was on his way to the airport now to go back home, but he decided to simply surrender to his agent instead. One, because his business here was a subject Raygene didn't want to raise before Stanley again, and two, because Stanley was not going to be denied now, no matter what Raygene said or did to avoid him. He'd flown 2,700 miles to chase after Raygene like a bounty hunter running down a bail jumper, and Raygene knew it would be just as pointless to try to duck him as it would be to ask him over the phone who this person was he was so hot for Raygene to meet.

He told his agent he'd be at the Four Seasons in thirty minutes, then ordered his driver to take no less than forty-five to get there, wanting all the time he could get to prepare himself for the Q and A Stanley no doubt had in mind for him.

"**YOU WANNA** write a book about *me?*" Raygene asked Aeneas Charles just short of an hour later.

"Actually, the way it would work, I'd be helping you write it. The book would bear your byline, with me as just your coauthor."

"Yeah?"

Aeneas nodded. "All you'd really have to do is talk to me. Answer a lot of questions, tell me your life story. I'd do all the rest."

"You mean the typin', and all that."

"Yeah. The technical stuff."

They were sitting at a table in the Four Seasons main bar with Stanley Winston, all of them fingering drink glasses only Stanley was actively emptying. The agent's nerves were still on edge, but not so much now that he saw how well Aeneas was pulling off their little charade. The man was good. They'd beaten out a general outline of his journalist cover story during the course of their flight out from New York, a thoroughly backward, writer-before-the-athlete book deal only someone as clueless as Raygene would take seriously, but what Aeneas had just told Raygene about his imaginary autobiography's byline—Raygene would be credited with writing it, with Aeneas's mere assistance as his coauthor—was an ad-lib, and a brilliant one at that. Raygene was already convinced he could do anything; suggesting he could actually "write" a book, as opposed to simply providing the material for one, played perfectly into his delusions of grandeur.

Still, just as his agent might have feared, Raygene was not yet convinced that all this book business Stanley and his friend were handing him was for real. Primarily because this brother with the same weird, unpronounceable first name as Aeneas Williams, the safety for the Rams—*Eye-nee-ass,* was that how you said it?—didn't look like any writer, sports- or otherwise, Raygene had ever met before. What he looked like was a big corner or a small outside linebacker, somebody whose arm tackle Raygene might have had a little trouble breaking had their paths ever intersected on a football field somewhere. And dog seemed too *smooth* to be a writer, his movements fluid and his attire damn near as immaculate as Raygene's own.

"Who'd you say you write for again?" Raygene asked him, preparing to conduct a little Q and A session of his own.

"I'm a freelancer. I've done pieces for everybody. *SI, Newsweek, Esquire* . . . Maybe you saw the last one I did for *Esquire,* last October. On Keyshawn Johnson?"

Raygene shook his head. "Naw. I must'a missed that one." Stanley damn near gagged on his drink, because Gene the Dream's interest in the act of reading was precisely nil, and his interest in the press of professional athletes not lucky enough to be him was equally nonexistent. "What about books? What other books you done?"

"I've ghosted on three previous sports bios. Two basketball, one football. But this would be my first with a cowriting credit."

" 'Ghosted.' What's that mean?"

"It means he helped write the books but he didn't get credit," Stanley said.

"So your name wasn't on the cover?"

Aeneas shook his head.

"So . . ."

"Why don't we do this one that way? Well, you could, if that's what you want. But—"

"But not with him," Stanley said, cutting in. "Aeneas is all through ghosting for other people, Raygene. I've read his stuff, he's too good for that. He's ready to do a book with his byline on it, and he wants it to be a book about you. It's a great opportunity for us, we really should be flattered."

"Flattered?" Raygene didn't know how to be flattered.

"He's already got a six-figure contract from St. Martin's in place, and for a book about any one of five pro athletes of their choosing. Michael Vick, Jeremy Shockey, Terrell Owens . . ."

"Terrell? Puh-lease," Raygene said, nose crunching up as if catching a whiff of something foul. He and the 49ers' Terrell Owens were mirror images of one another, supreme physical talents with egos of incalculable dimension, so naturally there was no love lost between them.

"Exactly," Aeneas said. "It's the same old list of usual suspects, with one exception: you. Nobody's ever done you before, Raygene, your story's uncharted territory. I could do another book on Owens, sure. Maybe even one unlike any of the others that've already been written. But I'd rather write a book about somebody the fans don't really know yet. There'd be more of a challenge in that, and that's what I'm really looking for here. A challenge."

"Jesus," Stanley said, accidentally marveling at Aeneas's genius aloud. The man was playing Raygene like a violin, talking up the love of a challenge to somebody who had no time for anything that didn't promise to test him in some substantial way.

Aeneas and Raygene looked at the sports agent expectantly, assuming some elaboration for his exclamation was forthcoming.

"Oh. I was just . . . agreeing with your assessment," he said to Aeneas. "About the fans not really knowing Raygene yet. They may think they do, after all the fluff pieces that have been written about him, but they don't. Not by a long shot." He shifted his gaze over to Raygene. "Do they?"

"They think I'm all flash and no substance," Raygene said forlornly, addressing Aeneas. "Just 'cause I got abilities most players can only dream about, and I ain't afraid to admit it, they call me a clown. If they knew what I was really all about, the kinda man I really am . . ."

"It'd blow their minds," Aeneas said. "I'm sure."

"This is our chance to change the public's perception of you once and for all, Raygene," Stanley said, playing charades with their distant waiter to order another round of drinks for the table. "And if the book were to take off and make the best-seller lists, the money wouldn't be bad for us, either."

"Yeah?" Raygene perked up. "What kinda money we talkin' about?"

Here, as they had anticipated, was where the absurdity of Stanley and Aeneas's big lie was bound to get a little sticky. The two men traded glances, quietly negotiating who should respond to Raygene's inquiry, before Aeneas said, "Well, my advance on the book was a hundred and twenty-five, and I'm prepared to offer you two-thirds of that."

"Two-thirds . . ." Raygene ran the numbers through his head, working hard not to allow the exertion to bring a frown to his face. He looked to Stanley, disillusioned: "Ninety thousand? That's all?"

"Actually, it's closer to eighty," Stanley said. "But that's a fair amount for a deal of this kind, and it's payable to us almost immediately upon signing the contract."

"What do you mean, 'almost' immediately? What's wrong with immediately?"

"Before the publisher will sign off on the book, they're going to want to see something in the way of a few sample chapters, or a rough outline," Aeneas said. "An outline will probably be sufficient, but I'll need to spend a few days with you, at least, to knock one out."

"And what if I ain't got a few days?"

The question froze time at the table like a Polaroid snapshot.

"What?" Stanley asked.

Raygene readjusted himself in his chair, as if suddenly irked by the confines of it, and said, "I'm sayin', like, makin' me wait to get paid is an insult. Like they don't really think I got a story to tell, or somethin'."

"It's not about you having a story to tell. It's about them being sure your story's worth a hundred and twenty-five grand. They're only covering their asses, Raygene. It's nothing personal."

As their waiter appeared to set fresh drinks before them, Raygene made use of the timely interruption to silently wonder if there was any way in hell he could make Trip wait a week or so just to get eighty G's. Raygene seriously doubted it, but as things stood at present, he didn't have one thin dime to offer the white boy, having just botched his attempt to con Reece out of the Super Bowl betting slip that could have been the answer to all his problems. Perhaps compared to nothing, eighty grand, even delayed by several days, wouldn't sound so bad to Trip.

"Tell me again what I'd have to do," Raygene said to Aeneas.

And Stanley smiled, unseen, his worries fading into the distance right in time with his sobriety. Life was good again.

His big fish was on the hook.

"**SOMEBODY NEEDS** to clean the mosquitoes out this goddamn pool," Trip said.

His houseguest watched him lean over the side of his patio chair to scoop some of the filthy water into a cupped palm, toss it onto the lawn behind him with disgust.

"Never mind the pool, man. Tell me what happened. You just let the nigga's momma throw you an' E out the house?"

"Didn't nobody throw nobody out, fool. Mrs. Milbourne asked us to leave, so we left, end of story."

"Yeah, but—"

"Raygene's moms and I go way back, I owe her some respect. If you can't understand that, there's somethin' wrong with your ass."

"I understand it. I'm just sayin'—"

"Shut the fuck up, Weezer," E.Y. cut in, nursing a tall glass of lemonade from the next patio table over. "You wasn't there, so you don't know."

Trip inched his head to one side to look at his driver/bodyguard, the pity in his gaze almost equal to the repugnance in it. "Shit. If anybody needs to shut the fuck up, bitch, it's you. And I *was* there, so I guess I *do* know." He turned to the other man, said, "Weez, you wearin' a cup? Or are you just as stupid as he is?"

"A cup? What kinda cup?"

"The kind ballplayers wear to protect their nuts. Damn, don't you niggas know anything?" He shook his head and rapped the knuckles of one hand on the hardshell athletic supporter he was wearing under his briefs. "You grew up where I grew up, you'd know: A baller don't wear a cup is just askin' to get his shit kicked in. Ain't that right, E.Y.?" He laughed heartily. "I bet you'll be wearin' one'a these bad boys tomorrow, won't you?"

"I'm gonna kill that motherfucka," E.Y. said, still feeling the residual effects of Brew's indelicate handling of his groin.

"When the time comes, you damn straight you are. Raygene's little homie done fin'ly got on my last nerve. But we ain't gonna mess with 'im 'til Raygene comes back from Cali and gives me my ducats. Dog's actin' squirrelly 'nough as it is, we whack his boy now, ain't no tellin' what he'll do." He glanced at the swimming pool again and scowled. "Shit, E, go get that net over there and clean this motherfucka out, I might wanna go swimmin' later today." He was renting the three-bedroom home in the Richland Hills area of Dallas for $2,600 a month, and every shortcoming of the house and grounds made him suspect its owner was taking him for a ride.

Though he had no desire to leave his seat, let alone drag the pool for mosquitoes, E.Y. pulled himself gingerly to his feet and proceeded to do as Trip had instructed. He'd already earned his employer's contempt once this week, and he didn't want to tempt the fates by voicing a complaint about anything that the white boy wouldn't want to hear.

"So who you think the bitch is the nigga went out to Cali to see?" the man they called Weezer asked Trip.

"I don't know. Homeboy's prob'ly got all kinds'a Hollywood connections, could be any one of 'em."

Weezer nodded his head, liking the sound of that. "Yeah, Hollywood. There's a shitload'a money out there."

" 'Cept, he said the chedda he was goin' to get is his, he ain't gonna borrow it. What the hell you s'pose he meant by that?"

Weezer moved his head from side to side to say he had no clue. Something about Trip seemed different to him today. The white boy was acting as if he were distracted, dividing his attention between what was and something that might be. If it had been anybody else, Weezer would have said the man was nervous. But Trip Stiles was never nervous.

Ever.

Trip threw back the last of his seven-and-seven and craned his neck to deliver an order—"Come on, E, we out"—before standing up to leave. He yawned and stretched luxuriously as E.Y. tossed the pool net aside, relieved. Addressing Weezer again, Trip asked, "You all right? You got everything you need?"

"Yeah, I'm cool. But I was thinkin'—"

"Uh-uh. Don't start that shit again, a'right? You don't leave this motherfuckin' house 'til I say so."

"What, not even to see my girl? She don't live but two—"

"I don't care if the bitch lives next door," Trip said, cutting the other man off for the second straight time. "Your ass is stayin' right here."

"But Raygene's in fuckin' Los Angeles, man. How's he gonna see me from way the fuck out there?"

"We don't know he's in Los Angeles. We didn't see the nigga get on the plane, did we? If he was just playin' us and he's still here, and he saw you fuckin' around somewhere . . . Why I gotta keep explainin' this to you, fool?"

Trip's reluctant houseguest looked away and sighed, signaling an end to his side of the argument. "Okay, okay, I'll stay in the crib."

"Goddamn right you will. Or else I'll have to whack your ass for real." Trip let that sink in, then turned to E.Y. "Let's go, dog."

The two men left without another word.

In their absence, the wild-haired Hispanic with the truck tire gut they'd left behind remained rooted to his patio chair by the pool for a good fifteen minutes, trying to decide what pissed him off more: being cooped up in Trip's rented house like a pet in a kennel, or the dumb-ass nickname the white boy had given him that even his useless bodyguard was starting to use for him now. *Weezer.* Luis Ortiz didn't mind people calling him Louie, or even 'Uis (as in "Weese") for short. But Weezer? That was the wackest moniker he'd ever heard.

Even for a man who was supposed to be dead.

9

IMMEDIATELY AFTER their meeting with Raygene at the Four Seasons Hotel, when they had settled into the taxi taking them back to their own far less ostentatious lodgings in Los Angeles, Stanley had asked Aeneas what he thought. And Aeneas had given it to him straight.

"I think you were right. Looks to me like Stiles, or somebody, has already put their hooks in him."

It was what Stanley had both most expected and least wanted to hear the private investigator say. "Why do you say that?"

"He's hurting for money. You saw how he reacted when I told him he'd have to spend a few days talking to me before he could see his piece of the advance. He basically told me he didn't have a few days to wait. And as for his explanation for why he's out here in L.A. . . . ."

"What? You don't think he could've been asked to sing backup on a rap record?"

"Well, anything is possible, of course. But he says he did the recording session this morning, and intends to fly right back home tonight. Even if we believed he could get in and out of a recording studio in less than three hours, if he went to all the trouble of jumping on a plane at a moment's notice to do a homie in the music business a favor . . ."

"You'd think he'd want to do a little partying after. Yeah, you're right. Raygene would. *Damnit!*" Stanley bounced a fist off the taxi's door glass.

"He left the hotel in a limousine. Would you happen to know what service he uses when he's in town?"

"Not off the top of my head. But I'm sure with a call back to the office I could find out."

"Good. Once I have the name of the service, assuming he's been using the limo the whole time he's been here, figuring out where he's been, if not who he's been seeing, should be fairly easy."

And it was. Four hours later, when the two men huddled up again in the lobby of their hotel just prior to Stanley's late afternoon taxi ride back to the airport, Aeneas had a copy of Raygene's Los Angeles itinerary in hand. It was mercifully brief. The Dallas Cowboy had done a little club-hopping shortly after his Wednesday night arrival in town, then retired to the Four Seasons around 2 A.M. Thursday morning. Alone. As he had remained, according to the driver Aeneas had spoken to, up to that point on Thursday, when he'd only used the limo to cruise West L.A. after making a single stop that morning.

"'Solaris Studios'?" Stanley asked. "Then he really did come out to sing backup on a rap record."

Aeneas shook his head before the agent's smile of relief could become fully formed, said, "I don't think so. It's Solaris

Studios as in 'movie' studios. They make porno films there, from what I understand."

"Oh, no. You're not gonna tell me—"

"No." Aeneas laughed. "No. At least, I have no reason to believe that's what he was doing there."

"Then?"

"They tape music videos at Solaris as well. They were taping one of JAXsun today on the specific sound stage Raygene visited. Are he and Raygene friends, by any chance?"

"Not that I know of. Which Jackson are we talking about?"

"It's 'Jackson' with an *X,* and a *U,* and he's unrelated to Michael. Anyway, the good news is, if he and Raygene *are* homies, Raygene might have gone there to do a cameo in his video. Which isn't the same thing as singing backup on one of his records, mind you, but I guess you could argue that it's close."

"So what's the bad news?"

Aeneas paused briefly to soften the blow. "The person who left the drive-on at the gate for Raygene was a lady named Reece Germaine. And 'Reece' is often shorthand for—"

"Clarice." Stanley didn't swoon, exactly, but he did do a slow wobble on his feet, as if riding out a small temblor only he could feel. "Jesus. You don't suppose . . ."

"He cut a deal with her? There's no way to know. But if he did, and I'm right about his hurting for cash, what would have been the point? Settling with Germaine now would only seem to put him deeper in the hole, not help him get out of it."

Raygene's agent nodded, agreeing.

"Could there be some connection between Germaine and Stiles I haven't heard about yet?"

"Germaine and Trip? What kind of connection?"

"I don't know. But if she and Raygene didn't meet to talk about Stiles or money . . . What was it? Her baby?"

"It had to be the baby." Stanley's eyes narrowed with worry. "Oh, God . . ."

"Maybe something happened to it?"

"It's not inconceivable. She's too far along for an abortion, her due date's early next month. But she could have suffered a miscarriage. I'm told she's a major player out here in public relations, and that line of work can be highly stressful at times. You throw in a months-long battle with Raygene's lawyers over paternity and child support . . . That's arguably a heart attack waiting to happen."

"And if she had lost the baby, Raygene would have felt responsible?"

"Absolutely. He's got a real soft spot for Germaine, he'd have run out here on the next plane available to beg her forgiveness. That, and offer her the moon as compensation."

"Which could explain his sudden anxieties about money."

"Yes. Yes, it could." Stanley began to visibly brighten. "Because Lord knows, he couldn't ask Shirelle for a dime intended for Clarice Germaine. Anything he promised her, he'd have to come up with on his own." He fell silent for a moment, testing the seams of his logic for tensile strength. "God, if that's it—if that's really why he came out here—Shirelle is positively gonna *strangle* him."

It was only a halfhearted complaint. Stanley was so encouraged to learn that Trip Stiles had had nothing to do with Raygene's jaunt to Los Angeles, seeing his client run over by a truck was the only thing that could have slowed the wave of relief that was presently rushing over him.

Until Aeneas said, "And you?"

Stanley's eyes fluttered with bewilderment. "Me?"

"If Raygene has cut a deal with Germaine, are you going to strangle him too? Or will you be okay with it?"

The sports agent didn't understand the relevance of the question, but he paused a moment to consider a proper answer for it nonetheless. "Frankly? I'd be happy to see it. I've only had very limited exposure to the lady myself, but from what little I've had, I can understand why Raygene's so fond of her. She's sharp as a tack, and a real straight shooter. And she's only been asking Raygene for a fraction of what most people would consider to be fair."

"And Raygene knows that's what you think of her?"

"I suppose so. Why?"

"Well, I don't mean to be a cynic, or anything, but . . . I'm wondering why he wouldn't just tell you the truth. About why he flew out here, that is. If he had no reason to think coming correct with Germaine would piss you off, why make up a lame story about singing backup on a rap record?"

It was a conundrum that stopped Stanley's rising spirits cold. While he was Raygene's agent and not his confidante, the pair's relationship was close enough that Raygene seemed to have no qualms about telling Stanley things he often kept hidden from everyone else, including his mother Shirelle. That he had found it necessary to lie to Stanley about the purpose of his trip to Los Angeles could only mean one thing, just as Aeneas was now insinuating: The truth wasn't something Raygene wanted Stanley to know.

"I think I need a drink," Stanley said.

"It was just a question, Mr. Winston. They come to me, I ask them. We've seen no sign of Stiles since we've been here, nor anything to indicate he's the reason Raygene came, so tell you what: Let's wait until I've rejoined Raygene in Dallas tomorrow to start connecting the two, all right?"

It was a request that only slightly allayed the agent's reinvigorated angst. The damage had been done. From the moment his impending taxi ride to LAX began, to the instant his flight touched down in New York six hours later, Stanley would think of nothing but Trip Stiles, and all the terrible news related to him Aeneas Charles might soon have to deliver to Stanley's ear from Raygene's home in Dallas.

Not once having any clue that Aeneas was never going to rejoin Raygene in Dallas as planned.

NO ONE knew it—not Weezer, his old cellmate, nor even his boy E.Y., whom he trusted above all others—but Trip Stiles wasn't trying to blackmail Raygene Price just for the 200 grand. He was doing it to save his ass.

Trip owed almost a half million dollars to a man named Pierce, a supplier out of Memphis he'd made the mistake of using four months ago and not compensating in a timely manner, and the primary reason "Pierce" was the only name the player needed—no first, last, or middle goddamn initial required—was that his reputation rendered all other identifiers unnecessary. Pierce was a psycho's psycho, the kind who hurt friends and enemies alike with equal indifference, and legend had it he was connected in his home state of Tennessee all the way up to the Capitol building. Thus, he was both insane and fearless, a duality that demanded all but the most suicidal fool's respect. Even a thug like Trip had to pause on occasion to consider the possible consequences of an action he was contemplating—injury, death, incarceration—but not Pierce.

Pierce was politically immune from consequences, so it was said he hurt people as he pleased, recklessly and without hesitation.

Trip wasn't fearful of him, exactly, but neither was he in denial about the danger the man represented. If he didn't make good on his promise to pay the supplier $450,000 by next Tuesday, Trip was a dead man walking. That was a bona fide fact.

Up to now, Trip had been living under the weight of this threat with substantial composure. He only had 250 grand to offer Pierce, and rather than do something stupid and impulsive to raise the other two hundred, he'd hit on the idea of extracting it from his old homie Raygene, whom he suspected had millions just lying around loose in banks all over the globe. He'd tried simply asking Raygene for the money first, presenting the request like an innocent solicitation to invest in something only marginally illegal, but when Raygene had refused to bite, Trip had had no choice but to resort to blackmail. His mother really had, God bless her crazy, worthless ass, kept Raygene's old piece in a box in a closet back home, along with everything else Trip had left behind upon going off to Florida State Prison eight years ago, so the means for blackmail had indeed been at Trip's disposal. The gun hadn't been sealed up in any goddamn sandwich bag, however; Trip had made that shit up, demonstrating an uncharacteristic flash of imagination. If Raygene's prints were still anywhere to be found on the chrome Charter Arms .38, he would be more stunned than Raygene to learn of it.

As for the remaining elements of the game Trip was running on his old Riviera Beach partner in crime, these had been provided by Weezer. Luis Ortiz, before he'd fucked up a carjacking intended to feed his crack habit and spent three years sleeping on the bunk above Trip's at FSP, had been a part-time stunt man in the movies. Low-budget, direct-to-video, sorry-ass horror movies, where people got their throats slashed, skulls crushed, and brains blown out in damn near every frame. The experience had taught Weezer not only how to fake taking a bullet to the forehead, but what props were required to make the whole effect look real, even to a live audience. A blank round, a large packet of artificial blood and brains, and a touch of makeup for hiding a phony bullet hole beneath the skin; a little flash powder, and some electronics to detonate it. Items you couldn't just walk into a corner drugstore and buy off the shelf, maybe, but nothing a resourceful man like Trip Stiles couldn't assemble.

The plan was ingenious, and had been executed without a hitch. In perfect synchronization, Trip had aimed and fired the Charter Arms at Weezer's forehead; E.Y. had fingered a remote to both blow a "hole" in Weezer's forehead and scatter his "brains" all over the walls; and Weezer had collapsed and played dead with astonishing realism. It all made for an act that should have shown Trip an immediate return, but for a single, almost unimaginable complication: Raygene didn't have the 200 grand.

He'd been telling Trip that all along. His finances were all fucked up, he said, and that kind of cash just wasn't within his easy reach. Trip had thought sure Raygene was full of shit, unable to understand how anybody who played in the NFL could not have thousand-dollar bills coming out of his fucking *ass*. But now Trip had little choice but to believe Raygene's claims of poverty were at least partially based on fact. Because here it was three days later, and Raygene had still not anted up. He'd gone all the way out to L.A. and come back without a goddamn dime, save for the promise of some pissant eighty grand he said he was going to get in a couple of weeks from a book deal.

A *book deal*?

"I'm sorry, Trip. But right now, that's the best I can do for you," Raygene said.

Trip would have fucked him up right then and there had they been sitting anywhere else, but here in Raygene's sky-box at Reunion Arena, midway through the third quarter of a Dallas Mavericks–San Antonio Spurs basketball game, Trip couldn't touch the fucker without being seen by at least a hundred people, and maybe even a live television audience. Which, no doubt, was exactly why his old friend had insisted on the site for this impromptu meeting.

"No. It ain't," Trip said.

"It is, Trip. I swear it is."

"A lady was holdin' some money for you, you said. You was just goin' out there to get it, you said."

Raygene was silent.

"So what the fuck happened?"

"Didn't nothin' happen. We just"—Raygene shrugged—"couldn't work things out, that's all."

"You couldn't work things out? What the hell was there to work out, it was your fuckin' money, wasn't it?"

"Well, yeah. Sort of. But—"

"But what? Nigga, stop fuckin' around and make some sense! Did the bitch have some benjamins belonged to you or not?"

Raygene was trapped. He'd already told Trip more about his business in L.A. than he should have, and now there was no turning back. Trip was all out of patience, and was ready to stop talking and start kicking ass. The mere fact that he'd forced this meeting on Raygene immediately upon his return from Cali, rather than wait to do it Friday morning, was evidence enough that things between the two men had reached critical mass. Raygene had to tell the white boy the truth, or brace himself for a throwdown that, win or lose, would probably cost Raygene everything he had.

Suddenly, he was sorry that he'd left Brew back home as agreed, just as Trip had allegedly done with his own man E.Y.

With great reluctance, and a considerable amount of editing to protect his pride, Raygene told Trip about Reece and the Super Bowl betting slip. Assuring himself that whatever happened after this was really on the lady's head, and not his own, because all this drama could have been avoided if she had just been reasonable and played ball with him this morning.

He prayed her lack of judgment wouldn't prove to be fatal.

SHORTLY AFTER 10 P.M. Thursday night, Pacific standard time, Aeneas Charles returned to his hotel in Los Angeles to find the message light blinking on the phone in his room.

Raygene Price had called, and his agent Stanley Winston wasn't going to like the reason why: He was changing the plan. Instead of hooking back up with Raygene in Dallas the next day, as the three had agreed, Raygene wanted the "journalist" to fly out to Las Vegas and meet him there. He mumbled something about the "mad fun" of Super Bowl weekend as a way of explanation, and told Aeneas not to worry about finding a place to stay, he had that angle covered. Then he named a casino and a rendezvous time before hanging up: The

Bellagio, one o'clock, under the seventy-foot chandelier hovering over the main lobby.

Judging from the time stamp on the recorded message, Aeneas determined the call had come in no earlier than 11:30 P.M., Dallas time. So it had been late. An observation that suggested this wasn't a premeditated request on Raygene's part, but a spur-of-the-moment one. Just as his one-day jaunt to Los Angeles had seemed to be.

Aeneas called the airline to change his reservations and was immediately put on hold. Something foul was in the air, and he suspected it would only get worse once he got to Las Vegas.

Especially if a man he'd never met named Trip Stiles had something to do with it.

10

"WHAT DO YOU MEAN, you're going to Las Vegas?" Shirelle Milbourne asked.

"Just what I said. I'm goin' out to Vegas. What's wrong with that?"

"You just got back from Los Angeles, Raygene. And you still haven't told me what you flew out *there* for."

"I told you. I had to see some people." Then, an inspired afterthought: "About a movie."

"What movie?"

"One they was shootin' out there. At Solaris Studios."

"I've never heard of Solaris Studios."

Rather than admit that, prior to today, he hadn't either, Raygene put his sandwich down and, spewing lettuce, said, "Momma, why you sweatin' me like this? And what you doin' out here, anyway?"

"I came to see my son," Shirelle said, fighting back the urge to reach a napkin across the table and wipe the mustard off Raygene's churning mouth. "What's wrong with that?"

The man still ate like he had as a boy. The only thing different between this 1 A.M. kitchen moment and all the ones he and Shirelle had shared back in Riviera Beach was the kitchen itself. Whereas Shirelle's old one in Florida had been a cold, black pit of destitution, this one in Raygene's Dallas home was like a dream: all bright metalwork and white tile, in a space that looked to be the size of a three-car garage.

"Shit," Raygene laughed. "You came to check up on me. That's why you didn't even call first to say you was comin'."

"You *need* checking up on. Flying out to California for God knows what, then talking about flying to Las Vegas as soon as you get back. And you see what I find the moment I walk into your house, don't you? Four niggas having a gunfight in the living room!"

"Trip ain't no 'nigga,'" Raygene said.

"Let me tell you something. As much as it pains me to say it, he's more nigga than half the black men who ever have, or ever will, live to be called one. Including you."

You got no idea how right you are, Momma, Raygene thought to himself.

He was going out to Vegas today to try to find Reece again, and Trip was coming with him. That was the plan. Trip, of course, wanted to handle the "hardheaded bitch" alone, his way, once she turned up, but Raygene, after much debate, finally disabused him of this idea. He'd simply approached the girl all wrong Thursday morning in L.A., Raygene said; tried to run a game on her instead of just keeping it real, and pissed her off. But he still believed there was a chance he could bring Reece around, if she really did have the betting slip he so desperately needed.

Because she still had a detectable vibe for Raygene. Before

he'd put his foot in his mouth and run her off, that much had been obvious to him. Besides which, as indifferent to the honor as his actions suggested he was, he was and always would be the father of the child Reece was carrying inside her. The magic of DNA testing had ultimately proven that without a doubt. With a bond like parenthood connecting them, surely there was no way the lady could have hate for Raygene forever.

With any luck, then, Reece and Trip would never even have to meet. All Raygene had to do was hunt her down before Sunday, then take a completely different tack with her. Show her more respect, more honesty than he'd ever found it necessary to show her before. Let her taste just enough of the terrible truth driving him to command her sympathy, and then commence with the renegotiations. And this time, she would go along with the program. She had to. Otherwise, Trip Stiles would take matters into his own hands, and both she and Raygene would, from that point forward, be in a world of hurt.

Not that Raygene was worried he couldn't take Trip on *mano a mano* if it came to that. On the contrary, Raygene was certain he could snap the psychotic white boy and his bodyguard E.Y. both like a pair of frozen drinking straws if Trip were fool enough to force that issue. But there was still Trip's blackmail threat to consider.

Though he remained doubtful Trip could successfully frame him for murder, Raygene continued to fear the fallout if the police were to merely question him as a material witness to a homicide. He could not afford to have his past scrutinized that closely by the general media. Knowing what little they knew about him now, the guardians of the NFL's sacred public image already looked upon him as a player who only barely met the league's guidelines for personal conduct. Were the adventures of his misspent youth to come to their attention, and that of the league's fickle fans, the Cowboys and every other team in the NFL would cut him adrift without ever looking back.

So Raygene had to keep the lid on the boiling pot that was his old homie Trip until he could find a way to pay the white boy and make him go away. He could not allow Trip's impatience and impulsive nature to spur a confrontation of any kind out in Vegas. Which was why he'd just invited Stanley's writer friend, Aeneas Charles, to the party. There was no guarantee that having Charles around at Raygene's side 24/7 would encourage Trip to behave himself in Nevada, but Raygene didn't think the journalist's presence could hurt. Anything that might inhibit Trip's more violent tendencies was worth a try.

STILL SCARFING down his late-night sandwich, Raygene studied Shirelle's face as she scowled at him, ever the skeptic where her son's intentions were concerned, and tried to find something, *anything* there that might encourage him to come correct with her. To tell her all about the bind he was in, and ask for her help in resolving it. Lying to Shirelle always gave Raygene a headache, and having to tell her lie after lie only turned that headache into a migraine. If he could only trust her with his confidence, just this once, the knots his life had been tied in over the last three days might loosen up and give him the respite necessary to devise a way to undo them altogether.

But he was dreaming. There was nothing to see in Shirelle's face tonight but the same old question: *What in the hell've you done now, fool?*

"I don't want you hanging with that boy anymore, Raygene," Shirelle said. "He can't bring you anything now but trouble."

"I *ain't* been hangin' with 'im. He's been hangin' with *me*."

"You went to that basketball game tonight with him, didn't you?"

"No! What—"

"That wasn't Trip you were talking to on the phone before you left?"

"It was him on the phone, yeah. But he wasn't at the game with me."

"No matter. Any man who can't leave your house when he's asked to leave, without having Brew or somebody else pull a gun on him first, is somebody you don't need to be associating with."

"Yes, ma'am."

"You can 'yes ma'am' me if you want. But I mean it. You stay away from Thomas Stiles." Raygene nodded, looking for the fastest end possible to this conversation. "Okay. Now. One more time: Tell me why you went to Los Angeles today. Then we'll talk about why you *think* you're going out to Las Vegas tomorrow."

Raygene threw up his hands, faking the frustration of someone who had to keep repeating a simple fact to a dunce. "Momma, I already told you . . ."

"You said something about a movie."

"At Solaris Studios. Right."

"And? You went out there to act in this movie, or what?"

"Act? Naw, naw, I wasn't doin' no actin'. I was just like, in the scene. With the star."

"You mean, you were an extra?"

"An extra? Hell— I mean, no, ma'am, I wasn't no extra. I was a *guest* star. I was playin' myself."

"I don't understand."

"It was a music video, Momma. For this JAXsun joint called 'U Can't Play a Playa.'"

Raygene had figured out that much just by passing through the sound stage as they were taping, on his way out to the lunch area where Reece was waiting for him. From what he'd been able to see of the set, the video was going to be seriously wack, but it was making for an ideal cover story now; even if, by some miracle, Shirelle happened to catch the Raygene-less music video on the tube later, he could always explain his absence by saying his part had been cut out. Bigger people than he were left on the cutting room floor out in Hollywood all the time.

"'Jackson'? Are you talking about *Michael* Jackson?"

"No, just 'JAXsun.' Capital J-A-X, small S-U-N. All one word. Damn, Momma, you tellin' me you ain't never heard'a JAXsun?"

"Never. I take it you got *paid* to be in this video?"

"Paid?" Finally, a trick question. Shirelle would have heard through Stanley of any deal for a music video appearance long ago. "Naw, I didn't get paid. I did it as a favor. Like, for a friend."

"A friend? What friend?"

"JAXsun. Who else? He's a dog'a mine. He called me up an' asked me to be in his video, and I said sure, why not." He pushed his chair away from the table. "I'm tired, I'm goin' to bed."

"Clarice Germaine lives in Los Angeles, Raygene," Shirelle said. "Are you sure you didn't just go out there to see her?"

"Clarice who?"

He was overplaying the ignorance bit with that one, but he didn't know what else to say. His mother frowned.

"Clarice Germaine. The mother of your next child. Don't act stupid with me, Raygene."

"You mean Reece? Puh-lease . . ." He got up and took his empty plate to the sink, vying for time. Stanley had asked him this exact same question in California this morning, catching him equally off guard. Was everybody around Raygene a damn psychic, or something? "Why the hell would I wanna go see her?"

"Because you like her, and you think we've been treating her unfairly. Maybe you thought, if you went down there and talked to her alone, charmed her the way you charmed her in Las Vegas when you and she got all hot and bothered, you could come to some agreement on a support settlement."

"I already tried talkin' to her. Ain't no way I'm gonna fly all the way out to Cali just to try again." He busied himself washing his plate, preferring to keep his back to Shirelle until the subject of Reece had come and gone.

"Look at me, Raygene."

"What?"

"I said turn around and look at me."

Raygene set the plate down in the sink, turned off the water. Braced himself for a moment, and then turned on a heel to face his mother again.

"Damn, Momma. There just ain't no keepin' secrets 'round you, is there?"

He was grinning.

"What kind of secret are you talking about, Raygene?"

Raygene said nothing for a long beat, his smile expanding with simulated pride. "I'm gonna write a book," he said.

ON ITS most ordinary day, Las Vegas was a zoo, but during the week of the Super Bowl, it was a zoo without a keeper.

In the seven days leading up to the NFL's hallowed championship game, Nevada's "Diamond in the Desert" was virtually overrun with a lava-like flow of crazy people, most of them armed with too much money to spend and not enough common sense with which to spend it. The drunks were drunker, the boors more boorish, and the painted ladies easier to find than at any other time of the year. It didn't seem possible, but this Las Vegas made its normal self look like a rest home by comparison.

By all rights, only three days before the big game, Reece never should have been able to find a room within a sixty-mile radius of the Strip. Every hotel and motel in the city proper had been booked solid for weeks, all but a few of their paying guests having made their reservations months, if not a full year, ahead of time. But Reece Germaine was not a woman without connections. One of her former clients, an R & B crooner named Romeo Ali, was a Las Vegas junkie, a regular visitor nearly as ubiquitous on the scene as Wayne Newton, and he loved Reece like a big sister. The suite at the Hard Rock Hotel and Casino he held in reserve year-round had been hers just for the asking, as Ali had only in the last day or so sadly determined that his tour schedule would prevent him from occupying it himself.

While another hotel might have been considered more suitable to a woman only a week away from childbirth, Reece adored the Hard Rock. There was a youthful vitality here that few other Vegas hotel/casinos could match. The median age of its clientele hovered around the mid-thirties, well below that of the Winnebago set who frequented many other establishments, and an explicit threat of carnal mischief permeated everything. Moreover, people actually laughed out loud here, adding a welcome touch of cheer to the bell-and-whistle din of the wagering machines and the *real* music—Rolling Stones, Pearl Jam, Nirvana—that throbbed down upon the masses from an army of unseen speakers.

The place was invigorating, and Reece was badly in need of invigoration.

It was only Friday morning, but she wanted Sunday afternoon and the game to come, and come quickly, because she no longer doubted that Raygene was coming after her Super Bowl betting slip. She'd had almost twenty-four hours to reflect on their meeting in Los Angeles, and the desperation to claim the ticket as his own all his bullshit had betrayed, and his arrival in Vegas now appeared not only likely but imminent. And she hadn't made this trip to spend all her time watching and waiting for some sign of Raygene Price. She was here to have fun, and to enjoy being a lady with varied prospects for impending wealth. Planning for another go-round with Raygene was seriously cramping her style.

Fortunately, Reece thought she may have already devised a method for dealing with the Dallas Cowboy. Desperate or otherwise, Raygene was still Raygene, and she could outmaneuver his like even on her slowest and least inspired day.

Besides, there was a far more pressing piece of business demanding Reece's attention: What to do with her Caesars

Palace wagering ticket before Sunday at three o'clock? Keep it, or sell it off?

Marching across the Hard Rock's game floor on her way out to her rental car, she set a deadline of Saturday at high noon for determining the matter, after she'd thoroughly tested the waters of possible buyers. Then she bravely set out to throw herself headlong into the crush of pagans jarring the teeth of Las Vegas.

Once, that was, she had run a few simple errands for the sake of Raygene Price.

IT HAD taken all of six months for Carmen Oliveras to hate Las Vegas. She had known her love for the city would eventually wane as a consequence of living here, but she hadn't been prepared for how quickly and completely her change of heart would come. Once a great fan of the blinding, unremitting light shows that were downtown and the Strip, Carmen could now imagine nowhere else in the world she would be unhappier making her home, with the possible exception of Newark, New Jersey.

Newark was the reason she was here.

As of her arrival two years ago, Carmen was a casino security flak, a professional fly on the wall who spent all her time cruising game floors incognito, watching people do one, or sometimes all, of three things: lose money, win money, or try to cheat the house in lieu of the latter. There was an art to what she did, sure; it wasn't everybody who could effectively spy on three players sitting in a row of dollar slot machines while realistically appearing to be a busy fourth. Truly invisible surveillance took talent. But this wasn't rocket science, and, more important to Carmen, it wasn't police work. It was grunt work, what people who used to be cops, and others who simply wanted to be, had to settle for when no legitimate police force would return their phone calls or give their résumés a second look.

This wasn't the direction Carmen's life was supposed to take.

At thirty-four, she should have been a Newark P.D. detective by now. A seasoned vet with a long list of commendations and a big, fat pension waiting in the wings for the moment she chose to start collecting it. She should have owned a three-bedroom colonial in Somerville or Whippany, an Acura to park in the driveway, and maybe even had a family to share it all with. Carmen had always wanted kids. But none of this was hers, or was ever likely to be; it was just a dream that had all turned to dust in a single day.

And why? Because the lady's name was Carmen, not Carmine. Or Jorge, or Stan, or Hank, or any one of a thousand names people gave their sons but not their daughters. Carmen Oliveras was a woman, not a man, and an attractive one on top of it, and for someone whose only ambition in life was to wear a badge, a real badge bearing the stamp of a major metropolitan police force, this combination had proven to be as deadly a drawback as two eyes that could not see. Because nobody wanted a female cop to succeed but the female cop herself. From her first day at the Newark police academy, to her last hour in uniform, this reality had been impressed upon her in a multitude of ways. Vulgar jokes and snide remarks, hands forever groping and pinching her, and a playing field of career achievement tilted so far and so brazenly to the side of men, it was damn near vertical. Every minute of her

NPD experience had been a nightmare of harassment and obstruction, molestation and injustice.

And yet Carmen would have survived it all, every insult and indignity, had it not been for one additional dynamic to the institutionalized sexism of her chosen profession: The boys not only didn't want you to be a girl, they didn't want you to be another one of the boys, either. It was the ultimate catch-22.

On the one hand, they dared you to operate by their own set of rules, convinced that by virtue of your femininity, you'd never measure up; then on the other, got all bent out of whack when you did. Called you a dyke and a lesbo, a freak of nature who could only be as hard and capable as they if your sexual preference was all ass-backwards. No other explanation was possible.

The official ruling of the NPD's Board of Review had branded Carmen Oliveras a "rogue cop," a cowgirl whose violent impulses were a threat to both her fellow officers and the good people of Newark, but that was total bullshit. In her mind, Carmen's only real crime had been to perform her duties with the same contempt for the law, and for the citizens for whom they were supposed to be upholding it, as all the males around her. The only difference was, she had done it without a dick dangling between her legs.

So yes, she was bitter now, five years after her humiliating dismissal from the department. Perhaps she was even a little insane. The last shrink she'd talked to here in Vegas certainly thought she was. But she had no compulsion about being deranged, if that was what she was, because she wasn't the one to blame for her condition. If it was true that, sometimes, in her darkest hours of self-hatred and depression, when the aural and visual overload of her pitiful Las Vegas existence filled her brain with the dead weight of wet sand, she fantasized about killing somebody, the Newark Police Department was responsible, not her. The NPD in general, and one NPD cop in particular, the same one she always put to death in her black flights of fancy whenever the spirit moved her.

It was the uniform she'd been partnered with when she blew off all the fingers of Hector Ramirez's raised left hand, and who, months later, had then led the charge of witnesses against her at her tribunal. Mr. Above-All-Corruption-and-Temptation, he of the perfect conduct record and, hence, unassailable credibility. Without him, the case against Carmen would have folded like a bad tent, because, irony of irony, the all-boys club she so detested would have saved her skin otherwise. No other cop on the scene would have spoken a word against her, "dyke" or no "dyke," had Carmen's partner not broken ranks and started singing, leaving them no other choice but to follow suit.

He claimed he would have done the same to nail ANY bad cop, man or woman, but that was hardly relevant. The damage to Carmen's life had been done, no matter how pure the self-righteous asshole's motives had been.

She understood he was no longer a cop himself, and was not surprised to hear it. No one served their partner up to the brass on a silver platter and remained a cop for long. He was doing private investigation work in New York these days, and was making out rather well. While she rotted here in Sin City, watching trailer trash old ladies dip their hands into other people's coin cups, and wise guy college kids work in pairs to snatch purses and duffels from their inattentive owners. In short, protecting the billionaire owners of Las Vegas's great hotel/casino empire from the scourge of the earth.

It was a dichotomy that burned a hole in Carmen's gut like a hot rivet.

Taking a cigarette break out in front of her latest place of employment, the Hard Rock Hotel and Casino, she watched a gorgeous, bronze-skinned pregnant woman exit the lobby and walk past, heading for the street, and thought about the baby inside her. The baby Carmen herself might have been carrying at this very minute, had Officer Aeneas Charles of the Newark Police Department not derailed all the plans she had ever made for her future. She dared not think, let alone hope, that their paths might someday cross again, but imagining such an improbable occurrence was the only relief she could ever find from the pain he had doomed her to endure.

That, and how she would go about properly thanking him for it.

11

LIKE REECE, Raygene had had no business finding a place to stay in Las Vegas only two days before the Super Bowl, but if Reece had connections in this town, Gene the Dream had more of them, and in higher places. He was famous, he had money, and his annual losses in Vegas could have paid the Strip's electric bill for six months. The first two characteristics made him popular among casino owners, but the third made him an object of desire to them, somebody they would order locked in chains if he dared walk into their establishment and then attempt to leave again, taking his deep pockets and losing ways elsewhere. For luckless high rollers like Raygene, there was always a room somewhere in Vegas waiting, even when there wasn't so much as a space in the parking lot available to anyone else.

On this particular occasion, Raygene and his four-man entourage of Brew, Trip, Aeneas Charles, and Trip's man E.Y., all ended up at the Bellagio. The Dallas Cowboy normally preferred the more exotic ambiance of the Mandalay Bay, but management at the Bellagio was quicker to comp, and despite the lavish spending he'd been doing over the last several days, Raygene was still supposed to be operating on a budget. If he didn't want Shirelle to cancel all his credit cards before the weekend was out, he had to start taking his freebies where he could find them.

Aeneas had arrived in Vegas first, just before noon, followed shortly thereafter by everyone else, flying in out of Dallas on the same late Friday morning flight. The plane had only been in the air two hours, but it had felt like six to Raygene, so thick was the tension between the two bodyguards. They were sitting rows apart, Brew next to his employer and E.Y. beside his, yet the mad hate they had for each other moved through the cabin space between them like a poisonous gas. Neither man ever made a move toward the other, but that was coming. Raygene was sure of it. He only hoped they could keep their shit together until his business in Vegas was complete.

Little did he know that Brew and E.Y. were only the undercard to the main event he would soon be anticipating with even greater dread: Trip Stiles versus Aeneas Charles. Because the two men despised each other at first sight, without a single word from either needing to be spoken. It was uncanny. Raygene had seen the same thing happen with some ballers, total strangers who disliked each other from day one of training camp for no apparent reason, and it was always a pain in the ass to deal with, like a bomb that could go off in your face at any moment.

Not that Raygene hadn't been expecting some drama between the pair. He'd told Trip the writer would be meeting them here before they'd left Dallas, and Trip had been pissed as hell to hear it. How were he and Raygene supposed to do what they were going out to Vegas to do with a goddamn reporter hanging around? he wanted to know.

"First off, 'we' ain't goin' out to Vegas to do nothin'," Raygene had told him. "I'm goin' out there to get my bettin' slip, and you and your boy're just comin' along for the ride. And secondly—"

"I don't give a shit about 'secondly'!"

"And secondly," Raygene pressed on, "the man's only gonna be around when I want 'im around. He's gonna hang with us some, yeah, but he ain't gonna be ridin' my jock all day'n night. That ain't part of the deal."

Trip had no way of knowing that Raygene was lying to him—the deal Raygene had in fact made with Aeneas and Stanley Winston Thursday called for total, around-the-clock access—but the white boy rejected his story just as flatly as if he had.

"First time I want that motherfucker gone, he ain't gone, both of your asses gonna be in trouble," Trip said.

And now that he and Aeneas had actually met, here in the middle of the Bellagio's crowded lobby where discretion on everyone's part was a must, Raygene had no doubt that Trip's threat was more valid than ever.

Two days, he told himself as he appraised the quartet of grim-faced men he was bound to share his weekend with. *All I gotta do is keep these four fools from killin' each other for two days . . .*

AENEAS'S FIRST thought, upon laying eyes on the blacked-up white man sauntering into the hotel at Raygene's side, was one of pity. He just couldn't imagine Stanley Winston surviving the news that Raygene and Trip Stiles were here in Las Vegas together.

And this *was* Trip Stiles, without question. Aeneas didn't need to see a name tag on the man's chest to know that much. Raygene's homie looked exactly the way Stanley had described him four days ago: pink skin, black leather coat, black porkpie hat, all moving alongside Raygene and two other unidentified black men with the pimp-walk gait of a thug on parade. Blond ponytail swaying behind his head, left side of his throat festooned with a dragon tattoo, gold chains flashing. If Kid Rock had an older brother, this was him. Aeneas would have laughed out loud had he not been standing in everyone's clear view.

Raygene made a big production out of greeting him warmly, shaking his hand and hugging him tight to his chest like they'd known each other for ten years, instead of a mere twenty-four hours, and then introduced him to his crew, identifying Aeneas as "the best-selling author" who was there to interview Raygene for his next book. Shirelle's son couldn't have appeared more proud had Aeneas been the Pope, here in town to canonize him.

Meanwhile, Brew was his "security chief," and "Trip" and "E.Y." were homies from the old neighborhood, Raygene said. Brew shook Aeneas's hand and offered an easy "Pleased t'meet you," while the other two men made do with the handshake and little else, E.Y. mumbling, "How you doin'?," Stiles just nodding his head and smirking, amused by Raygene's writer friend for reasons he chose not to share with the group.

"What? Did I say something funny?" Aeneas asked, grinning right back at the white boy. Just to let him know how things were going to be: He might only be a "journalist," but

Aeneas wasn't going to let anybody punk him for a laugh. That wasn't the kind of writer he was prepared to play.

Stiles just looked at him and kept on smirking.

Sensing disaster brewing, and not caring to be shown the door of the Bellagio before he'd come a full fifteen steps inside, Raygene said, "Well, we better hurry up and get checked in 'fore they give our rooms away," and ushered everyone over to the front desk, careful to keep Brew and himself between Aeneas and Trip the whole way.

Aeneas still had no idea what this sudden jaunt to Vegas was about, but he did know one thing he didn't need to be told: E.Y. was Stiles's muscle, not just a fellow homeboy of Raygene's from Riviera Beach. This was obvious from the way the big man hovered at the white boy's elbow as they crossed the Bellagio's marbled floor. That, and the fact that E.Y. seemed to be carrying all the bags he and Stiles had between them.

Again, Aeneas's thoughts drifted off in the easterly direction of poor, unsuspecting Stanley Winston. His client was in Las Vegas, he'd brought Trip Stiles along with him, and Stiles had found it necessary to add a bodyguard/enforcer of his own to their traveling party.

The telephoned report Aeneas would soon have to give Raygene's agent was getting worse by the minute.

"SO YOU'RE a writer, huh?" Brew asked. Not with a hint of suspicion, but with innocent curiosity.

"That's right," Aeneas said.

"Just a sportswriter, or do you write about other stuff too? Like"—Brew shrugged to show this next was coming off the top of his head—"like maybe religion?"

"Religion? No. I've done a Hollywood profile or two, but I've never written about religion. At least, not yet."

Given the same room to share at the Bellagio, the two men had hit it off almost immediately. They didn't have much in common, a high school dropout from Texas and a top-dollar private investigator from New York, but the one thing they did share was both vitally important and instantly apparent to each of them: a genuine fondness for Raygene Price.

Brew was professionally obligated to care on some level for Raygene, but Aeneas was not; all Aeneas was supposed to be was a man writing a book about the Dallas Cowboy, somebody with no more interest in Raygene's safety than the tailor who made all his clothes. Yet Brew's natural instincts had told him right away that the New Yorker not only posed no threat to Raygene, but was actually inclined to look out for him. Brew couldn't imagine why.

Aeneas, meanwhile, recognized the very same inclination in Raygene's bodyguard, only more so. He had seen his share of security men for whom the protection of their employer was a job and nothing else, a task they had no personal stake in whatsoever, and Brew wasn't of that ilk. Brew truly liked Raygene. Nothing Aeneas had seen him do since they'd been introduced was outside the realm of a bodyguard's normal duties, yet his affection for Raygene was apparent to Aeneas all the same. And Aeneas was touched by it. Brew was more than just a consummate professional, he was a professional with a good heart, something Aeneas came across about as often these days as a Porsche without a vanity plate.

They were waiting for Raygene. He and his four guests had been checked in to the hotel now for a little over an hour, long enough for everybody to shower and change and gear up for the partying this Nevada escapade was ostensibly all about, and Raygene had promised to give Aeneas thirty minutes of his time here in the "writer's" and Brew's room before they headed out onto the Strip. The TV was on as they talked, but neither of them was paying much attention to it.

"You a religious man yourself?" Aeneas asked.

"Me? Naw." Brew shrugged again. "I've just been . . . wonderin' about some things lately, that's all."

"Like whether there is or isn't a God, you mean?"

"Oh, I know there's a God. That ain't the question. The question I've been tryin' to answer is, who is he, and why should I care about 'im? Why should anybody?"

"That's a good question," Aeneas said.

"Yeah." Brew's head bobbed up and down in agreement. "So what do *you* think?"

"What do *I* think?" Aeneas had to pause a moment to consider the question, not sure whether he should give the man an honest answer, or just a quick and facile one. "I think there is a God, yes. And I think, on some level, he has an interest in our welfare. But I also think his intervention in our lives is fairly minimal, that he pretty much leaves us to do all the damage to ourselves we like."

"So there ain't no point, really, in prayin' every day, and studyin' the Bible, and all that. That what you mean?"

"No, not quite. I'm just saying, there are no guarantees. You can do those things and a lot more, and never see a single dividend. Or you can do them once, and watch your cancer go into permanent remission. Sometimes, the water's going to turn to wine, and sometimes it's not. You never know."

"Then why bother with God at all? If he ain't gonna listen when you ask 'im for somethin'—"

"You bother because sometimes he *does* listen. And because the alternative is to believe in nothing. Atheism can be very liberating, and it's more easily explained than faith in something that can't be seen, but it doesn't give you much reason to hope for the future of humanity. For me personally, I find it's better to have a superficial belief in a God that gives a damn than to think our only chance of survival hinges on our collective conscience. Because our collective conscience, as history has clearly proven, isn't worth a shit."

Aeneas had said far more than he had intended to. Religion was a subject he generally felt uncomfortable debating with anyone; it was too subjective an issue to discuss without going around and around in circles with people. But something about Raygene's bodyguard had inspired him to open up a little and reveal a part of himself he ordinarily looked upon as no one else's business. They had barely known each other an hour, yet he had the sense Brew was actually seeking his counsel, a show of respect for an older man's wisdom Aeneas could not help but respond to favorably.

"If you don't mind my asking, why is all this on your mind? You in some kind of trouble?"

"Trouble? How you mean trouble?"

"Terminal illness. A death in the family. Impending divorce . . ."

Brew shook his head. "Naw. It ain't like that at all. I just . . . heard a man on the radio last week, and he's got me wonderin' 'bout some things. Things I ain't thought much about since I was a little boy."

"Such as?"

"Such as, whether this shit I do for a livin' is right. Bustin' people up for money. Didn't never used to bother me, but now . . . Since I heard this preacher on the radio . . ."

"He must be some preacher. Who is it?"

Brew was about to tell him, but then Raygene walked in from the hallway, using his copy of the cardkey without knocking because he was paying for the room, and that made his right to enter more important than their right to privacy.

"Come on, Brew, let's go," he said. He was dressed in fine silk from head to foot, giving him the look of a monarch's son about to go hunting for a bride.

"Go? I thought—"

"We were going to do thirty minutes to get started, Raygene," Aeneas said.

"Yeah, I know. I did say that. But somethin' came up, we gonna have to do it after Brew and me get back."

"Back from where?" Brew asked, immediately suspecting Trip's hand in this. He still hadn't moved from his chair.

"There's somebody we gotta go see. Lady frienda mine I hear is in town. Come on, come on, we gotta jet."

"Is Trip going with you?" Aeneas asked.

Raygene didn't like the question. "No. Why do you ask?"

"I thought maybe I'd hang with him and—'E.Y.,' is it?—until you get back. He grew up with you in Florida, right? I bet he could give me some fairly interesting background material, if he'd be willing to talk to me."

Raygene's face told Aeneas he had no love for this idea. "I think Trip's got other plans. They just ain't with me."

"So what time will you be back?"

"I dunno. We gonna be gone a couple'a hours, maybe more. I'd ask you to come along, 'cept this girl we gonna see don't take to strangers right away. I'm takin' a chance of spookin' her just bringin' Brew."

"Fine. But you can't make a habit out of this, Raygene. The deal was, I go where you go for the next fourteen days. I don't have a book otherwise."

"Sure, sure. I just gotta make this one run, then it's you and me, for long as you want." He turned his head again toward Brew, who was finally on his feet. "You ready?"

REECE WAS doing a late Italian lunch at the New York, New York casino, going over a list of baby names—"Raygene Junior" most definitely not among them—when she broke down crying for the second time today.

Her hormones were making her crazy. Her feet were swollen, her back ached if she sat in a chair for longer than ten minutes, and she was perpetually tired. Dog tired. Reece wasn't prone to self-pity, and even less to public displays of emotional breakdown, but this pregnancy business was proving to be more stressful than anything she'd ever tackled in her life.

It seemed like there was always something else to plan for or worry about. Doctors, hospitals, dietary restrictions, maternity clothes, baby clothes, breastfeeding, diaper services, nurseries, and baby furniture . . . Reece never did anything halfway, and motherhood wasn't going to be any exception. If everything about her delivery, and her baby's life immediately thereafter, didn't go down perfectly, it wasn't going to be because she'd overlooked something. She wanted this child, and there was nothing it could demand of her she wasn't willing to give.

But Jesus, doing it all alone was hard.

Her only saving grace was that she was used to it. She'd been alone essentially all her life. A drunk driver floating all over the road on U.S. 90 in Louisiana one rainy night in 1978 had pretty much seen to that. Living under the same roof as her maternal grandparents, Troy and Betty Patterson, for the next nine years hadn't been the same thing as growing up alone, exactly, but it hadn't been far off. The Pattersons had both been in their late sixties when fate had dropped their only grandchild in their laps to raise as their own, and neither had had much energy to spare for parenting a precocious nine-year-old.

The closest her Grandpa Troy could come was to show Reece from time to time how to defend herself against boys or men who might try to exert their will upon her. He was an ex-Navy man who'd done a little boxing in the service, so he knew a thing or two about using one's fists, and whatever else might be handy, to put bullies, muggers, and drunks in their proper place. Which, in his book, was either facedown on the ground, or six feet under it, whatever the sonofabitch made necessary.

It was an ethic that, by the time she left her grandparents' South Carolina home for good in exchange for a dorm room at Georgia Tech, had permeated Reece's approach to everything: school, friendship, even romance. Every challenge was a threat to be countered, every person a foe to be watched with a suspicious eye. She would work hard for the things she wanted, and defend her right to keep them with a pit bull's tenacity. Nobody was ever going to catch Reece Germaine napping.

And so far, no one had, with the possible exception of Raygene Price. Dropping her guard against Raygene had definitely been the high-water mark for her in terms of stupid mistakes. It was all going to come out right in the end—that was still a given—but by the time it did, she was going to have paid an infuriatingly exorbitant price in anxiety and aggravation. And like it or not, she was going to be stuck with having Raygene around as the father of her child, even if it was only for birthdays and holidays. It was either that, or go to battle with him all over again for visitation rights.

Sex. Why was it always so damn *expensive*?

Reece wiped her eyes and looked over the list of baby names again. Dante, Antoine, Jason, Baldwin. And for the girls: Nina, Alexis, Haley, Vivian. They were all nice, but none of them struck her as a perfect complement to "Price"; they were simply okay. To halve the task at hand, she almost wished now that she knew the baby's gender; she could have requested this information when Raygene took the paternity test she'd forced upon him, but had decided against it. She wanted to be surprised in the delivery room.

Much to her amazement, Reece was actually starting to cry again when her cell phone rang.

"I need you, Reecie," Peter Crockett said.

12

AENEAS MADE SOME EXCUSE to join Raygene and Brew when they went downstairs to leave, and spotted Trip Stiles's man E.Y. on the gaming floor immediately. Just as he thought he might.

He hadn't figured Stiles would let Raygene go off somewhere alone, unsupervised, and finding the white man's hired hand loitering near the hotel elevators, behind a bank of $10 poker slots, seemed proof enough that he'd been right. Especially when the big man tried to duck farther out of view the minute Raygene, Brew, and Aeneas stepped out of the elevator car.

Aeneas bid his two companions a quick and pointedly conspicuous farewell, then went off on his own, hoping to resemble a man in search of a friendly gambling table somewhere. But all he did in reality was circle back around in a large loop to come alongside E.Y., just as Stiles's man fell in behind Raygene and Brew on their way out to the street, maintaining what he must have thought was a safe distance.

Aeneas let him go for a while, continuing along the circuitous route he was cutting through the casino, then stepped straight into the hired muscle's path, blocking his view of the two men he was trying to follow.

"Hey, E.Y. You seen Raygene around?"

There was only one answer the other man could give without all but revealing what he was doing. "No. Scuse me."

Raygene and Brew were melting fast into the swarm of bodies on the gaming floor. Desperate, E.Y. tried to get around Aeneas, but Aeneas took a single side step to counter the move, turning up the wattage on the smile he was wearing to show he meant no harm. "Whoa, hold up. What about Trip? Hell, dog, I've got to interview somebody here soon, or my publisher's going to call me back home."

"Mr. Stiles is up in our room, takin' a nap. You gonna get outta my way, or what?"

"Out of your way?" Aeneas feigned surprise. "Oh, sure, sure. I didn't realize." He turned his body to let E.Y. slip by.

Trip Stiles's boy started forward, stopped after taking three steps, searching in vain for some sign of two people long since gone. He turned around, set his maddog on Aeneas at full power.

"The fuck you didn't."

Aeneas waited until he was too far away to hear, then allowed himself a good laugh.

"YOU NEED ME? Impossible," Reece said. "You told me you could handle any emergency while I was gone, Peter. You put me on the plane *swearing* you could."

"Reecie, I've tried, believe me. But I'm in over my head with this one, I need you to tell me what to do."

Reece let out a sigh so expansive it nearly knocked the cell phone from her hand and into her pasta. She'd *known* she'd never get out of Vegas without the wheels falling off of something back in L.A. "All right. What happened?"

"B-Candy got another tattoo," Peter said.

Janet "B-Candy" Williams (the "B" stood for "boy") was the lead singer of an all-girl grunge band Reece represented called NightBleeder, and she collected tattoos and body piercings the way a dust mop collected lint. Reece had long ago decided the twenty-year-old could no more go a month without buying another tatt then Anna Nicole Smith could resist buying another donut.

"Okay. So she got another tattoo. What—"

"It's an addendum to one she already had. The little *W* on her left breast, remember?"

"I remember. It's for Wicked Sly, her fiancé. Don't tell me they broke up again?"

"Not 'again.' For good this time. Her band mates tell me she caught him in the ladies' room at some club in Hollywood Tuesday night doing a male DJ and the coat-check girl at the same time. My God, can you imagine?"

Reece didn't *want* to imagine. "What did she do, Peter? Let's cut to the chase here."

"She added 'fuck' to the *W*, Reecie. That's what she did. The little twit's left tit is now clearly emblazoned with the epitaph 'Fuck W,' you could read it from across the street."

Reece lowered her head into her free hand, closed her eyes. "Oh, my Lord . . ."

"And in case you've forgotten what the girls are scheduled to do Monday morning—"

"The Victoria's Secret special. Of course," Reece said.

Getting the three members of NightBleeder the prime-time CBS gig had been a major coup for Reece, she couldn't have forgotten about it had she tried. For this year's annual television event, the lingerie giant was mixing things up a bit, signing female celebrities of various stripe to wear its scandalous attire right alongside its trademark stable of drop-dead gorgeous professional models, and Reece's clients were to be the youngest and most exotic of the invitees.

But now? Assuming Peter wasn't grossly exaggerating the conspicuousness of Janet's new tattoo, the deal was sure to be off. Victoria's Secret made push-up bras and thong panties, not flak jackets, and there wasn't a stitch in their entire product line that could reliably hide a *mole* on a woman's breast, let alone the word "FUCK" in giant caps. With a lead singer so labeled, the NightBleeder trio now had about as much chance of walking the runways on the company's one-hour show as a fat man with brown teeth.

"Peter, are you sure—"

"That it can't just be covered up somehow? I'm positive, Reecie. This thing looks like the animated message board on the Goodyear blimp, we'd have to wrap the girl up like Queen Tiy to fully obscure it."

"Who?"

"Queen Tiy. Amenhotep's wife. The Egyptian mummy?"

"Oh."

"Anyway, I thought about having it removed, of course, but that can't be done so soon after it was laid down, and even if it could, the combination of the two processes would scar the girl for life. Have you ever seen what an erased tattoo looks like?"

"Yes. Peter, what about makeup? Couldn't we—"

"Makeup's a possibility, sure, except that it would take hours to do, and Miss Candy says the area still hurts like hell, there's no way we could get her to stand still for the pain that long. Especially since the little idiot doesn't think she's done anything wrong, it's all Simon and I have been able to do just to keep her and the others under house arrest until I could speak to you." "Simon" was Simon Spencer of Triple Platinum Enterprises, the band's New York–based management company. "You've got to tell me what to do here, Reecie. Old Peter's plum out of fresh ideas."

"Okay, okay. Give me a minute to think," Reece said.

Out in L.A., Peter waited dutifully, calmed by the knowledge that giving Reece Germaine a minute to think almost always paid huge dividends.

Reece looked out across the packed house of the New York, New York bistro as she frantically brainstormed, seeking inspiration anywhere she could find it. As was the case all over Las Vegas this weekend, Raiders fans sporting silver-and-black faces were everywhere, most of them loud, rude, and carrying enough liquor to stock an Irish pub on St. Patrick's Day. Many were women, like the matching pair of blondes that was sitting at a table off to Reece's left. From hairline to halter top, they were mirror images of the same vertical-split motif, all silver war paint on the left, all black on the right. Oddly, the two men they were with were dressed like castoffs from a cruise ship, their Hawaiian shirts almost as loud as their Hee Haw brand of laughter.

Reece turned away, shaking her head, and started to examine the lineup at the bar, hoping to see some characters there less inexplicable and more thought-provoking. But then her gaze swung back to the silver-and-black twin blondes, and the idea she'd been fishing for came to her in an instant.

"All right, Peter, here's what we're going to do," she said into the phone. "Call Helen Parsons and make an appointment with her right away. Pay her whatever she wants to see us before noon tomorrow, price is no object."

"Helen Parsons? The makeup artist? But I just told you—"

"It's not B.C. she's going to work on. It's Darlene and Vida."

Darlene and Vida were the other two members of Night-Bleeder.

"Darlene and Vida? Okay, you've lost me."

"It's very simple. Helen's going to put a fake tattoo on each of them to match Janet's new one exactly, except that Darlene's is going to read 'Fuck A' and Vida's is going to read 'Fuck R.' Or vice versa, it doesn't matter, you can let them decide who gets what if they want."

"Sorry, but I still don't get it. 'Fuck A' and 'Fuck—'" Peter fell silent. But only for a moment. *Oh, father!* He broke out laughing. "W-A-R, 'war'! Reecie, you are too much!"

"There's an old saying in the P.R. business, Peter: 'When you can't get your client to shut up, get him to talk about politics.' Because that's the one form of speech in this country people consider most untouchable. Victoria's Secret can kick the girls off their show for being vulgar without any concern for a fallout, but if it looks like what they're really doing is trying to censor the band's anti-war beliefs, well . . . That would be downright un-American, wouldn't it?"

"And nobody likes to be called un-American. It takes too big a bite out of your quarterly dividend."

"Exactly. They might still cancel the girls' appearance anyway, but I'd be willing to bet they'd work with us instead. Play with camera angles and choreography to keep the tattoos hidden from view, or maybe even do some on-screen overlays in post-production to obscure them completely. The show's being taped, it's not running live, so that shouldn't be a problem."

Peter was still chuckling. "God, if this actually works . . ."

"It'll only work if the press gets word of the tattoos early, well before the girls go in for their taping Monday, and we back the tattoos up with action. It's not going to be enough to *say* 'fuck war,' they're going to have to demonstrate some actual conviction in that concept."

"What did you have in mind?"

"Photo shoots and interviews. Lots of them, as many as we can arrange before Monday. Make a visit to the V.A. hospital in Westwood your first stop the minute the paint's dry on Helen's work. And whatever you do, Peter, don't rehearse them. The dumber and less informed they sound about world peace, the more sincere they'll strike people."

"But what if they don't actually *have* an anti-war position? I've never heard any of them discuss the subject, have you?"

"I don't have to. I've heard their music. What those kids know about the justifiable rationales for war wouldn't make a complete newspaper headline. Besides—damn near every American male they might care to have sex with over the next ten years is eligible for induction. If only to keep getting laid, they'd *have* to be down on war."

"All right. I'm on it. Reecie, you've done it again. If you were here, I'd give you a big, fat wet one."

"Save it for the baby," Reece said. "And tell B-Candy I said the next time she wants to stick it to a philandering boyfriend, try marking up *his* body, and not her own."

"**GODDAMNIT**! You see that?" Trip railed. "That's why you don't send a fool to do a man's job—'cause the motherfucka's only gonna fuck it all up!"

"Wasn't my fault, T. That goddamn writer—"

"Follow two people, that's all I asked your simple ass to do. So the man got in your way, so what? You're bigger than him, ain't'cha? You know what *I* do when people get in my fuckin' way?" Trip stuck a hand in E.Y.'s chest and shoved, throwing him backward onto the couch of their suite. "I *move* their ass, that's what!"

Trip walked away before he could really lose his temper, started pacing the floor as his bodyguard rearranged himself on the couch, trying to recover what was left of his fleeting dignity.

"Somethin' ain't right about that man," E.Y. said. "He don't act like no writer I ever seen."

"Uh-huh. And how many writers you ever seen? Exactly?"

"Well . . ."

"Shit. The answer's 'zero,' bitch, same as it is for me. You ain't never met a writer before, and neither have I." Trip came back over to him in a rush, only to stop and hover right above him, leaving the threat of further admonishment unrealized. "But you're right. That ain't what the man is. I don't know what he is yet, but I know he ain't no writer."

E.Y. blinked up at him, surprised.

"He carries too much heat. You can feel it. You learn to do that shit inside. Man ain't Five-Oh, but it's somethin' like that. Ain't no doubt about it."

"So what're we gonna do?"

"For now? We ain't gonna do nothin'. Long as Raygene takes care'a bus'ness, Brother Aeneas—is that how you say the nigga's name, *Uh-nye-us?*—don't matter."

"And if Raygene don't?"

"Then you an' me gotta do it ourselves. And anybody tries to stop us gets fucked up. Raygene, Brew, Aeneas . . . Goddamn, what kinda name is that for a nigga anyway, Aeneas?"

"I think it's Greek," E.Y. said. "Some shit like that. But you pronounce it Uh-nay-us, not Ee-nye-us."

"Greek, huh?" Trip chortled. "Well, ain't that sophisticated. Come on, let's get the hell outta here, I didn't come to Vegas to sit in this goddamn hotel room all day."

"But I ain't got no bread t'spend."

"So I'll loan you some. Damn, dog, you sound like a little girl sometimes."

Outside in the hall, as they waited for an elevator, Trip said, "You know the funny thing 'bout fancy-ass names like 'Aeneas'?"

E.Y. shook his head.

"Aeneas, Jack, Joe, Bill—they all look the same on a headstone when you're dead."

The elevator arrived, and the two men stepped inside, laughing.

FOR SEVERAL days, Carmen Oliveras had been wooing someone who worked in food service over at the Bellagio. They'd been introduced by a mutual friend at a wedding and hit it off in a mild, understated kind of way. For now, their relationship was just a fling, nothing to lose any sleep over, but she was infatuated enough to make a point out of dropping in on her new lover at work every couple of days or so, if only to say hello.

Today, they'd chatted over coffee here at the hotel, traded silly innuendos about the sex games they would play the next time they spent the evening together, and said good-bye with a simple kiss. It was a short and sweet respite from the disappointment and rage that normally filled Carmen's days, and it had ended too soon. Before she knew it, she was on her way out of the Bellagio and headed back to the grind waiting for her at the Hard Rock.

Then, only thirty feet from the exit doors, she saw Little Rodney, hitting what sounded like a fifty-coin payout on a dime slot.

Little Rodney was a local nuisance, a fourteen-year-old black kid with cab door ears and a patch of peach fuzz on his chin who liked to dive into various casinos, throw some coins into a slot near the door, then run out again before security could grab him and haul his ass out by force. Most times he got away with less than he'd come in with, but every now and then, he made a few dollars he wasn't legally entitled to. Carmen knew for a fact that he'd once taken the Flamingo Hilton for fifty dollars in quarters.

"Shit," Carmen said.

Throwing Little Rodney out of the Bellagio wasn't her job, and the hotel's own security people would spot him and do the honors soon enough, but catching sight of the kid stopped her in her tracks just the same. She hated his bony, scruffy-looking little ass. She'd had to chase him out of the Hard Rock herself twice in the last ten months alone, and though she'd caught him on both occasions, his contempt for her authority, and everyone else's, galled her to no end.

He hadn't yet taken note of her. If Carmen wanted to, she could grab a handful of his nappy hair and snatch him off his stool before he had time to blink.

This isn't my hotel, she reminded herself.

But it didn't do any good. Eschewing the exit doors for some small shot at revenge, she made a sharp right turn and moved in on the kid, itching for a fight.

"Nice work, Rodney," she said, startling him.

He stopped shoveling dimes into his pockets, took a quick look around, then grinned at her. "Thanks."

"That's all you've got to say? 'Thanks'?"

He shrugged. "What you want me to say? 'Thanks, bitch'?" He laughed. "This ain't your hotel. This here's the Bellagio."

"So?"

"So you don't work here, so I ain't gotta talk to you. Do I?"

But Carmen knew that wasn't really what the little fuck meant. What he really meant was, *You aren't a cop, a real cop, wherever you are, so kiss my black ass.*

He was starting to laugh again when she snatched him off his stool and dragged him by the front of his shirt to the exit door only a few feet away, out into the Bellagio's parking garage. He screamed like a stuck pig, but they were outside the casino in mere seconds, not enough time to create much more than a minor scene.

"Lemme go, bitch! My money!" the boy cried, trying in vain to break her iron grip on his shirt.

There were security cameras all over the garage, and Carmen did a quick inventory of the ones she could see, searching for a blind spot among the array. She thought she found one behind a broad support column and pulled Little Rodney into it, then quickly broke the kid's nose with a forearm shiv that might have made gravel of a concrete block. His face was a bloody mask as he fell to the cold garage floor, his eyes alight with fear and shock. He tried to speak but couldn't; a horrified groan was the best he could do.

"What do you think now, asshole?" Carmen asked him, absently rubbing her blood-smeared elbow. "Think you have to talk to me now?"

Little Rodney was only fourteen years old, just a child with the mouth of a man she should have known better than to touch, but it wasn't Little Rodney Carmen saw lying there at her feet. It was Aeneas Charles. Him, and every disrespectful, condescending sonofabitch who had ever looked down upon his fucking nose at her since she'd lost her badge.

Carmen stepped forward to set her right foot down upon Little Rodney's throat . . .

. . . and caught herself. Sanity slowly taking hold of her again, and not a moment too soon.

"Anybody asks you how that happened, you say you threw down on me first," she told the kid. "Otherwise, I'll finish what I started. That's a promise. Do you understand me, you little prick?"

Little Rodney nodded, lacking the courage to do anything else. Carmen glared at him awhile longer, testing his sincerity, then walked away, through the garage.

Had she reentered the casino instead, via the same door she had used to exit it, she would have encountered a man crossing the casino floor she had been dreaming of killing for more than five years. But their meeting wasn't meant to be.

She and Aeneas Charles never saw each other, and in all likelihood, they never would again.

13

"WELL?" STANLEY WINSTON ASKED. Aeneas had briefed him over the phone just over two hours ago, but here Raygene's agent was already, calling him on his cell to see if anything out in Vegas had changed, hopefully for the better.

"Sorry, Mr. Winston. Still nothing to report."

"What? You mean Raygene isn't back *yet*?"

"I'm afraid not, no."

"But it's been three hours!"

"Actually, it's been closer to two. But you know how it is. Time just flies in the City of Gold."

Winston fell silent, but Aeneas could both hear his heavy breathing and visualize the sweat rolling languidly down his shiny brow in time to it. "To hell with this, I'm coming out there," Winston said.

"For what? Nothing's happened yet."

"Maybe not, but something's about to. I can feel it."

"You're paying me good money to keep Raygene out of

trouble, Mr. Winston. I've got things under control here, don't worry."

"How? You don't even know where the hell he is!"

"At this very moment, that's true. But as of fifteen minutes ago, he was over at the MGM Grand playing roulette."

Winston's silence spoke volumes about his confusion. He'd been trying to reach Raygene on *his* cell phone all afternoon, and Raygene hadn't answered one of his calls yet. "You've spoken to him?"

"No, but I've got eyes and ears everywhere. That's why you hired me, remember?"

The P.I.'s "eyes and ears" all belonged to Raygene's man Brew, whose cell phone number Aeneas had been clever enough to ask for before the bodyguard and his employer had departed the hotel this afternoon. He'd told Brew he might check in with him from time to time, just to make sure Raygene hadn't left the city limits, and Brew had generously agreed to take his calls, feeling empathy for a man who was only trying to do his job without any kind of assistance from Raygene.

"Really, there's no need to panic. It's only Friday, and we've been here less than four hours. If Stiles has something un-toward planned for Raygene, it isn't likely to go down until Sunday sometime. At least, that's my guess."

"Sunday? Why Sunday?"

"Because that's when the game is. This is—"

"Super Bowl weekend. Of course."

"It's damn near the craziest three days of the year out here. There may be no connection to the two, but I'm betting what-ever Raygene and Stiles came out here to do, it's connected to the game somehow."

"Oh, no. Please don't tell me you think they intend to bet on it?"

"That's one possibility, certainly. But it's not the only one. We'll just have to wait and see."

Aeneas sounded to Stanley like an oncologist discussing the five hundredth malignant tumor of his career; he'd seen this all before, and knew how to deal with it. Such unflappability was reassuring on some level, but it was troubling to Stanley too. Was the investigator merely the coolest customer Stanley had ever met, or was he simply failing to grasp the full gravity of the situation?

"Okay. Okay," Raygene's agent said. "We'll wait and see. But if Raygene doesn't show up soon—"

"I'll go out and look for him. Sure thing."

Stanley hesitated a moment, seemingly searching for one more salient question to ask before letting Aeneas go, then just said a lifeless good-bye and hung up. Leaving little doubt in Aeneas's mind that he'd be calling back in another two hours or less if Aeneas or Raygene didn't call him with some kind of good news first.

A FEW minutes shy of five-thirty that evening, Reece spotted Raygene before he could spot her, even though he was the one doing all the looking. She was playing blackjack at the Mirage, and Raygene and another man, who she suspected was his bodyguard, were cruising the game floor together, heads turning this way and that as they combed the house for her. She had been sitting at this same table for almost an hour now, and was up $60 and counting. She didn't want to leave, but whether Raygene caught sight of her at this point or not, her luck had just gone south, and she knew it.

She played briefly with the idea of running away, then rapped a hard nail on the table for the dealer, requesting a hit on the feeble 14 she was holding.

When Raygene inevitably saw her, he had to shake the hand of one effusive fan, and leave another pair for his bodyguard to deflect, before he could make his way through the crowd to reach her. By that time, a four of hearts had increased Reece's 14 to 18, the dealer had dealt himself 20, and Reece's night was already moving in the downward spiral she had predicted.

"Well, well. This really must be a small world, mustn't it?" she said, scooping her remaining chips off the table as Raygene slid up behind her.

"Reecie. I know what you're thinkin' . . ."

"But you didn't come out here to see me. No, of course you didn't." She eased herself off her stool and started walking as soon as her feet hit the floor, leaving Raygene and his man to trail after her like paparazzi chasing a movie star.

"No, no, I did. I'm all through playin' you, Reece, I'm gonna be completely honest with you from now on, I swear to God."

"It's a nice gesture, Raygene, but it's too late. I'm not interested."

A waitress carrying a tray full of drinks tried to slice between them, moving at full tilt, and Raygene had to slam on the brakes to avoid colliding with her, showing more concern for her safety than she apparently had for her own. Reece kept on walking and never turned around. She was almost at the lobby doors when her pursuer and his shadow caught up with her again, Raygene leaping ahead in a single bound to physically halt her forward progress.

"Reecie, this ain't funny anymore. I'm in trouble here. Life-or-death kinda trouble. You gotta listen to me, please!"

He was pleading with her, an act his lack of humility usually prevented Gene the Dream from even faking with any semblance of authenticity. Reece sighed, already tired of arguing, and studied his face, prepared to slap it at the first sign of disingenuousness. But all his face reflected back was need, and the barest hint of something she would have taken for fear had the man before her been anyone other than Raygene Price.

"I'll give you five minutes," Reece said.

They stayed at the Mirage and found the nearest bar. In Vegas's pre–Super Bowl state of human gridlock, they had to wait almost half an hour to get a table, but it was either that or seek one elsewhere, and Reece wasn't eager to follow Raygene even as far as across the street. She was looking for this meeting to be the only one they would have before late Sunday evening, if then, and the sooner it was over, the happier she was going to be.

"So who's your friend?" Reece asked when she and Raygene were finally seated, gesturing toward Brew, who stood guardian-like just outside the bar's perimeter, well beyond earshot.

"My security chief. Brew. He's a good man, you ain't gotta worry 'bout him."

"'Chief'? You mean, you need more than one?"

"Right now, I could use about a hundred boys like Brew. Though he has been actin' kinda funny lately." Raygene turned thoughtful. "Been readin' the Bible, askin' me questions 'bout God, and shit." He blushed at his use of profanity, another anomaly. "Sorry."

"Okay, Raygene. Tell me what you came here to tell me. If anybody's acting funny around here, it's you, and I'd like to know why before I bed down for the night."

It was all the invitation he needed to tell her everything. More or less. Naturally, he said nothing of Luis Ortiz's murder, choosing to claim instead that Trip's only blackmail weapon against him was the white boy's firsthand knowledge of Raygene's checkered past in Riviera Beach. But aside from that half-truth, the story he related to Reece was an honest one. A crazy childhood homie of his was threatening to besmirch Raygene's public image, and thereby destroy his football career, if Raygene didn't pay him 200 grand in four days. And Reece's Super Bowl betting slip was Raygene's only hope of paying him.

"Call the police," Reece said.

"I can't call the police. I'm right in the middle of contract negotiations, I gotta keep my name out the papers 'til I can sign a new deal."

"To hell with a new deal, Raygene, this is life or death. Remember?"

"I remember. But football *is* my life, and if I call Five-Oh, Trip'll put all my bus'ness in the street, and football ain't gonna be an option for me no more. You understand?"

"What he has to say about you is that damaging?"

"Let me put it to you like this: If the Cowboys or the league office hear just *half*'a what this fool could tell 'em if he wanted to . . ." He swiped the index fingers of both hands across his throat, showing her the modern baller's de rigueur gesture for death on the field of battle.

"And if I give you the ticket to give to him, and it doesn't pay off? What happens then?" Reece asked.

"Don't nothin' happen then. If he takes the ticket, game's over. Win or lose, I don't owe him nothin' after that."

"Wrong. If this guy's as bad as you say he is, he's just going to come back for more. That's how blackmailers work, Raygene."

"So? Long as he don't come back 'fore I get a new contract, let him come."

"I don't understand."

"See, Reecie, once somebody commits to payin' me—the Cowboys or whoever—they ain't gonna wanna renege on the deal just 'cause of some bad publicity. They'd know I'd sue their asses blind if they did. Too many ballers in the game today done things in the past they're ashamed of to make me the only one worth cancelin' a contract on. But if Trip starts talkin' before I'm signed, when I'm still a free agent . . . That's a whole different story. My market value's gonna go to hell, I might not get signed by anybody, for no amount of money."

Especially if I'm a suspect in a murder investigation, Raygene could have added but didn't.

"So you're asking me to hand this man a chance at one and a half million dollars just to keep him quiet for a month or so. Is that right?"

"He ain't gonna win no million dollars, Reecie. The Cardinals've gone as far as they gonna go, Oakland's gonna beat them boys by three touchdowns on Sunday. I played against 'em the third week of the season, I know."

"But the line's only Oakland minus-seventeen."

"Don't matter. Raiders are a lock, you can take that to the bank."

"Okay. If we assume your friend Trip—is that his name?—is just as certain of that as you are, you're still asking me to hand the bastard a shot at selling the ticket before game time for a hundred grand or more. Why the hell should I want to do that? Other than to help you out, I mean?"

"That ain't enough reason? To help me out?"

Reece wasn't falling for the faux self-pity. "I don't want to see you get hurt, Raygene, but you've put me through too much these last few months to want to do you any large favors. You essentially accused me of getting pregnant all by myself yesterday, remember?"

"Yeah, I remember. That was stupid, I'm sorry."

"It was worse than stupid. It was cruel." Reece stroked her abdomen with her right hand, already trying to keep her baby at arm's length from the seemingly clueless, overgrown child who had fathered it. "Now, I didn't want to have to bargain with you over a support agreement you should have signed off on willingly, on your own, six months ago, but if that's the only way I can get you to act like a responsible parent, so be it. Make it worth my while to give you the ticket, and we can go on talking. Otherwise, this conversation is over, and there won't be another one."

Goddamn, Raygene thought. *What the hell'd I ever see in this evil-ass woman?*

"My offer from yesterday still stands," he said. "I'll give you eighteen-five a month."

"Your offer was two grand a month, and it wasn't your final one. Your final offer was, I could name my price, I believe."

"Name your price? I said that?"

"Yes, you did. Are you going to sit there and deny it?"

"No, no, if you say I said it, I guess I musta said it." He

drained half of what remained of his drink in one swallow, put his glass back down. "So what's your price, Reece? We gonna finally cut a deal here, or what?"

"That's something I'm going to have to give a good deal of thought to, Raygene. This is an important decision for me to make, needless to say, and I don't want to rush into it."

"Reece, come on . . ."

"But before I'll even consider giving you the ticket, I'll have to see this homeboy of yours for myself. Trip . . . ?"

"Stiles. And that's a deal breaker, Reecie, I ain't lettin' you come within a hundred miles of Trip Stiles." *Oh, hell no.* Raygene had more reasons to keep the two apart than he could admit to, starting with all the things Trip might tell Reece that she wasn't supposed to know, and ending with Raygene's concern for Reece's health. Though he couldn't help but wonder if it wasn't really *Trip's* health he was looking out for.

"What, you can't fly him out tomorrow so we can talk?"

"I don't have to fly 'im out. He's already here. But that ain't the point. Point is, this man ain't nobody you need to meet. 'Cause he ain't just a blackmailer, Reecie. Trip's a whole lotta things, and every one of 'em's somethin' *bad.*"

"I do P.R. in the music business, Raygene. I deal with bad people who can sing and dance every day."

"It ain't funny, Reece. You ain't meetin' 'im, I'm sorry."

"Then I'll see you after the game on Sunday. Either a very, very rich lady, or a slightly disappointed one." She pushed away from the table to stand.

"Goddamnit, what the hell you wanna talk to 'im for?" Raygene asked, incensed.

"It's very simple, Raygene. If I give him that betting slip and the Cardinals win Sunday, I'm going to be thinking about him, and what he's doing with all my money, for a long, long time. I just want to know how hard I might be kicking myself, that's all."

There were a million arguments she could have made to support her case, but if there was a less disputable one than the one she chose, Raygene couldn't bring it to mind. The lady was right. Had their positions been reversed, he, too, would have wanted to know who he was being asked to make a possible millionaire. There wouldn't be any deal otherwise.

Still, bringing Reece Germaine and Trip Stiles together was something Raygene was loath to do. They were both highly combustible individuals, and mixing the two, even for five minutes, was likely to have disastrous consequences. Raygene spent a whole twenty seconds looking for a way around Reece's demand . . . and then gave up. Because as near as he could tell, absolutely nothing about the balance of power between them had changed since yesterday afternoon. The lady was still calling all the shots.

"I'll see what I can do," he said.

14

JUST LIKE IBM, Eldon Hawkins was in the information business. He bought it, he sold it, and he traded it in kind. Why some cops thought he was just a snitch, he couldn't imagine.

Dropping dimes on people for personal gain was only one of Eldon's numerous occupations. First and foremost, he was an entry-level bagman, just a guy who moved illicit packages from place to place all over Broward County, Florida, without ever being told—or caring to know—what was in them. But by night, he was self-employed, a pusher of all the 411 on the street he was able to gather. And a professional bagman, even one as low down on the food chain as Eldon was, was always able to gather plenty.

Longtime associates like Aeneas Charles understood this. Aeneas had been a client of Eldon's for years, or ever since the investigator had saved Eldon's life while working a stolen-child case in Pompano Beach.

Aeneas had come to Florida looking for Fernando Acuna, a speed freak and parole violator who'd kidnapped his four-year-old daughter from her mother in New York five weeks earlier, and when Aeneas eventually found him, he was only moments away from cutting Eldon's throat. Eldon had been making a drop at Acuna's apartment building, and Acuna had randomly chosen him as the benefactor of his next meth buy, whether Eldon wanted to donate to the cause or not.

Eldon knew a lot of cops and ex-cops like Aeneas who would have stood by and allowed Acuna free reign to do with Eldon what he pleased, not wanting to interfere in a squabble between two presumed dirtbags. But Aeneas never hesitated. He stumbled upon Eldon's mugging out in the building's back alley and waded right in, first turning Acuna's attention from Eldon to himself, then knocking Acuna unconscious when he got it. Eldon hadn't believed in heroes prior to that point, and he still didn't, but Aeneas Charles had impressed him enough that day to warrant the closest thing to idolatry the twenty-something bagman had to offer.

Aeneas had been occasionally taking advantage of Eldon's information services, at decidedly cut-rate prices, ever since.

Sometimes, all the P.I. wanted was the answer to a simple question. Who was the biggest peddler of underage flesh in West Palm Beach? Or where was so-and-so holed up in Lake Park where Five-Oh and his jealous wife hadn't been able to find him for six weeks? But at other times, Aeneas's needs were a little more complex. The inquiry he'd called Eldon with this past Tuesday was a perfect example.

A white dealer with an Eminem complex named Trip Stiles, he had said. *Tell me everything you already know about him, and then find out all the rest.*

Most of what Eldon was able to tell him immediately, Aeneas already seemed to know. Like he'd seen a copy of the man's rap sheet, so the black-and-white details of his criminal history were old news to him. The data he was fishing for instead was all pertinent to Stiles's present, not his past: Since he'd been paroled from Florida State Prison ten months ago and come home to Riviera Beach, who had the man been hooking up with? Who were his friends, and who were his enemies?

Eldon had known checking Stiles out would be tough sledding—crazed psychopath that he reputedly was, people weren't going to be anxious to talk about him out of school. But after two days, Eldon's data-gathering efforts had proven even more fruitless than he had been anticipating. Stiles had emerged from FSP last March and hit the ground running, getting into the cocaine trade with almost reckless abandon; that was about all anybody felt comfortable saying about him.

Then tonight, straight out of the blue and quite by accident, Eldon heard something about Stiles he was certain Aeneas Charles would find interesting: Eldon wasn't the only person in Florida asking around about him. A heavyweight crack dealer up in Memphis named Pierce had informants dropping Stiles's name all over Broward County as well, and with good reason: Stiles, it was said, owed Pierce a mountain-sized slab of cheddar, and was suddenly nowhere to be found in the Sunshine State to pay off. Any information on his present whereabouts was worth two grand, a little bird named Billy Dutton had just told Eldon over a full glass of Glenlivet.

And tomorrow, it was likely to be worth even more easy money than that.

REECE'S MEETING with Trip Stiles was set for eight-thirty Friday night at Rosemary's, a popular but relatively quiet upscale restaurant not far off the Strip on Sahara Avenue. Reece chose the venue. Raygene had suggested several other casino-housed establishments somewhat less urbane, never feeling quite comfortable in settings that weren't specifically suited to a party-animal mentality, but Reece nixed them all. Rosemary's was her favorite restaurant in Vegas, and its placid tone was likely to discourage any ideas Stiles might get during the evening to create a public scene.

She stepped into the taxi that would take her in all of five minutes from her hotel to the restaurant still not having any idea why she was meeting with Raygene's alleged blackmailer, or what she intended to say to him when they met. She had insisted on the meeting out of impulse, as a way of buying some time before she had to either give Raygene the Caesars Palace betting slip he wanted, or conclusively refuse to do so. The possible risks involved in making Stiles's acquaintance had never even entered her mind.

Assuming such risks even existed. Just because Raygene said Stiles was dangerous didn't make it so. Which was perhaps the real reason she'd demanded this face-to-face with Raygene's "homeboy": She wanted to see for herself how scary he was. If she was going to hand Raygene a wagering ticket with a possible net worth of a million-plus to keep Stiles happy, hell if Stiles wasn't going to have to convince her of his potential to do Raygene some form of serious harm.

Her research this afternoon had determined that there were at least three people in Vegas who'd be willing to buy the ticket off her now for as much as ninety grand. The best odds anyone could get from a sports book on the Super Bowl at present were 12–1, which meant somebody would have to bet a minimum of $100,000 to approach the $1.25 million payoff of Reece's ticket if the Cardinals were to win on Sunday. Ninety thousand wasn't the windfall she'd come here hoping to see, but it wasn't chump change, either. If she wanted to, all she had to do to go home a sure winner was stiff Raygene and Stiles, go back to her room at the Hard Rock, and make a few phone calls.

"Scuse me?" Reece's taxi driver asked.

She looked up, saw the big Asian eyeing her in his rearview mirror. "What?"

"It sounded like you said 'turn around.' Were you talking to me?"

"Oh. No." Reece smiled, blushing. "I was just thinking out loud, sorry."

They rode the rest of the way to Rosemary's in silence.

THOUGH IT was Raygene's normal M.O. to be late for all dinner dates, he made it a point to be early to this one, determined to do whatever he could to keep Reece in a good, cooperative mood for the duration of the evening. Everything else about this meeting she'd insisted on had already gone to hell, and he didn't want to make things worse by making her wait so much as five minutes for his and Trip's arrival. Especially since he and the white boy weren't exactly going to be alone when they showed up.

Raygene wasn't about to hook up with Trip anywhere and not have Brew nearby, and Trip wasn't going to let Brew come and not have his own boy E.Y. come, too, so the dueling body-guards' attendance at this affair had been pretty much un-avoidable. But fucking Aeneas Charles . . . There had been nothing Raygene could say or do to make the writer remain back at the hotel, short of telling him their book deal was off. Raygene had committed himself to giving the man complete, around-the-clock access when they'd shaken hands on the deal out in Los Angeles Thursday, and Aeneas was going to hold him to his word or walk. Which Raygene was sorely tempted to let him do, except that he still had use of the five-figure book advance the writer was promising him—Raygene had to have *something* to offer Trip if all other avenues of pay-ing the white boy off failed him—and, only somewhat less im-portantly, the prospect of seeing a hardcover book with his gorgeous face on the jacket continued to hold great appeal to Raygene's massive ego.

Hence, Aeneas was going to be attending Reece's party too.

"But you gotta sit at a separate table with Brew and E.Y.," Raygene had told him back at the Bellagio.

Aeneas said that was bullshit.

"You seem to be confused about the nature of a biography, Raygene. You can't write one from a 'separate table.' If I'm not privy to who you hang with, and why you're hanging with them, at least in some general way, I don't have anything to write about. I may as well just go home."

"But this is a personal meeting, dog."

"Fine. So I'll sit with Brew and E.Y. *After* you introduce me to the lady you and Trip are hooking up with, and give me a rough idea at least of what your business is with her. This isn't some kind of ménage à trois thing, is it?"

"Ménage à— *Hell, no!*" Raygene cried, aghast. "Look, you want the lady's name? It's Reece Germaine. She's an old girl-friend'a mine, like I told you before, and me and Trip just wanna have a nice, quiet dinner with her to, like, catch up on ol' times." Raygene saw something change in Aeneas's face, as if Reece's name had somehow struck him as familiar. "What? You know Reece too?"

"No. But I know *of* her. She's expecting your baby, isn't she?"

Raygene winced at the accusation, peeved. "Yeah. Who told you that, Stanley?"

Aeneas nodded. "I asked him for some background on you, and she was included in it."

"Okay. So now you know who I'm gonna go see, and why I'm gonna see her. So—"

Aeneas shook his head. "Not good enough, Raygene. She's the mother of your unborn child, somebody a reader of any book purporting to tell your life story would want to know something about. I need to meet her. In person. I'm on the next plane back to New York if I don't, and this is the last time I'm going to say it."

Raygene had no choice but to concede the argument, though he did manage to add a caveat to his terms of surrender: Aeneas had to ride out to the restaurant alone, apart from Raygene and the others, so he'd already be there when they arrived, too late for Trip to object to the writer's invitation to the dance.

Of course, Trip pitched a bitch anyway.

"What the fuck's *he* doin' here?" he asked upon spying Aeneas in the restaurant's waiting area. Fifteen people standing there with them, they hadn't even been seated yet, and already the white boy was threatening to have Raygene and company respectfully asked to leave the premises.

One hour. That was all Raygene figured he had before his Friday night, and maybe his entire life, went up in flames.

AENEAS WASN'T sure he could take any more surprises. First Trip Stiles appears in Vegas, then Clarice Germaine. Was there anybody who could land him in a world of hurt Raygene didn't plan to come in contact with this weekend?

Trip still posed the more tangible danger to him, of course, but Germaine was a wild card. The very fact that she was an acquaintance of Trip's as well as Raygene's—or so Raygene would have Aeneas believe—led the P.I. to wonder if child support was the only thing the lady wanted from Stanley Winston's client. It was for certain her presence in Vegas was no coincidence, any more than Stiles's was. There had to be some connection between the two, and that automatically made Germaine's motives suspect. Without ever having met her, Aeneas was prepared to dislike the woman immediately.

And then he laid eyes on her.

She was waiting at one of the two tables she had reserved for herself and Raygene's entourage when Aeneas and his four companions were eventually seated. She was wearing a white sweater with a scoop neck, and a dark blue, ankle-length linen skirt. The shoes on her feet were comfortable black flats, and a single, narrow braid of gold adorned her throat. Her brown hair had been combed straight down to her shoulders and left unrestricted by bands or clips. It was all very demure and unpretentious, but combined with her caramel-colored skin and electric brown eyes, the latter set in a face that was both hard and inviting at the same time, it was a look that no one descriptive term could do justice. Simply saying she was "beautiful" would have been a criminal understatement.

And how much of her allure was aided by her being the most radiantly pregnant woman in the house, Aeneas was afraid to guess.

AFTER ALL the introductions were done, Reece was joined at her table by Raygene, Trip Stiles, and Raygene's intriguing new friend, Aeneas Charles, while Raygene's bodyguard and a second man she'd been left to assume was Stiles's, retreated to the other, situated almost halfway across the room. Per Raygene's instructions, Reece had asked that each table be visible to the other, but for reasons ostensibly related to privacy, not in close proximity. She watched the two bodyguards lumber off now, clearly not the best of friends, and asked, "Are they going to be all right together?"

Raygene followed her gaze. "Who? Brew and E.Y.? Oh, yeah. They're cool."

"They don't look cool. They look like two men in love with the same woman."

Trip Stiles laughed, genuinely tickled. "That's good. I like that," he said.

Reece studied him, trying to decide what about him already irritated her more: that dog-choking-on-a-bone laugh he'd just hacked out, or his clothes. Nobody had told him this was a formal dinner, so a tuxedo would have been uncalled for, but his black leather ensemble, complete with Kangol hat, was taking Rosemary's casual dress code far too literally. He looked like somebody auditioning for a Run-DMC impersonators act.

"It's the Super Bowl," Raygene said. "Brew's down with the Raiders, and E.Y. likes Arizona. Right now, they ain't got no love for each other, but all'l be forgiven once the game's over."

"Besides." Stiles clapped Aeneas Charles on the shoulder, grinning, and pinched the writer's trapezius with false affection, making sure to put more firmness in his grip than was necessary. "Aeneas here's gonna go over there to play referee for 'em in just a minute. He just wanted to say hello to the pretty lady 'fore you, me, and Raygene have to get down to bus'ness." He squeezed Aeneas's trapezius again. "Ain't that right, partner?"

Reece watched with some fascination as the man Raygene had described—in so many words, at least—as the cowriter of his upcoming autobiography, turned a benign little smile in Stiles's direction, seeming so oblivious to the white man's hand on his shoulder that Trip just let it fall away, mortified to have failed so miserably at bullying another man in front of a woman. Then, to Reece, Aeneas said, "I'm afraid it is. Raygene tells me your business here tonight is a private affair that doesn't belong in the book we're writing, so there's no reason for me to sit in on it. Aside from the sudden reluctance I feel to go, that is."

Okay, Reece thought. On a scale of one to ten, Charles was a solid nine in the physical department, and his rap was a commendable seven and a half. If Reece didn't watch herself, the man was going to have her head veering off in directions that had nothing to do with her reasons for being here.

"I wish I could say Raygene's mistaken, but for once, he's absolutely right," Reece said. "It probably would be better for everyone if our dinner conversation remained just among the three of us. I'm sorry."

"Please don't apologize. I understand completely."

"Of course, there's no rush. I'm sure the boys won't mind if you stay until our drinks are served, at least."

She waited for Raygene to agree.

"Huh? Oh, sure, sure, why not?"

A circle of smiles at the table was broken only by Stiles, who was looking at Raygene like a fool the world would be better off having dead.

"So you're writing a book about Raygene. How interesting," Reece said. "Will this be your first? Or have you done this sort of thing before?"

"He's done it lots'a times before," Raygene said, answering the question for Charles. "The man's a pro."

"Oh?" Her eyes were still on the writer. "What else have you done?"

Charles said he was a freelance journalist who'd ghosted on three previous sports bios and written a number of personality pieces for a host of male-oriented publications, including but not limited to *Esquire* magazine.

"*Esquire*? When was this?"

Charles seemed to need a moment to recall. "My last piece for them was in October."

"It was on Keyshawn Johnson," Raygene added proudly, as if he'd actually read the article, and every incredible word was still fresh in his mind.

"Then you must know Danny," Reece said.

"Danny?" Charles asked.

"Danny Tanaka. He's a senior editor at *Esquire*, we went to school together at Georgia Tech."

She couldn't tell if Charles himself was aware of it, but Stiles's eyes were suddenly affixed to him, the white man suddenly interested in a conversation that had appeared to be boring him stiff only moments ago.

"I'm afraid not," the writer said. "I'm only an occasional contributor, like I said. The editors I work with are all fairly low-level."

"I see." Reece smiled. "Well, that's a shame. Danny's a terrific guy."

A brief silence held sway at the table before the small talk resumed, turning now to other, less poignant matters: the health of Reece and her baby, Raygene's contract status, what entrees Reece might care to recommend. Finally, their orders taken, the waiter arrived with drinks, and the time had come for Charles to remove himself to Brew and E.Y.'s table.

He stood up and offered Reece his hand, his bald head literally glowing in the restaurant's soft light. "It was a pleasure meeting you, Ms. Germaine. Best of luck with that baby."

"Thanks. I'm sure I'll need it. But my name is Reece." She held onto his hand right up until the moment he felt the need to withdraw it, and then he moved smoothly away. Had Raygene had any real feelings for her, Reece knew, she would have just given him good reason to fly off in a jealous rage.

"All right, gentlemen," she said to her two remaining dinner companions, devoid of all humor now. "Let's talk."

15

AENEAS SAT DOWN with his drink at his new table and immediately got the sense that he hadn't missed a thing. The two men already seated there looked like stroke victims at a nursing home; straw dummies could not have done a more convincing job of ignoring each other. The bodyguards' chairs were diametrically opposed, but E.Y. had turned his 45 degrees to both afford him a better view of Trip Stiles and reduce the one he had of Brew to the bare minimum. Raygene's man didn't seem to mind.

"All right, fellas," Aeneas said. "You're going to have to bring the volume down before somebody complains to the manager."

E.Y. just glared at him, his unwanted company here having apparently just doubled, but Brew found something worth a smile in the joke. For the last ten minutes, while E.Y. had been struggling mightily to deny his existence, Raygene's bodyguard had been busy trying to answer for himself a deep philosophical question: In his present mental and spiritual condition, could he kill E.Y. if he had to? Did he still hold the potential to do such a thing?

The truth was, Brew wasn't sure, one way or the other.

The problem was Galvin Morrison. While following his employer from casino to casino this afternoon in search of Reece Germaine, Brew had been allowed to entertain himself by listening to his personal stereo, and somewhere around four-thirty, he'd managed to find the evangelist's program on a local FM station. He only caught the last twenty minutes, but that had been enough to fill his head anew with Scripture and all its attendant guilt trips.

Morrison's sermon today had specifically revolved around Judgment Day, and how a man would ultimately be held accountable for his actions here on Earth when God abruptly brought the world to an end. Several of the Gospel passages the evangelist had referred to had taken some measure of root in Brew's mind, but one in particular was proving impossible to shake. It was Ecclesiastes 12:14, which read: "For God shall bring every work into judgment, with every secret thing, whether it be good, or whether it be evil."

Every secret thing—that was the part that reverberated with Brew. The idea that nothing was hidden, that everything he ever did in life—every thought, every action, no matter how small or insignificant—would be taken into account when God came to assess the value of his eternal soul . . . Well, that was some daunting shit.

Because Brew could deal with the shame of his major sins, but not his minor ones. His minor transgressions were the ones that stayed with him the longest and, on those rare occasions when he looked back upon them, hurt him the most deeply. All the homeless people he'd passed on the street without so much as a sideways glance; the heartache his cynical view of the world had caused his mother and grandmother; the women he had used and discarded like disposable silverware. Imagining himself standing before God, made to listen to a list of every such incident, and then asked to explain them away, was almost enough to bring Brew to tears.

He had never thought of himself as an evil man, but now he had to wonder. Because Morrison had opened up for him a whole new universe of sins to be ashamed of. For the first time in his life, Brew was beginning to *feel* like a sinner, and though this mantle had never meant much to him before, he feared it always might from this point forward.

So here he'd been sitting prior to Aeneas's arrival, sharing a table at Rosemary's with Trip's man E.Y., trying to determine how much of what he'd always believed about himself was still true, and how much a smooth-talking radio Gospel peddler had perhaps changed forever. Like his capacity for murder, for example. As much as he despised E.Y.—his professional incompetence, his superior attitude—could Brew still kill the man if his *own* life depended on it, let alone Raygene's?

He looked over, saw Trip Stiles's boy frown down at the appetizer plate their waitress had just set down before him. "This ain't what I ordered," E.Y. told the girl. "This look like chicken to you?"

The waitress apologized profusely, her pink face flushing red to betray her humiliation, and withdrew the offending appetizer to the kitchen as fast as her feet would take her. And in that instant, Brew had his answer: Yeah, he could kill this asshole, and enjoy himself doing it.

At least, for one more day.

. . .

"SO," **TRIP STILES** said to Reece, "Raygene says you got somethin' belongs to us."

She smiled as if she'd just been complimented on her earrings. "If you're referring to the betting slip, it doesn't belong to either one of you. It belongs to me. I thought I set Raygene straight on that point yesterday."

"Well, it ain't straight to me."

"No? Well, Mr. Stiles, how would you like me to put it so that it is? I made the bet, the ticket's in my name, and it's in my possession. That doesn't sound like it's mine to you?"

She expected that grating laugh of his to come again, but he surprised her by letting his brown-toothed smile—which was almost as unsettling, but not quite—suffice. "Raygene said you was a real hard-ass. I can see now why he likes you."

"Come on, Trip, ease up," Raygene said, temperature rising. He'd given his old homie explicit instructions on how Reece was to be handled tonight, and right out of the gate, the white boy was operating counter to them all. "Let's not let this thing get pers'nal."

"Who, me? This ain't pers'nal. Hell, I kinda like the girl myself. Even in her 'delicate' condition."

He tried a leer on her to see if she'd squirm beneath it, but Reece was unfazed. A leather-bound appointment book and a thick-bodied fountain pen had been sitting on the table in front of her since they found her, and she picked up the pen now, started fingering its surfaces with both hands as she spoke. "Look," she said calmly, "I didn't come here to be dicked around, okay? I came here to discuss the terms of a deal that'll get you out of Raygene's hair, and mine, forever. Not for six months or a year, but forever. Is that understood?"

"Yeah, it's understood. You gimme that ticket, and neither one'a you will see my sorry white ass ever again. Guaranteed."

"And anything you could possibly tell the press or the police about Raygene's past will stay in the past."

"Yeah, yeah, sure. My lips'll be sealed." He turned a tiny grin and shrug toward Raygene—*What's with this bitch?* "So where's the ticket? You got it with you now?"

"We'll get to where the ticket is in a minute. After we're through."

"Through? Lady, we *are* through. All this conversation is bullshit."

"Hey, Trip . . ." Raygene said uneasily.

But Stiles waved him off, his gaze still affixed to Reece, his patience for negotiating that which should have needed no negotiating all but gone. "No, fuck this. Let's cut to the chase here, all right? Either you gimme that goddamn betting slip or a million and a quarter in cash, I don't give a damn which, or I burn Raygene's ass to the ground. How's that? You got the picture now, sister?"

Reece didn't say anything.

"Reece, tell the man you got it," Raygene implored her.

"Oh, I got it. Did *you* get it? Mr. Stiles here just threatened you with blackmail in the most unambiguous terms, and I heard every word." She turned to Stiles, eyes aflame. "Which means he has something he didn't have before, doesn't it?"

"Reecie, Jesus Christ, I *told* you—"

Stiles was dead silent.

"That's right. He has a *witness* now," Reece said. "Somebody who'll be happy to put your 'sorry white ass' away for thirty years if you make it necessary for me to do so."

"Yo, hold up. Both'a you," Raygene pleaded.

Trip shook his head, incredulous and livid at the same time. The dragon ingrained on his throat was crimson and pulsating. "Lady, what *is* it with you? Didn't Raygene tell you who I am? *What* I am? Do you think because you're pregnant I won't fuck you up? Take that goddamn pen in your hand and drive it straight through your fat ass and your baby's too? Shee-it . . ."

"Trip, I ain't gonna let you—"

"No, no, Raygene, it's okay," Reece said, reaching out to place a hand on his arm, holding him in his seat. She'd finally gotten Stiles to go where she needed him to go to give her the courage to do what she planned to do next, and Raygene's intervention at this point would serve no purpose. "Our friend's a little confused, that's all."

"Confused? Who the fuck's confused?" Stiles demanded.

"You are. You think this is a pen?" Reece coolly took the cap off the slender black instrument in her right hand, revealed what appeared to be a tiny white spray nozzle. "Wrong."

AENEAS SAW Reece rise from her seat, lean forward across their table to point something at Trip Stiles's face, and instantly recognized what he was watching. He was up and moving toward them before Stiles had even started to scream, the white boy all in black falling sideways out of his chair, clutching at his eyes with both hands.

"Awwww, fuck! You fuckin' . . . !"

E.Y. and Brew had witnessed the incident as well, but Brew

hadn't seen any need to hurry over, his employer not being in any apparent danger himself, and E.Y. was just plain slow to react. By the time Trip's man stood up to follow Aeneas, Brew had made up his mind to stop him, troubled by the thought of what such a brainless fool might do to Reece and her unborn baby under the circumstances.

With all eyes in the house fixed on Stiles, Brew jumped up, spun the other bodyguard around, and hit him with a straight left flush on the nose, then doubled him up with a right to the gut and caught him before his unconscious form could crash to the floor. If anybody noticed as he dumped E.Y. back into his seat at their table, freely allowing the big man's face to settle gently into his salad plate, nobody said a word.

Raygene was bellowing, "Reece, what the hell you doin'?" as Aeneas appeared, restaurant personnel beginning to swarm the area to watch Stiles's violent and invective-filled thrashing about continue unabated. Reece, for her part, was showing Trip no mind, returning the trick Mace dispenser and appointment book to her purse, displaying all the worry and distress of a woman who'd dropped one too many tabs of Valium before dinner.

"Come on, let's go," Aeneas said quietly, taking her arm to lead her out. His relief was profound when she went along without argument.

"Yo, where the hell—" Raygene tried to take off after the pair, but the sightless Trip clambered to his knees and grabbed him by the trousers, blindly reaching for Reece.

"*I'll kill that bitch! Awwwwww, where are you, you fuckin'* . . . *!*"

Aeneas kept Reece moving toward the door, all before them stepping aside for the woman who had apparently caused all this chaos, some out of fear, and others out of respect. She was trembling in Aeneas's hands all the way out to the taxi stand, but she didn't look back once, until the car they eventually loaded themselves into the back of was off and rolling.

Whisking them away from the scene of the crime.

SEVERAL MINUTES later, referring to their taxi driver, Aeneas said, "You know, eventually we're going to have to tell this man where to go."

"Just drive," was all the instruction the P.I. had given the operator when they'd jumped into the car, and the man behind the wheel had been doing exactly that ever since.

"Anywhere will be fine for me," Reece said. Then, to the driver: "Pull over, please."

"Scratch that," Aeneas countered. "The lady's had a bit of a scare, she needs a few more minutes to get her head straight."

"My head is fine. I want to get out." She called to the driver again, "Pull over, please."

The driver did as he was told this time, worked the taxi over to the curb as Aeneas rushed to produce their fare before Reece could take off on him. The car was still moving when she leapt out in front of the Aladdin Hotel and Casino, and in her haste dropped her purse, spilling half of its contents onto the sidewalk.

"Shit!"

She started the laborious process of getting down on one knee to gather everything up, feeling like a whale trying to fold itself in half, but Aeneas beat her to it. He had her belongings collected and loaded back in her purse faster than she could say a word to stop him.

"Before I hand this back," he said, getting to his feet again, "I'm going to need to know where you're staying."

"That would be a bad idea," she said, taking a stab at snatching the bag from his hand and coming up empty.

"Look, you're a lady who can take care of herself, I get that. But there's a time to do your fighting alone, and a time not to. I don't know Trip Stiles very well, but I think it's safe to say he's going to take what you did to him tonight pretty hard, whether he had it coming or not, and that's not good."

"So it's not good. Next time we meet, maybe I'll have more than a little Mace for him. Give me my purse, Mr. Charles." She snatched at it again, only to have him pull it out of her reach, same as before. Their act was starting to attract the attention of passersby, but Reece was oblivious, and Aeneas didn't give a damn.

"You're either going to tell me the name of your hotel and let me take you there, or I'm going to follow you over. It's your choice," he said, holding her bag out to her.

Reece jerked it from his grasp and glared at him, almost as taken by his chivalry as she was enraged by his old-school male effrontery. In the end, her decision came down to the little gold ringlet in the man's right ear; the lights of the Vegas Strip were flashing off it like sparks from an iron foundry furnace, and try as she might, she couldn't take her eyes off it.

"The Hard Rock," she said. "But if it's all the same to you, I'd rather not go back there just yet."

REECE STILL needed to eat, and she wanted to do it in a public place, but she didn't want to sit at another bar or restaurant. As the Super Bowl approached, every bar and restaurant in the city was increasingly overflowing with drunks and wackos, and even if you could find a seat somewhere without having to wait an hour for it, you didn't have the space on either side of you to take too deep a breath.

"Isn't there someplace in this godforsaken town that's relatively quiet and uncrowded?" she asked Aeneas.

"I think I can meet the 'uncrowded' requirement," he said. "But the 'relatively quiet' one will have to be a matter of interpretation."

He took her to the bowling alley atop the Gold Coast, off the Strip on the opposite side of Interstate 15 on Flamingo Road. At ten o'clock on a Friday night, the lanes were modestly populated with kids throwing gutter balls and bowling league diehards working the kinks out of their 5–10 spare, but there was ample seating throughout the viewing area, and the snack bar was still serving hamburgers and the like, which suited Reece just fine. She figured a little cheese and beef fat wouldn't hurt the baby for one night.

"You a regular here?" she asked Aeneas, popping three French fries into her mouth at once.

"Let's just say, when I used to bowl league, we ended our season here at least once a year."

"You? A bowler? I would've never guessed."

"Yes, well, it's a skeleton in my closet I don't often flash before strangers."

"So this league you were in." Reece took a draw off the straw in her chocolate shake, smiled. "I take it it was made up of other 'journalists' like yourself?"

Aeneas smiled right back. It was what he always did upon stumbling across a woman smarter than he. "Actually, it was a police league. Newark, New Jersey P.D., I was on the force there for nine years. You're going to tell me your friend Danny Tanaka doesn't really work for *Esquire*, aren't you?"

"He did. Right up until a delivery truck flattened him in the crosswalk on West Eighty-second Street, last May sometime."

"I didn't think you'd bought my story. But when you didn't out me at the table . . ."

"I couldn't. I didn't know if Raygene was in on the gag or not, and if he was, then it had to be Stiles you were both trying to fool, not me. And why would I want to tip that asshole off to anything?"

Aeneas had to laugh. He couldn't remember ever being smitten by a pregnant lady before, but this one was steadily growing on him. "So what'd the poor man do to get himself pepper-sprayed tonight, anyway? Make a pass?"

"He threatened my baby." Reece's face darkened. "Said if I didn't start seeing things his way, he'd take my pen and kill us both."

"And what was it he wanted you to see his way that badly? If you don't mind my asking."

"I'm afraid I do mind, Mr. Charles. Seeing as how I may know now what you *aren't,* and what you once *were,* but I still haven't heard what you *are* yet. Have I?"

She thought he would take at least a moment to mull over his options, but he surprised her. "I'm a private investigator. Or, in this case, 'security consultant.' Raygene's agent hired me to keep an eye on him for a while."

"You mean, to keep his association with Stiles from flushing his career down the toilet."

"That's as accurate a way of putting it as any, I suppose."

"Then Raygene *doesn't* know. He thinks you really are a writer doing research for a book about him."

"Mr. Winston suspected he wouldn't exactly welcome me into the fold of his daily entourage otherwise."

Reece thought about it, shook her head. "No. Of course he wouldn't."

"I don't imagine I have to tell you this is all strictly between you and me? Everything I've just said was pretty much spoken out of turn."

He was hoping she wouldn't ask him the obvious follow-up question: "So why tell *me,* then?" Because as of yet, he didn't know the why of it himself.

Reece detected his discomfort, found herself oddly touched by it. He'd known her for all of ninety minutes, yet here he'd gone and betrayed a professional confidence just because she'd asked him to. As near as she could recall, Reece had never earned a man's trust so quickly, nor as effortlessly.

"Not to worry. I understand," she said.

"All right. Now it's your turn. My question was, what was Stiles so determined to have you 'see his way' that he found it necessary to threaten your life, and your baby's?"

Reece stalled for time by taking a bite out of her hamburger and languidly munching on it like a cow chewing its cud. Bringing this relative stranger into her confidence would be taking a hell of a chance, but he'd been dead on back at the Aladdin, and there wasn't much point in denying it: She had just made the Number One slot on Trip Stiles's shit list, and that was no place for a lady to be all alone. Especially when she couldn't even bend down to touch her toes.

"I have something he wants to buy, and we're having trouble agreeing on a price. Which is to say, I think he should have to pay one, and he doesn't."

"And this something he wants to buy is . . . ?"

She wanted to reciprocate his openness with her in kind, without reservation, but despite herself, she had to hesitate before giving him an answer. "It's a Caesars Palace betting slip. For a wager I placed there last May. Twenty-five grand on the Arizona Cardinals to go all the way."

"The Cardinals?" Aeneas rolled the idea around in his head. "You bet the Cardinals to win the Super Bowl back in May? Jesus, the odds—"

"Were fifty-to-one. Yeah. If Arizona wins on Sunday, I'm a millionaire."

Outdated as it seemed in these modern times, the word still demanded a moment of silence from Aeneas: *millionaire.* "Wow. So why does Stiles think he's entitled to the ticket?"

"Because he has the same misconception about it that Raygene does. They both think it belongs to Raygene, not me."

"And where—" When she turned her head to avert his eyes, pretending to watch a gaggle of teenagers on the lanes directly in front of them wrestle for control of a single ball, he knew there was no need to finish the thought. "Oh, wait. Twenty-five grand, you said. Where else would you get that kind of bread?"

Reece spun back around to face him again, said, "He did it as a *lark*! He no more expected to make a dollar off that bet than that I was going to end up pregnant with his baby. So if you're thinking about reporting him to the league—"

"The league? Why the hell would I want to do that? I'm being paid to keep Raygene *out* of trouble, not find new ways to get him into it."

"That's what you say, sure. But how do I know it's true? How do I know you're not just another parasite like Stiles looking to take Raygene for all he's got?"

"Is that what Stiles is doing? Trying to take Raygene for all he's got?"

"Of course. Besides being a thug and a lousy dresser, he's a blackmailer. He and Raygene grew up in Florida together, and apparently Raygene did some things in his presence that could land him in jail, or ruin his career, or both, if word were to ever get out. You haven't answered my question yet, Mr. Charles."

"What question was that?"

"How do I know you aren't running the same game Stiles is? Even if you showed me a valid private investigator's license—which you haven't, by the way—that still wouldn't prove anything about your intentions toward Raygene. Would it?"

Aeneas took out his wallet, slid it open-faced across the counter so she could examine the operator's license she'd just referred to. "No, I don't imagine it would. But look at me—do I look stupid enough to blackmail a man who isn't worth much more than the clothes on his back?" He put his wallet away and went on. "The evidence of this little Super Bowl party weekend to the contrary, Ms. Germaine, our friend Raygene's all in the red these days. His last financial advisor took him to the cleaners, and his present one's got him on such a tight leash, he has to ask her permission just to pluck lint from his pocket. If Stiles is demanding more than fifty dollars for his silence, Raygene's going to offer him an I.O.U.

"But then, I suspect you already know all this, don't you? Because you would have told Raygene to stick it where the sun doesn't shine if he'd asked you to pay Stiles off with *your* betting slip without convincing you he was flat broke first. Or am I mistaken about that?"

Reece didn't say anything. Suddenly, the sound of pins crashing all around her was like a deafening roar in her ears.

"Let me repeat something I've already said, Ms. Germaine. I'm on Raygene's side here. Not Trip Stiles's, or the NFL's, but Raygene's. If you level with me, I can help him, and I can help you."

"Right. By picking up the phone and calling the police."

"That would be my first suggestion, yes."

Reece shook her head, said, "No. We bring the police in, and Raygene's screwed. Even if Stiles went away for fifty years, he'd spend every minute talking about Raygene, trashing his image beyond repair. Or worse, depending on what he's got to say, maybe fixing it so Raygene got a cell of his own right beside him."

"So what's the alternative? Give Stiles your ticket and trust him to disappear with it nice and quiet like?"

"The alternative is, hold the threat of prison over his head and see what happens. One of the reasons I agreed to meet with him tonight was to give Raygene a witness to his blackmailing. And I did, I got Stiles to articulate his demands for me beautifully."

"Which accomplishes what, exactly?"

"Maybe nothing. But at least now, Stiles understands the game has changed. If we ever do go to the police, it won't just be Raygene's word against his, it'll be mine and Raygene's together. Which is no guarantee they'd lock his ass up and throw away the key, I know, but it's something for him to think about."

Aeneas shook his head. "Won't matter. We're talking about a potential million-dollar payday for the man, he isn't going to be scared off of it by anything short of a machete to his throat. And even that probably wouldn't suffice."

"Perhaps not. But hoping he'll spook is about all Raygene and I can do at the moment. Because we aren't going to the authorities unless Stiles forces our hand, and that's final. Do I make myself clear?"

She locked her gaze onto his and kept it there. Waiting. "Mr. Charles?"

"With one condition," he finally said.

"No conditions."

"It's a simple one. You call me 'Aeneas,' and I'll call you 'Reece.'" He smiled. "Unless you'd prefer 'Clarice.'"

The shift of topic caught her off guard. He was working her, maneuvering for position, and she had every right to be wary of the attempt. But he was smiling again, and that made him difficult to treat harshly.

"I've always preferred 'Reece,'" she said, "but I used to be rather fond of 'Firecracker' as well."

"'Firecracker'?"

"It was what my grandfather liked to call me back in Conway." She did a flawless rendition of her Grandpa Troy's South Carolinian drawl: "'Hey theyuh, Fyuhcrackuh, what's shakin'?' 'Fyuhcrackuh, what I tell you 'bout goin' up in that toolshed without askin' somebody?'"

Aeneas laughed. "South Carolina?"

"Nice guess. Conway's a lovely little stick in the mud roughly fifteen miles northwest of Myrtle Beach. Do you know Myrtle Beach?"

"Of course. Big resort town. Very popular among East Coast college kids during spring break."

"That's the place. I used to beg my grandparents to take me down there at least once a month, right up until I went off to school. It was about as close to real life as you could get when you lived in Conway."

"That bad, was it?"

"Well, only if you needed more excitement than you could get watching Miss Hemingway put the arm back on her rocker every time it fell off on the porch."

They both cracked up.

" 'Firecracker,' huh? I wonder why he called you that?"

Reece thought he was serious, until she looked over and saw him smiling again.

"It's been a lovely evening, Mr.— Excuse me, Aeneas," she said. "But I'm going back to my room now and go to bed."

AENEAS INSISTED on escorting Reece all the way to her door at the Hard Rock, and she couldn't muster enough of an argument to stop him. She was registered with the hotel under an assumed name, and unless they'd just been followed here, no one knew this was where they could find her, but it felt good to have the P.I.'s company all the same.

On the taxi ride over, they agreed to go with her suggested plan of total inaction until Trip Stiles gave them no choice but to abandon it. Aeneas was staying at the same hotel as the white man, he said, so he'd do what he could to keep a close eye on him. He didn't add that he intended to fall on Stiles like a ton of bricks if he made one move in the Hard Rock's direction, but Reece got that impression from him nonetheless.

They bid a quiet good night to each other and Aeneas left, more distracted than he realized. He blinked, and he was walking through the Hard Rock's gaming area, unable to remember anything that had transpired between the time he'd turned away from Reece's door to this very moment. Cursing his carelessness, he spot-checked his surroundings for any sign of Stiles or E.Y., and decided with some relief that neither they nor Raygene were anywhere in the house. He then crossed the lobby and exited the hotel, unaware that he had just come within twenty feet of the same ghost from his past he had failed to see at the Bellagio earlier in the day.

This time, however, Carmen Oliveras did see *him*.

16

E.Y. WAS SITTING in the lobby waiting for him when Aeneas returned to the Bellagio just shortly before midnight. Had he been anywhere else, Aeneas would have been surprised.

"Mr. Stiles wants to see you," the bodyguard said. His mood was always surly, but now it was downright foul.

"Yeah. I thought he might," Aeneas said.

They went up to Trip's room together, Aeneas generously allowing E.Y. the illusion that he was only going because E.Y. said he had to. Trip was pacing the floor of his suite when they came in, a lion at the zoo waiting for feeding time, and Raygene was just watching him do it, sitting in a chair with an exhausted, hangdog look on his face. There was no sign of Brew.

"Where is she?" Trip said to Aeneas. "I want the name of the goddamn hotel, and I want a room number."

Aeneas made a modest attempt to appear confused by the order. "If you're referring to Ms. Germaine—"

"You goddamn right I'm talkin' 'bout 'Ms. Germaine'!"

"—I don't *know* the name of her hotel. What the hell did she do to you, anyway?"

Trip covered the distance between them in an instant, bringing his face mere inches from Aeneas's to give the P.I. a closer look at the red, tortured eyes still watering heavily in his head. "Motherfucka, you *know* what she did to me! She *Maced* my ass! Now, are you gonna tell me where she is, or am I gonna have to fuck you up too?"

" 'Too'?"

"Nigga . . ."

"I can't tell you what I don't know, Mr. Stiles. All I did was put the lady in a taxi. I've got no idea where it went."

"Bullshit!"

"No, it's the truth. Sorry."

Trip maddogged him for most of a minute, finally turned around to address Raygene. "Ray, you better talk to this fool. I ain't got no patience for this shit, all right?"

"Look here, Aeneas," Raygene said, sounding more like a pistol-whipped bank teller than a professional football star. "If you know where Reecie is, you need to tell us. Right now. I know you think you're protectin' her and all, but you ain't gotta worry 'bout that. I ain't gonna let nothin' happen to her, I promise."

He had said it as if he actually believed it, that he had the power to keep Stiles from doing whatever he pleased to Reece should the white man ever find her. Aeneas had to wonder how deluded the poor bastard could get.

"I appreciate that, Raygene," he said. "But I'm afraid it doesn't change the fact that I don't know where the lady's staying."

"Yeah? Then where the fuck you been all this time?" E.Y. asked, inserting himself into the conversation for the first time. "If you ain't been with her—"

Aeneas showed him a look he usually reserved for small, unwittingly funny children. "This is Las Vegas, dog. You'd be better off asking me where I *haven't* been."

"E," Trip said, exasperated. Not simply speaking the man's name, but giving him an order.

The bodyguard stepped forward to grab hold of Aeneas and the P.I. set himself to resist. In five seconds, the room was going to be the staging area for a full-scale mêlée.

"The man said he don't know nothin'!"

Raygene's outburst froze everybody, including Trip Stiles. The white boy blinked at him, startled.

Raygene was on his feet now, trembling with a rage all his own. "Leave 'im the fuck alone! I told you, I'll find Reece myself in the mornin'."

Another split-second of silence passed, and then Trip started laughing. By intent, feeding the tension in the room, rather than relieving it.

"Go ahead and laugh, Trip. But you touch one motherfuckin' hair on this man's head or hers, and I don't care what you threaten' to do t'me, I'm stickin' my *foot* up your ass."

Trip kept right on chuckling, looked over at his boy E.Y. to get him started too. Without warning, Raygene came at Trip in a rush, then veered to his left at the last instant to throw a booming right hand at Trip's bodyguard instead. Failing to consider the off-chance that Raygene might actually be gunning for him, E.Y. rushed to place himself between Raygene and his employer and stepped right into the blow. He took the brunt of Raygene's punch and folded up like a broken lawn chair, only conscious enough upon hitting the floor to roll his head this way and that while mumbling something completely incoherent.

Trip, of course, became homicidal at this point, but Raygene had him by the throat before he could move a muscle. And only then did the white man realize he'd made an old mistake: He'd forgotten how big Raygene was. Trip had always had the advantage against his old homeboy where matters of the will were concerned, and this was generally enough to overcome the black man's superior size and strength. But on those rare occasions when he slipped up and let Raygene strike the first blow, Trip was doomed to wind up like this: held fast in one unbreakable submission hold or another, struggling uselessly to escape as Raygene waited for him to either admit defeat or pass out.

Gazing into Trip's bulging red eyes, the fingers of his right hand bearing down so tightly on the white man's throat Aeneas feared they might break the skin, Raygene said, "This ain't no laughin' matter, Trip, all right? You wanna fuck with me, that's one thing, I can handle that. But you ain't gonna hurt none'a my friends. Not Reecie, not her baby—not *nobody*. You understand?"

Behind them, E.Y. had finally lost consciousness, and Trip was now losing his, his feeble attempts to break Raygene's grip petering down to nothing. Raygene lifted him another inch toward the ceiling to hold his attention, then went on. "Now, I told you I'm gonna get you your fuckin' money, and I will. But I'm gonna do it *my* way. If that ain't good enough for you"—he tossed Trip aside like a man dropping a trash bag into the garbage—"then I guess I'm just gonna have'ta kill somebody for *real.*"

He turned without another word and headed for the door, nodding for Aeneas to follow as he stepped over E.Y.'s supine form.

As Trip busied himself with the task of learning how to breathe again, Aeneas held back a grin, impressed with Raygene's sudden style, and said, "Hold up." He got down on one knee to pat E.Y. down, then took possession of the handgun he found holstered under the bodyguard's left arm. "Might be a good idea to take this."

Raygene nodded his assent and the two men disappeared out into the hall.

"**CAN'T NONE'A** this go in the book."

"No. I don't think it should, either."

"And ain't nobody callin' the police, neither, so don't even bother makin' the suggestion."

"Whatever you say, Raygene."

"You don't know the whole story, Aeneas. What you just heard in there . . . That ain't *half'a* what's really goin' on here."

Aeneas shrugged. "You're being blackmailed. Who needs the other half?"

Surprise wiped Raygene's face as clean as a slate. "Who told you that? Reecie?"

"You just told the man you didn't care what he threatened to do to you. What *else* could that mean?"

"Okay. So you figured it out. The important thing is, Trip's ass is straight now, he ain't gonna fuck with you again."

"And Ms. Germaine?"

"He ain't gonna fuck with her, neither. *Especially* not with her. But in order for me to *guarantee* that . . ."

"Sorry, Raygene, but I still can't help you. I just put her in a cab, like I said, I don't know where she's staying."

Raygene studied Aeneas's face for a long beat, eventually reached the conclusion that the "writer" was either telling the truth or was too good a liar to break down under further questioning.

"Damn," he sighed.

He and Aeneas were in the latter's hotel suite, along with Brew, who'd been sitting there reading a book when they came in. The book looked like a brand-new copy of the King James Version of the Bible, but Aeneas couldn't be sure. The body-guard had closed the big paperback up and set it beside him on the seat of his chair as soon as he'd realized he had com-pany.

"You should'a let me come with you," Brew said.

Raygene looked over at him and snorted. "Why? So we could'a *all* wound up dead? After what you did to that fool E.Y. back at the restaurant, I can't let you and him be in the same room together ever again."

"I did what I had to do. He was goin' over to your table to jack somebody up, I couldn't just let his ass go."

Aeneas said to Raygene, "You mean, you just—"

"Fucked homeboy up for the second time tonight. Yeah." His teeth flashed in a broad grin as he rubbed the knuckles on his right hand. "I don't know how that boy's s'posed to be guardin' Trip's body when he can't even guard his own."

All three men got a good laugh out of that, then quickly grew solemn again. "That was some smart thinkin', takin' his piece off 'im," Raygene told Aeneas. "I should'a thought'a that myself."

"It doesn't mean they won't come knocking on that door any minute, regardless." Aeneas popped the magazine from the hilt of E.Y.'s semiauto, tossed it over for Brew to catch like a baseball. "But assuming this was the only weapon they got past airport security this morning, I figured it might at least slow 'em down not to have it. Trip's not licensed to carry too, is he?"

"Hell no," Raygene said.

"Then unless they strapped up here in Vegas, they should both be unarmed. For now."

"Yeah. Still, I gotta find Reecie. You sure—"

"I'm sure. Look, what's she got to do with you and Trip anyway? Trip's not blackmailing her too, is he?"

Aeneas already knew the answer to both of these questions, but his facade of ignorance concerning Reece Germaine required him to ask them anyway. Plus, he was curious to see how Raygene would respond.

"Naw, naw," Raygene said. "If it wasn't for me, Trip wouldn't even know the girl was alive. She was just tryin' to do me a favor, is all, and now I got her knee deep in shit. If I don't find her 'fore Trip does—"

"I don't think you really have to worry about that. You know her better than I do, of course, but she doesn't strike me as a lady who'd *let* Trip find her after tonight."

"How do you mean?"

"He means she's gonna stay low for a while," Brew said, the servant catching on faster than his master. "Change her name at the hotel, hang in her room 'til tomorrow mornin', then go home, probably." He turned to Aeneas. "Right?"

"If she's smart," Aeneas said. "And she is smart, isn't she?"

Raygene thought about it, and came to the conclusion that Aeneas was right. He'd called around to the various major hotels in town today trying to locate Reece before he and Brew had begun to comb the streets for her, and no one named "Clarice Germaine" had been registered anywhere. Providing she stayed in her room like Brew was suggesting, wherever that room was, Trip had about as much chance of finding her in all of Vegas's pre–Super Bowl chaos as a vacant penthouse suite on the Strip going for just $35 a night.

"I'd still like to find her," Raygene said. "Just so I can have her back if she needs me."

"All right, I tell you what. I'm a journalist, aren't I? What we journalists don't know, we generally have a way of finding out. I'll make a few calls in the morning and see if I can't locate her. How's that?"

Raygene nodded. "Yeah, yeah. I'd really appreciate that, dog."

"And as for Trip . . . What do you intend to do about him? Surely you aren't going to pay him like you said?"

Raygene could only wish it were that simple. Whatever Aeneas thought the white boy had on him that was worth being blackmailed over, it couldn't be as bad as the reality of it. When a man could frame you for murder, there weren't a whole lot of things you *could* do with him other than pay him off and hope for the best.

"I ain't quite figured that out yet. But I'll think of somethin'. You just concentrate on findin' Reecie for me, and leave Trip and E.Y. up to me."

"And me," Brew added, lest his loyalty be overlooked. "I'm sleepin' on the couch in your room tonight. Just in case."

THE FIRST thing Aeneas did when Brew and Raygene left him was check his cell phone messages. He'd received two calls while he'd been out tonight, and he'd left them both unheeded until now, certain that a still frantic Stanley Winston was behind each. But he was wrong. It turned out that only the first call was from Winston; the other had been made by Aeneas's Florida informant Eldon Hawkins. He'd come up with some interesting info on Stiles, Eldon said succinctly, and he thought Aeneas should call him back to hear what it was right away.

Aeneas checked his watch, saw that it was well after 1 A.M. here, 4 A.M. out in Florida. Like most useful snitches, Eldon didn't have much use for sleep, but four in the morning was a less than optimum time to try reaching anyone by phone. Aeneas almost put off calling Eldon back until morning. But then his cautious side told him too much had gone down tonight to take anything for granted, so he rang Eldon's number before retiring to bed.

Minutes later, he drifted off to sleep feeling grateful that he did, as visions of a luminously beautiful pregnant woman danced playfully in his head.

TRIP STILES, meanwhile, did not sleep at all that night. He was too busy scheming.

He still had the ominous Mr. Pierce of Memphis, Tennessee, to worry about, of course, and getting the cheddar to pay the dealer by Tuesday morning remained at the very top of Trip's priority list. But now the little matter of revenge was demanding the white boy's attention as well, and its voice would not be stilled. There were just too many people who needed killing to ignore. In one day alone, Raygene's cunt girlfriend Reece Germaine had sprayed Mace into Trip's face in a crowded restaurant; Aeneas Charles, the so-called sports journalist, had helped the fat bitch escape afterward; and fucking Raygene himself had thrown down not only on E.Y., but on Trip too, leaving them both seeing stars and counting teeth without having suffered so much as a scratch of his own. Try as he might, Trip couldn't remember the last time he'd been so dissed and abused within a single twenty-four-hour period.

Raygene and his two associates were going to have to answer to Trip, and answer him with their lives.

First, however, Trip had to get that million-dollar betting slip off Reece. Obscured by rage as his vision was, he could still see that much clearly enough. And there was no way he could trust Raygene to get the slip for him, either; Raygene was too big of a fuck-up, and his alliances could no longer be taken for granted. No, Trip had to find Reece, and relieve her of the ticket, all by himself. And *fast*.

The question was, how? Before Charles had shown up in Trip's suite Friday night, and Raygene started throwing punches, Raygene had *sworn* he didn't have any idea where Reece was staying, and Trip, despite himself, had believed him. He didn't want to, but he did. All Raygene knew, he said, was that he'd found Reece at a gambling table at the Mirage, after someone at the front desk had already told him over the phone no guest by the name of "Clarice Germaine" was registered there. He'd called more than two dozen Vegas hotels that morning, Raygene said, and was told the same thing at each one, an almost ironclad indication that wherever Reece was staying, she was checked in under a phony name.

Which, if true, reduced Trip's chances of finding the bitch before Sunday's game to one man: Aeneas Charles. Because, whereas Raygene's claims of ignorance regarding Reece's hotel accommodations might be genuine, Trip was utterly convinced that Charles's were bogus. Just as his sportswriter front was. Trip had no doubt about this last point now, though he still couldn't figure out what Charles *was*. Dog walked the walk of the personal secuirty professional E.Y.'s sorry ass was supposed to be, but Raygene already had one of those. What the hell did he need with two?

In any case, who- or whatever Aeneas Charles really was, other than a writer of some kind, he probably had the 411 Trip needed. He was a Boy Scout; a knight in shining armor who fancied rescuing damsels in distress. He hadn't just put the bitch in a cab and waved good-bye, he'd jumped in the cab right alongside her and shown her to her goddamn door. So he knew where Reece was staying, all right, hell yes. He just wasn't likely to ever share the information, no matter what Trip tried to threaten him with. Trip knew a hard-ass when he saw one, the kind of man whose grip on something you could waste half your life trying to break, and Aeneas Charles was a hard-ass.

If he'd still had access to E.Y.'s nine, Trip might have thought it worth a shot to ask Charles where he could find Reece anyway. But he didn't. As if Charles hadn't been impediment enough to Trip's business, Charles was strapped now, and that rendered him all but untouchable, at least until Trip and E.Y. could get strapped up again themselves.

The sun was almost on the rise over the Nevada desert Saturday morning, and Trip was still rolling around in his bed, trying to devise a method for finding Reece Germaine that didn't involve Aeneas Charles's cooperation. Then, just before 6 A.M., it all came together for him. As plans went, it was complicated as hell, and every stage would take time, but with a little luck, it would probably work.

Trip didn't ordinarily care to rely on luck. But after Friday, he had to think he was way overdue to get lucky.

17

MUCH LIKE MICHAEL BREWSTER, Carmen Oliveras was suffering a crisis of conscience. Or she had been, anyway. Come the end of her own sleepless Friday night, any worries about whether or not she could kill Aeneas Charles and live with herself afterward were gone, reduced to vapor by the hatred she still harbored for the man.

Naturally, her resolve to see Aeneas dead may have been the direct result of her eventual decision to let somebody else commit his murder for her. Guilt was always easier to work around if you could put a surrogate between yourself and the act that produced it, especially when the surrogate you had in mind was a crazy like Lenny. Asking Lenny to kill somebody wasn't so much conspiring to commit murder as it was lending some purpose to an inevitable, and otherwise pointless, event.

Lenny and Carmen had once been a hot item. Carmen had been looking for somebody easy on the eye who was good for a few laughs, and there Lenny had been. The fireworks lasted almost three months. But then the toll of having a lover who had both a heroin habit and a hair-trigger temper that seemed to turn every disagreement into an aggravated assault got to be too much for Carmen, and she broke the relationship off.

Lenny took their split hard, but did nothing more in the way of complaint than call Carmen several times a week in the middle of the night for a month to demand, then plead for a reconciliation. Neither approach worked. Though she felt sorry for the self-destructive dumbshit, Carmen held her ground, and after a while, her hotheaded ex got the picture and let her be. Still, Lenny made it clear that if Carmen ever wanted to try again, all she had to do was call.

It was a call Carmen had never thought twice about making until now.

They met at Lenny's place in Meadows Village early Saturday morning. Both the apartment and its owner looked exactly the way Carmen remembered them: tired, disheveled, and in need of a thorough cleaning. But Lenny still had the magic physically; Carmen could feel the draw of those hard, lean muscles, and the grin that promised untold pleasures, like a bull to the toreador's cape.

"So what is it that you need?" Lenny asked, right off.

"Who said I needed anything?"

"Come on, baby. You left me because I'm fucking insane, not because I'm stupid, remember?"

Carmen spelled it out, seeing no point in further denials, spinning things so it sounded like she had a reason to fear Aeneas, and not the other way around.

"So what is it you want me to do, exactly? Kill him?" Lenny had asked the question while lighting a Kool, treating the subject of murder with all the gravity and respect as the score of last night's UNLV game.

"Yes," Carmen said.

Lenny made a show of thinking it over, blue eyes rolling upward to the ceiling, then produced a little shrug. "Hell, for you? Why not?"

"Just like that? 'Why not?'"

"What do you want me to say? No?"

"You haven't asked me for anything in return yet, Lenny."

"Haven't I? Maybe that's 'cause I don't want anything in return. You ever think of that?"

"No," Carmen said flatly.

And her old flame's laughter threatened to bring the walls straight down upon them.

INCREDIBLY, with everything else that was going on around him, Raygene awoke Saturday morning finally ready to work with Aeneas Charles on his biography. But the writer wasn't in his room when Raygene and Brew went to look for him, shortly after 9 A.M.

Just as Aeneas had told Trip the night before, this was Las Vegas, after all, where a man could find a million places to eat a good meal and have a good time, so there shouldn't have been anything suspicious about his being gone. But Raygene thought he knew where Aeneas was, all the same. He was either out looking for Reece, or he was already with her. Raygene had seen the way the man had looked at his former one-night stand at dinner Friday night, and had recognized the gaze as one of something other than innocent admiration. Aeneas had been taken by Reecie, and she him, and if Raygene had been just a little more emotionally invested in the woman who was due in less than a month to deliver his third child, he would have been pissed as hell at them both.

But all Raygene could do was *like* Reecie, just as he was learning to like Æneas, so if the two wanted to hook up after the baby was born, get married and have six kids of their own someday, Raygene had no problem with it. As long as Reece gave him that Super Bowl betting slip before tomorrow. That was all he really wanted from either one of them. Because after last night, nothing but the slip was going to keep Trip from hurting somebody. Raygene's old homie had finally pushed him hard enough to make Raygene push back, and nothing ever made Trip more dangerous than having somebody he was trying to bitch, bitch *him* up instead.

It wasn't that Raygene had any regrets about what he'd done last night. He merely understood that it was likely to have consequences. To keep those consequences to a minimum, he had to throw Trip a bone. Give him his goddamn wagering ticket and let him cool off for a while. It wouldn't be enough of an appeasement to make the white boy forgive and forget, Raygene knew, but it might buy Raygene a little time to think.

And Raygene was relatively certain that if he could just get that, he could figure out a way to make Trip Stiles disappear forever.

THE MAN who went by the name of "Pierce" was fairly certain that Luis Ortiz really *didn't* know where his friend Trip Stiles was after Ortiz lost both the index and ring fingers of his right hand, but Pierce ordered his associate with the garden shears to relieve the dumbshit of his pinkie as well, just to make sure.

And Ortiz was most definitely a dumbshit, that much they knew for certain. He'd just admitted to leaving the safe house Trip had apparently put him up in, where they would have had little or no chance of finding him, to visit his old lady, whose crib was of course the first place they went to look for him. Like he couldn't have imagined beforehand that if they couldn't find Trip, they'd do the next best thing and find some of his homeboys, one of whom was almost certain to know something about the white boy's present whereabouts.

Sadly for Pierce, however, even three severed fingers later, Ortiz was not that homeboy. He simply didn't have the information they were seeking. All he had to tell them was some bullshit story about a fake murder, and Raygene Price—yeah, *that* Raygene Price, Ortiz had said—and some kind of extortion scheme Trip was trying to run on him. Which was all very fascinating, sure, but of no fucking interest to Pierce whatsoever, so all this screaming and bloodletting, which Pierce wasn't nearly as fond of as people thought, was for nothing.

He should have stayed home in Memphis.

Finally weary of it all, Pierce was about to tell his man to put a bullet in Ortiz's ear, and his girl's back in the bedroom after that, when the cell phone in his pocket rang.

"Yeah?"

It was his oldest son, Thurman, who knew better than to call his father on the road unless it was something vitally important. "You find what you're lookin' for yet, Daddy?"

"No. What is it, boy?"

"We just got a call from somebody down in Florida. Man said his name was Eldon Hawkins."

"And?"

"I thought you might wanna hear what he had to say right away."

"I'M NOT going to put up with this all day, you know," Reece said.

Aeneas gave her a blank stare. "Put up with what?"

"Being treated like a participant in the Witness Protection Program. Having you control where I go, what I do . . ."

"Is that what I've been doing? I thought I was just keeping you company."

She smirked at that, confident that no further refutation was needed. He had called her room at 8 A.M., before she'd had any chance to get out on her own, and said, "So where would you like to go first?" He was already down in the hotel lobby, and it would have done her no good to resist. She gave him a hard time for a few minutes, then cheerfully followed his lead.

But she hadn't done so for the pull of his charm alone. She'd done it because she'd had almost twelve hours by that time to reflect on her present circumstances, and there was simply no denying the danger she was in. The danger she had *put* herself in. After what she'd done to Trip Stiles last night, Raygene's imbalanced friend would be looking for her, and if she allowed him to find her, this time around a Mace-dispensing pen would not be enough to stop him.

For that reason alone, having a man like Aeneas Charles close by was a good idea. But only in moderation. Reece wasn't going to let Stiles chase her back to L.A. with her tail between her legs, and she wasn't going to let him force her into hiding in Charles's shadow for the remainder of the weekend, either. She had too much pride for that. For the sake of her baby, she was going to take advantage of Charles's protection at intervals of her choosing, and spend the rest of her time in Vegas alone, doing the town just the way she'd planned to all along. If that made her a fool, it was the only kind of fool she knew how to be.

It was almost noon. She and Aeneas had had breakfast at the Hard Rock, played some slots there and a little blackjack at the MGM Grand, and now they were playing arcade games at the ESPN Zone: NASCAR racing, skeeball, computerized football. All the simulated sports a pregnant lady could try her hand at without risking premature delivery.

At the moment, they were shooting miniature baskets at adjacent machines. Six dollars in, Reece was up 64 to 40, and she didn't think Aeneas was deliberately tanking it.

"If my stalking bothers you, I would suggest again that we call the police," he said.

"No. Concentrate on your follow-through."

"Stiles isn't going to quit, Reece. He wants that ticket, now more than ever." He'd told her how Raygene had left the white man and his bodyguard in two separate piles in their hotel room the night before, so she had reason to know what kind of mood Stiles was likely to be in this afternoon.

"So you say."

"Men like Stiles are not complicated. They want something, they come after it. And the more you tell them they can't have it, the more they're willing to risk to get it."

"I'm not giving the asshole my ticket, Aeneas."

"Nobody's asking you to. If you'd let the authorities handle this—"

"I can 'handle' it myself, if you'd let me."

Whereas Aeneas had stopped playing minutes ago, Reece was still firing balls at her hoop, though now she was bounding shots off the rim more than anything else.

She didn't know it, but Aeneas's insistence on calling the authorities was only halfhearted. A nearly hysterical Stanley Winston had threatened to do this very thing himself this morning, after finally receiving a bare-bones status report from the investigator, and Aeneas had summarily talked him out of it. Aeneas wasn't ready to see the lid blown off Raygene's blackmailing and the history behind Reece's Super Bowl betting slip just yet. As he'd told Winston, he still had hope that he could prevent both events from occurring, if he could just be left to manage the situation in his own inimitable way.

And yet as long as Trip Stiles was on the loose, and remained even a remote threat to Reece Germaine's health, Aeneas felt obligated to push a call to the authorities on her as best he could.

"You're still under the delusion you scared him off at dinner last night with that 'mess with me and I'll testify against you' routine? Come on, Reece."

Reece's game ended, finally giving her an excuse to face the P.I. directly. "Okay. So maybe he is more determined than ever to have the ticket. When and if he comes for it, I'll be ready, Aeneas."

"Ready how? You going to try Macing him again?"

"No. I'll be ready for him with *cash*. Proceeds from a sale of the ticket I intend to make later this afternoon."

"You're going to sell it?"

"That's the only way I'm sure to get something out of it.

I've given the matter a lot of thought, and I've come to the conclusion that I agree with you: I probably can't hold Stiles off until tomorrow. So—"

"Excuse me? Hello?"

Reece turned, saw that she and Charles were keeping a couple of teenage boys with spiked hair from reaching the basketball machines.

"Oh, sorry." She and Aeneas found a niche where they wouldn't be in anyone else's way, and picked up their conversation where they'd left it.

"So if you can't hold Stiles off until tomorrow . . ." Aeneas said.

"Then as much as I'd love to, I can't take the shot at winning the whole enchilada I've been thinking about taking. I've got to get something for the ticket now, before I have to give it to Stiles and, God forbid, he goes for broke with it and winds up with nothing when the Raiders win. If that were to happen . . . Well, let's just say I don't know what I'd do."

"And if Stiles takes the ticket and the Raiders *lose?*"

"Please. *That* I don't even want to *think* about!"

Aeneas shook his head. "Any way you look at it, you're still talking about giving in to a blackmailer's demands. And that almost never proves to be a permanent solution to the problem, Reece."

"You mean they always come back for more."

"Yes."

"Well, again, I have to agree with you. Except in those cases where the blackmailer's been given a reason *not* to come back for more. Ever."

"What kind of 'reason'?"

"The same one as before. The threat of prosecution on a

blackmailing charge. Only this time, it wouldn't just be based on hearsay. It'd be based on that, plus videotape of an actual payoff."

"Videotape?"

"I'd arrange things so the money would change hands in a very public place. Like this one, for instance. Have you ever counted the number of video cameras there are in a place like this?" She turned her eyes skyward, directing his attention to one of the many such devices that were visible overhead, mounted to the arcade's ceiling and walls. "It has to be a dozen at least, no?"

Aeneas didn't need to look to know it was true. Video surveillance cameras had become a commonplace fixture of life in America in general, but in a city such as Vegas, where almost every edifice was a repository of millions, they were nearly as ubiquitous as slot machines.

"How would you retrieve the tape?"

"If it came to that, the same way I do everything in my business. With beauty and guile. And if neither of those worked, cold hard cash."

For most people, this would have been a ridiculous suggestion. The people in charge of security videos were not usually in the habit of being massaged out of them, nor bribed into selling them. But coming from Reece Germaine . . . Well, though he'd known the woman for less than twenty-four hours, Aeneas could see her pulling it off. With ease.

"I'm hungry," he said. "Are you hungry?"

"No," Reece said, smiling. "But the baby is famished."

THEY WENT up to the top of the Stratosphere Hotel/Casino and had lunch at the revolving restaurant there, gazing down upon the hustle and bustle of Vegas from a height of 1,149 feet while the floor beneath them did a slow, clockwise crawl. Aeneas still had his guard up for Stiles, but Reece had no such compulsion, content to let the P.I. do all the fretting for them both.

Somewhere between their drinks being served and appetizers arriving at their table, their conversation turned to the origins of Aeneas's first name.

"He was the son of Aphrodite," he said, grinning sheepishly. "The Trojan warrior who founded the state of Rome. My father was a Roman mythology buff, and he thought 'Aeneas' went better with 'Charles' than 'Poseidon.' You weren't thinking about using it?"

"For the baby?" Reece laughed. "Thanks for the offer, but no."

"Do we know what we're having yet? Boy or girl?"

"No. I want to be surprised."

"But that makes it harder to plan for things, doesn't it? The color of clothes, wallpaper in the nursery . . ."

"You know what I think? I think planning is overrated. That's what partners are for."

"You mean business partners?"

"Yes. What other—" She answered her own question. "Oh. Right. Yes, I meant *business* partners. Surely you didn't think Raygene—"

"It didn't seem very likely. But one never wants to make assumptions about such things."

"Raygene is the momentary lapse in judgment that just keeps on giving. He's gorgeous, funny, and well intended, but if you put the poor devil on 'Jeopardy,' he wouldn't know the question if the answer under 'Grammar' for two hundred was 'C-A-T.'"

"Damn," Aeneas said, chuckling.

"Was that harsh? I'm sorry. But besides the baby, he's caused me no end of grief. Had he faced up to his obligations and given me the child support I've been asking for, none of us would even be here, worrying over Trip Stiles. I'd have given him his betting slip the first time he asked for it, no sweat."

"Even though it has the potential to be worth a million-plus in"—he checked his watch—"a little over twenty-four hours?"

"Fair is fair, Aeneas. That's been my credo all my life. I may be a kick-ass broad, but if you deal with me on the square, we'll get along. Raygene bankrolled the bet, and he should reap the rewards of it, if there are any. The only reason I've ever laid claim to the ticket at all is his reluctance to give me what *is* mine."

A loud roar from the patrons in the bar rolled through the dining area, not unlike the communal groan that would no doubt follow every dropped pass and fumbled handoff that occurred in tomorrow's game.

"It's a little early for a tailgate party, isn't it?" Reece asked.

"Somebody probably just missed a big payout on a five-dollar slot."

Their waiter appeared with their appetizer tray, having come from the direction of the bar. He was shaking his head.

"What's all the excitement?" Aeneas asked.

"ESPN news flash. Hope neither of you had Oakland to-morrow," the guy said.

PROFESSIONAL FOOTBALL was a violent game. The men who played it collected physical injuries like kids gathered shells at the seashore. Broken bones, ruptured tendons, lost teeth, sprained ligaments—it all came with the territory. No one ever ended their career walking quite as straight as when they started it.

But pro football was also a crazy game, sometimes played by crazy people. Throughout the 134-year history of the National Football League, men suffering from all forms of mental illness had been employed by its various franchises: alcoholics, schizophrenics, sociopaths, manic-depressives—and, of course, drug addicts of every stripe. Their unstable behavior often went totally undetected, but some made no secret of it, lending the press a hook upon which to hang colorful stories about their "wacky" and "nonconformist" ways. Alonzo Spellman of the Chicago Bears once barricaded himself inside his publicist's home; the Dallas Cowboys' Thomas "Hollywood" Henderson played the 1978 NFC Championship game stoned out of his mind on cocaine; Oakland Raider John Matuszak routinely liked to eat glass.

For all the unpredictability and volatility of such characters, however, none was ever known to have had an appreciably adverse effect upon a given game, and certainly not a game as significant as the Super Bowl. Elbert "Ickey" Woods, then of the Cincinnati Bengals, had come closest, going on a career-ending cocaine binge the night before the 1988 NFL championship game that rendered him a nonparticipant, but almost everyone who witnessed the San Francisco 49ers' ensuing 20–16 victory over the Bengals agreed that Woods's absence from Cincinnati's backfield had had little or nothing to do with the contest's outcome. The distractions they presented to their respective teams notwithstanding, then, the impact of head cases like Woods on the sport's biggest game had always been the stuff of newspaper sidebars, not headlines.

Until now.

If any one NFL franchise could claim more than its fair share of crazies, it was the Oakland/sometimes Los Angeles Raiders. The Raiders *liked* crazies. Crazies fit the team's angry, free-spirit mystique like a glove, and they generally came cheap, having often been discarded by every other league franchise as too stubborn or eccentric to coach.

Omar Robertson was the Raiders' latest crazy.

A six-foot nine-inch, 366-pound defensive end out of Southern Mississippi State, Robertson was an emerging All-Pro with the moves of Deacon Jones and the insecurities of Pee-wee Herman. Fans and reporters thought he was just a talented but excitable player who got flagged for too many roughing-the-passer penalties and bragged too gleefully about it afterward, but this was merely the lone side of Robertson they could see. Raider doctors knew something about the man no one else but his roommate on the squad did, which was that he often cried himself to sleep over an incident of sexual abuse he'd suffered as a child that was only now rising to the surface of his consciousness, and he was taking a hefty daily dose of antidepressants just to hold himself together.

If more of his teammates had been privy to this information, Omar Robertson may have played in his first Super Bowl without incident. But they weren't. Just as the Raiders' team doctors weren't privy to the knowledge that Robertson had last taken his "daily" dosage of Zoloft two days earlier, disenchanted with its wilting effect on his libido. What happened that Saturday afternoon in Miami Beach, Florida, then, at 4:14 P.M., Eastern standard time, in the course of what should have been a completely harmless team photo shoot, was perhaps as unavoidable as it was catastrophic.

Robertson and another Raider named Kenny Edwards, positioned one above the other in the team photo that had yet to be taken, engaged in some innocent trash talk, as grown men who play little boy games for a living so often do, and the barbs began to fly. Edwards said something about Robertson's breath, Robertson returned serve with a comment about Edwards's teeth . . . and then Edwards came back with a joke about the possible *cause* of Robertson's breath, which amounted to an act of fellatio on a Raider assistant coach.

End of trash talk.

Robertson, in row three, dove for the throat of the smaller Edwards, in row two, and both men went down to the grassy field in a heap, taking several other players down with them. They were separated before any actual punches could be thrown, but Edwards had put his right arm out to break his fall and, bearing the brunt of Robertson's weight as well as his own, broke his wrist in three places.

Which was immediately a newsworthy event, because Kenny Edwards was the Raiders' starting quarterback, and his right hand was the one he threw the football with.

"**OH . . . MY . . . GOD**," Reece said.

She and Aeneas were standing in the Top of the World bar, watching an ESPN talking head deliver details of the freak accident on one of several TVs overhead, and the room, the entire restaurant, was still abuzz with shock and disbelief.

"In case you don't know, Edwards's backup is a journeyman named Cal Schroeder," Aeneas said. "He's been around forever, played for practically every team in the league at least once, and I believe the last time he won a game as a starter was three years ago, for Denver or Minnesota, I don't recall which. If he completed more than six passes, I'd be amazed to hear it."

"So?"

"So the sound you just heard was the value of that ticket of yours going through the roof, Reece. Look around. The Raider Nation is in ruins. They've got no more chance of winning that game tomorrow now than the Sisters of the Poor."

And as if to prove his point, Reece's cell phone chose that moment to start ringing. She and Aeneas made a face at each other, then she answered the call.

"Yes?"

"Ms. Germaine? This is Dick Montecito. You haven't sold that betting slip of yours yet, have you?"

"Who?"

"Dick Montecito, ma'am. Caesars Palace race and sports book, remember?"

"Oh, yes, yes, of course." Montecito was one of several local sports book managers Reece had talked to on Friday about potential buyers for her wagering ticket. He'd told her then he could already guarantee her at least one possible buyer, and had promised to be on the lookout for others. "No, I haven't sold it yet. What—"

"I've just found another buyer for you, ma'am. And he wants to meet with you here at the hotel right away. Within the hour, if that would be possible."

Interesting, Reece thought. Was Montecito making no mention of Kenny Edwards's injury because he was hoping she hadn't heard about it, or because he thought she was a woman too stupid to know its monumental effect on the ticket's worth?

"What's he offering?" Reece asked.

"I'll quote the man directly. 'Tell the lady she can name her own price,' he said. That offer sound sweet enough for you?"

BY THE time Reece arrived at Caesars Palace twenty minutes later, Super Bowl XXXVIII had been yanked off the board at every major sports book in Las Vegas. Nobody in their right mind would take a dime from anybody on the Cardinals now, and there wasn't a fool in the city big enough to bet the Raiders with an old plow horse like Cal Schroeder at quarterback. Whatever money was going to be wagered on the game had already been collected, and nobody, it seemed, was holding a higher hand at the moment than Reece Germaine.

She walked into Caesars alone, having extricated herself from Aeneas Charles's smothering protection with no small amount of difficulty. She had already trusted him with more information about her personal affairs here than reasonable caution should have allowed, knowing as little about him as she still did, and there was no way she was going to have him looking over her shoulder now, at what could be the most critical juncture of her entire Las Vegas weekend. This was Reece's show to run, and she was going to run it her way, without Charles, Raygene, or anyone else whispering in her ear, trying to advise her on how to go about it.

Aeneas had given her his word he wouldn't follow her, but she'd made him leave the Stratosphere first, watched his taxi go left as she ordered the driver of hers to go right, just to make the task of tailing her as impossible for him as she could. If he was watching her now, it could only be because he'd taken a wild guess as to where she was going, and guessed right, which seemed extremely unlikely.

Dick Montecito, the broad-shouldered victim of a bad hair transplant, saw her coming his way before she could reach his station behind the wagering counter, and sprinted out to greet her like a parish priest welcoming the Pope to his humble little house of worship.

"Did you bring the ticket with you?" he asked anxiously, pumping her hand.

"Come on, Mr. Montecito. What do you think?"

"Sorry. That was a stupid question, wasn't it?"

Reece scanned the busy wagering area. "So where's your buyer?"

"Mr. Dvorak asked me to tell you he's waiting for you up in his suite. He thought you might be more comfortable discussing things there, in private, over lunch. He hopes you don't mind."

"His suite? Why would I want to go up there?"

"It's perfectly safe, Ms. Germaine, I assure you. Mr. Dvorak is a harmless old gentleman who's a regular and treasured guest here at Caesars, I can vouch for his honesty and credibility implicitly."

Reece took a moment to consider this. "And I take it he's a *filthy rich* 'harmless old gentleman'? He can pay me the kind of money I'm looking for?"

"Oh, shi— I mean, absolutely." Montecito laughed. "He's a regular here, like I said. I'm not really supposed to tell you this, but if he's ever stayed with us and not dropped twenty grand a day, it would've had to be while my back was turned. One look at his suite here and you'll see what I mean. It's one of our Duplex units in the Forum tower, the one he always gets when he's here. Number twenty-eight-oh-two. Should I call to say you're on your way up?"

A career in the entertainment P.R. business had taught Reece to be wary of all people who vouched for the veracity of things "implicitly," but it had also endowed her with an uncanny knack for recognizing most liars on sight. Montecito was a sexist boor and a hustler, to be sure, but he wasn't lying. He really did know this fellow Dvorak, and firmly believed in the man's good character.

"Sure," Reece said, "go ahead."

AENEAS HAD thought he could let Reece go without soon feeling compelled to find her again, but he proved himself wrong. The minute her gambit to ditch him at the Stratosphere left him sitting in a taxi moving north while hers rapidly disappeared to the south, his mind went to work seeking ways to track her down.

"That taxi that was in line behind us back at the hotel," he said to his driver. "I don't suppose you'd know who it was?"

"What taxi?" the guy asked, not even bothering to make eye contact with him in the mirror.

Aeneas had him circle the block anyway, cruise south down Las Vegas Boulevard for a couple of blocks before the futility of his mission set in. He was going to need help. He couldn't canvass the entire Strip on his own, and time was of the essence. He had a plan for dealing with Trip Stiles already in motion, but it could take another ten minutes to come together, or it could take all day, if it ever came together at all, and Stiles couldn't be trusted to leave Reece be until it did. The man was just too big a crazy.

Aeneas had to finally tell Raygene the truth.

He rang Brew's cell phone, and the bodyguard picked up on the second ring.

"We was wonderin' when you was gonna call," Brew said.

"Then Raygene *is* with you. Good. Do me a favor and put him on."

"Sure. I guess you're gonna come correct with 'im now, huh?"

Aeneas started to ask him what he meant, then thought better of it. Obviously, unlike his boss, Brew hadn't bought into a minute of the P.I.'s subterfuge yet, and playing stupid with him now wasn't going to change that.

"Yeah. I'm gonna come correct with him," Aeneas said.

WALKING THROUGH Caesars Palace was like crossing the state of Texas on foot, but Reece found the hotel/casino's Forum tower soon enough. She rode in the air-conditioned hush of an elevator up to the twenty-eighth floor, wondering if she wouldn't come down in the same car later almost a million dollars wealthier than she was now. It was a nice thought.

Irving Dvorak answered her knock on the door to suite 2802 himself, and Reece immediately felt better about Dick Montecito's credibility. Dvorak could not have appeared less menacing had he been wearing a shocking-pink tutu. He was a silver-haired white man in his early sixties, as plump as a ripe tomato and as fair-skinned as a forties pinup girl. Wearing a Western-style blue denim shirt, diamond-studded bolo tie, black jeans, and snakeskin boots, he showed Reece a smile upon opening the door he had to have borrowed from his favorite aunt.

"Ms. Germaine?"

"Yes."

"I'm Irving Dvorak. Please come in."

He shook her hand and waved her into his suite, then closed the door behind her when she entered. His grip had been soft and slightly moist, and his voice had carried just a hint of Southwestern drawl.

Montecito had inferred that Dvorak's accommodations here would speak volumes about his personal worth, and the sports book manager hadn't been exaggerating. Reece was stunned. The suite she found herself taking in almost seemed to have no end; were this a movie, it might have taken up an entire sound stage. It was furnished like a billionaire's Beverly Hills mansion, golden floor columns competing with rich tapestries and alabaster nudes for the eye's attention, and every possible amenity—full kitchen, wet bar, even a baby grand piano—seemed to be part of the package. If the room's nightly rate didn't equal Reece's monthly mortgage, it had to come awfully close.

"My God. This is unbelievable," she said, moving in for a closer look.

What appeared to be a ten-course meal for two was spread out across a large oak dining table nearby, sterling silver service pieces polished to a high luster all around. Reece saw a mammoth slab of prime rib, broiled to perfection and already carved, occupying center stage of the arrangement, along with an overflowing salad bowl, trays filled with potatoes and assorted vegetables, and a bottle of wine chilling in a silver ice bucket. It was the lunch Montecito had promised her. Reece had just eaten with Aeneas, but perhaps motivated more by the baby's hunger than her own, she was drawn to the waiting feast nonetheless.

And then she saw the two plates.

They were sitting at two different places at the table, and there was food on both of them. Not portions of a meal to come, but fragments of one interrupted. She knew what the distinction meant immediately, but she couldn't bring herself to believe it until she'd spun around toward Dvorak again and seen the man suddenly standing behind him, pushing the point of a steak knife into his soft, pink neck, just under the right ear.

"You make a sound, little lady," Trip Stiles said, grinning with tremendous satisfaction, "and good ol' Irving here bleeds first."

18

CARMEN HAD SAID the man Lenny was looking for was staying here at the Bellagio. Room 1912, as a member of the Raygene Price party. Carmen had friends all over Vegas, so getting this info and more out of somebody on the Bellagio's staff had probably been fairly easy for her. She didn't know who Price was, though; Lenny had to tell her. Gene the Dream, Dallas Cowboys; blinding speed, great hands, et cetera, et cetera. Why Charles even knew him, Carmen claimed she couldn't guess, and didn't care, and Lenny was inclined to agree. Still, the junkie was hoping Price wouldn't get in the way when the time came to take Charles out. That could make things pretty messy for everybody.

Carmen had given her ex-lover a rather exhaustive physical description of Charles, so it wasn't going to be particularly difficult to recognize the man when he finally showed up. But Lenny had been cruising the Bellagio for over three hours now, and there'd been no sign of Charles yet. Nor Raygene Price, for that matter. Obviously, the two men were spending their money elsewhere, which was the way it always seemed to go in Vegas. The poor bastards who owned these hotel/casinos spared no expense to keep guests entertained on the grounds, determined to hold onto every dollar to come within their reach, and still, people refused to gamble and sleep in the same place. For all Lenny knew, Aeneas Charles wouldn't reappear at the Bellagio until long after midnight.

Fortunately for Carmen, however, the former Marine she had assigned the task of Charles's murder had unlimited patience. Lenny was a real anomaly in that way, an intravenous drug user who could sit all day in one spot, waiting for something to happen, without becoming a howling, spasmodic basket case. But it took real willpower, and the proper motivation. Like the possibility, however remote, of sharing Carmen's bed again, even if it were only for one night.

For that, Lenny could wait to kill Aeneas Charles forever.

IRVING DVORAK was old, gay, and lonely, and Trip had spotted him as such the second he'd set eyes upon him. He knew the type.

Trip was no faggot himself, but life back at Florida State Prison had on occasion forced certain compromises upon him, so it couldn't honestly be said he didn't know his way around men who liked other men. He had seen dozens of old queens like Dvorak in the pen, and had learned to make good use of them. All you had to do was show them a little phony attention, give them the idea they still had something worth wanting, and they'd service you for days on end without demanding a thing in return. Bitches should have been so easy to seduce.

Still, arousing the desire of pathetic fudge packers like Irving Dvorak wasn't something Trip had been counting on doing much of once he got out. He had other options now, after all. But today he'd had the need for a hotel room to sucker Reece into, and a hostage to ensure her silence once she got there, and as hard as he tried, Trip just couldn't find a woman, young or old, better suited for his purposes than Dvorak.

The poor bastard was sitting before the main keno board at Caesars Palace when Trip found him, surrounded by empty seats and deep in the funk of a practically visible pall of loneliness. He was dressed in full cowboy regalia: hat, pointy-toed boots, belt buckle as big as a china saucer. Trip watched him for thirty minutes from a seat on the opposite side of the keno area, and no one but their waitress ever came near him. No wife, no girl- or boyfriend, nothing. So he seemed to be alone, check. And he was well heeled, double check, because, one, he never played a keno slip that he hadn't appeared to mark up with multiple-way bets, and, two, he was tipping the waitress like he intended to pay her way through college.

But was he gay?

Trip needed him to be gay, because he knew his chances would be nil of working his way up to a cowboy's room simply as a new drinking buddy, rather than a fresh young stallion the man was hot to break in bed. He studied Dvorak's mannerisms closely, detected nothing in the way of the telltale effeminacy that might have made the man's sexual preference an easier call for Trip to make. But soon enough, other clues to Dvorak's homosexuality became crystal clear, and they all began and ended with Dvorak's eyes: what they followed, where they lingered, and what they failed to notice altogether.

Their waitress, for example, was a buxom brunette in a smaller girl's uniform who was flashing her tits in Dvorak's face every time she served him, perhaps sizing the heavy tipper up for a fleecing of her own, and Dvorak seemed to look right through her, like the fleshy mounds she was offering up to him weren't even there. And when his gaze chanced upon a body in motion worth tracking, which wasn't often, it was always a man's, not a woman's. His head would turn ever so slightly to trace his target's path across his field of vision, and the self-pity that was already evident on his face would turn even darker, something Trip had seen happen many times to the queens back in the pen whenever the fear of dying alone came over them.

So, yeah, the cowboy was gay. Triple check.

It took Trip all of thirty minutes to catch his interest, and keep it. He slithered over to a seat nearby, broke the ice with some bullshit request to borrow Dvorak's keno brochure, and the rest fell into place as if Jesus Christ himself were pulling the strings. Trip hadn't lost his touch. He still knew how to draw a fag in when he had to. Especially when he made the extra effort of leaving all his customary black leather behind and actually prettied himself up for a change. Maybe the bitches couldn't see it, but geared up in conventional attire—silk shirt, twill pants, even tassels on his goddamn shoes—Trip Stiles was a fucking stud. Lean, hard, and tattooed just enough to promise a dancing partner the right mix of pleasure and pain.

Poor old Irving Dvorak hadn't had a prayer.

"**BET YOU** didn't know I could dress like this, did you?" Trip asked Reece, so proud of himself he could burst.

"What, like a human being? No, I must confess, the thought never occurred to me." She turned to E.Y., standing guard with the knife over Dvorak now, said, "Did you do it all yourself, or did he help you?"

Trip smiled, taking the shot like the ineffectual little thing it was. "Y'know, for a lady could be dead in the next five minutes, you sure talk a lotta shit." Nibbling at the lunch Reece's arrival had forced him to abandon, he opened her handbag and turned it upside down, dumping its contents all over the dining table where he sat. "Or don't you know what kinda trouble your ass is in here?"

Reece didn't answer him, just watched with mock indifference as he aimlessly picked through the items from her bag with a steak knife.

"It ain't here," he said eventually. And this time, he waited for her to respond.

Reece shrugged. "I like to travel light."

Trip stood up and moved in on her, bringing the steak knife with him.

"You ain't asked me how I found you yet."

"I don't really care."

"I read your mind, that's how. I asked myself what I would do if I was you, and I was here in Vegas with that bettin' slip of yours, two days before the Super Bowl. And you know what I figured out?"

"Don't touch me with that knife, you—"

"E! Stick a hole in that ol' faggot's ass for me, will you?"

"No, wait . . . !"

But E.Y. was already on it, clamping his left hand over Dvorak's mouth as he stabbed the older man in the buttock with his right. Dvorak screamed and wriggled like a stuck pig, but his cries were as muted as his struggle was pointless.

"Stiles, goddamn you!" Reece snapped.

"Who, me? You think *I* did that? That shit was on *you*, bitch! *You* control what happens to that man over there, not me. Do you get that now? Or has dog gotta cut 'im again?" He glanced over at his bodyguard, gave the nod for E.Y. to demonstrate.

"No! Don't!"

E.Y. watched his employer for another sign, Dvorak again flailing uselessly against him.

"Okay," Trip said to Reece. "That's better. We got an understandin' now, don't we?"

Reece nodded, her blood boiling, her fear for the baby inside her rising steadily. *She had to remain calm.* This close to her delivery date, any overload of stress could send her careening into labor, and she did *not* want that to happen here, with this monster watching. If she let him push her emotions too far . . .

"Anyway, as I was sayin'," Trip went on. "I asked myself what I would do if I was you, and I decided I'd look around for a buyer. Somebody to sell the ticket to *now*, before the game, in case I wanted to go for the sure money instead'a the bigger money I might or might not get, dependin' on who wins tomorrow." He prodded Reece's belly with the tip of his knife, gently, playfully, and it took everything she had to let him do it, even with Dvorak's life, as well as her own, on the line. "And that's just what you did, ain't it? Looked around for a buyer?"

"Okay. You're ingenious. You found somebody who knew how to contact me with an offer, then tricked me into pursuing it. So what? You know what all of this is going to buy you once Raygene finds out about it? Try 'your head on a *stick*.'"

"Raygene? You think I give a *fuck* about Raygene?"

"Yes, I know. He's a lot more flash than substance. But he's still two hundred and forty pounds' worth of substance, and this baby's still half his, and if you think he isn't going to break you into a thousand pieces after what you've done here today, you're delusional."

Trip maddogged her, seething. Long seconds ticked by as his mind worked an unspoken problem. Then he went back to the dining table, rammed the blade of the steak knife deep into its polished surface, and took one of the items he'd poured from Reece's purse earlier up in his right hand: the pen-shaped Mace dispenser she'd used on him the night before.

"This shit burns like hell, you know it?" he said, looking the trick weapon over like a kid examining a new toy. "I must'a washed my eyes out fifty times last night, and they was *still* fucked up this mornin'."

Reece said nothing, afraid even to exhale now.

"But that's only part of it. Shit fucks your stomach all up, too." He popped the pen's cap off and finally turned to look at her again. "But I guess that's why they call it 'toxic,' huh?"

"Stiles. Don't."

He walked back over to where she was standing, said, "I want that fucking betting slip, Reecie. Ain't that what Raygene calls you, 'Reecie'? And I'm gonna do whatever I gotta do to get it." He turned to E.Y. "Take that motherfucka in the bedroom and tie 'im up, then get back in here and help me with this bitch."

"Sure thing." E.Y. started off with Dvorak.

Reece swallowed hard, closed her eyes. "It's in my room at

the hotel. Room eleven-sixteen at the Hard Rock, the key's over there on the table."

E.Y. froze in his tracks, and Trip grinned, unable to believe his sudden turn of fortune. "Say again?"

"You heard me. Eleven-sixteen at the Hard Rock, it's curled up inside the toilet paper roll in the bathroom."

From Trip's perspective, the pain on the lady's face was exquisite. It was one of his favorite highs, moving people to turn the fire on themselves.

"That right? Inside the shitter paper roll?" He beamed with admiration. "Damn, where'd you get that from? That's fuckin' brilliant!"

And then he laughed that god-awful laugh of his, just as Reece had suspected he would.

MORE THAN forty minutes after Aeneas had confessed all, Raygene was still burning over the game both the P.I. and Stanley Winston had been running on him.

"Man, I can't believe that shit," he said again.

"Come on, boss," Brew said, trying not to sound as tired of Raygene's bitching as he felt. "Let it go."

"Dog, how'm I gonna let it go? They was punkin' me! There ain't no book, there ain't no contract—"

"They were worried about you. They were tryin' to protect you from a man they knew was gonna jack you up."

" 'Protect' me? Hell, I'm already protected. That's what *you're* here for, ain't it?"

Brew refrained from answering, preferring to concentrate on what he and Raygene both were supposed to be doing from their moving rental car: looking for any combination of

Reece, Trip, or E.Y. Raygene, driving, saw he'd lost the body-guard's attention and, reminded of the task at hand, decided to *follow* his lead, eyeballing the road and the northbound side of Las Vegas Boulevard in equal measure.

"Shit, this is crazy. How we gonna find anybody in all this?"

"We prob'ly can't. But we gotta try. We found Ms. Germaine yesterday, didn't we?"

"Yeah, we did. And we was damn lucky to do it too. Tryin' to do it two days in a damn row . . ." He let his voice trail off, his mood growing dimmer by the second. "You really think Trip might hurt the girl?"

"You know the fool better than I do. What do *you* think?"

Raygene shook his head and sighed, unable to deny the obvious. "I think I really fucked up, gettin' Reecie involved in this shit. That's what I think."

Brew let his silence provide all the agreement that needed to be said.

"I still say we should split up."

"Ugh-uh. I told you, chief, I ain't goin' no place today without you."

"But—"

"You wanna stop for a minute? Pull in here at the Flamingo, sit in the carport 'til they make us move? We might be able to see better if we're sittin' still."

It was a good idea, but even as he pulled over to make the turn, Raygene was shamed by the fact that Brew had thought of it first, more focused on what was truly important here than the man who was paying him was.

The Flamingo Hilton's carport was jammed with vehicles, but Raygene stopped the car way at the back, near the end of the taxi line, to keep them as out of the way and inconspicuous to the hotel staff as possible. Raygene told his bodyguard to get out of the car, see what he could see on foot for a while, but before Brew could close the door behind him, his cell phone rang.

"I'll answer that," Raygene said, reaching out for the instrument.

As he expected, it was Aeneas, checking status.

"Anything?"

"Hell, no. You?"

"Nothing. And I just checked her room again, she's not in there."

"You already been to all the sports books?"

Reece hadn't said, of course, but Aeneas was guessing that the caller up at the Top of the World restaurant who'd drawn her away with an offer for her betting slip had been somebody attached to one of the casino's sports books.

"Not all, but most of the major ones," he said. "And I've spoken to the men in charge of some of the others by phone. A couple of people admit they spoke to her yesterday about finding a buyer, but that's it, they say they haven't seen or heard from her since." He could have added that any or all of these people could have been lying, tight-lipped and security-conscious as sports book managers tended to be about even the most innocuous subject, but he didn't bother.

"So what do we do now?" Raygene asked.

"Nothing we can do but more of the same. You and Brew keep cruising the Strip in and out of the car. Me, I think I'll go back to the Stratosphere, see if I can't find the hack she left with. He probably didn't return there right away, but you never know."

"You sure it wouldn't help to call Five-Oh?" It had been a hard step to take, but Raygene had finally reached the point where he was willing to risk the fallout from Trip's blackmail threat if it meant sparing the lives of Reece and the baby.

"We could try that, but there'd be no guarantee that they'd make finding Reece or Trip a priority. Right now, Trip's just an alleged blackmailer, and Reece hasn't been missing two hours yet. But if that's what you want to do . . ."

Raygene said no. If the cops weren't likely to make a greater effort to find Reece than he, Brew, and Aeneas already were, then he didn't see the point in calling them in.

"Let's get back to it, then," Aeneas said, and hung up.

Raygene turned to hand the phone back to Brew, but the bodyguard was gone. While Raygene had been talking to Aeneas, Brew had wandered off from the car to take a look around, just as he'd been about to when the private investigator's call had come in. Raygene couldn't see him anywhere.

He sat in the idling car for several minutes, time passing like molasses through the eye of a needle, and was about to get out and go look for him when Brew reappeared from the direction of the street out front, face flushed with excitement.

"I got 'im," he said, jumping back in the car.

"Who?"

"Trip. I just seen 'im walk outta Caesars Palace, come on, let's go!"

Raygene put the car in gear, burned rubber exiting the carport.

"There! See 'im?" Brew pointed across the street as they waited for the thick northbound traffic to clear and allow them back onto the Strip.

Just outside Caesars Palace, Trip Stiles was walking away

from them on the southbound side of the boulevard, strutting among the sea of bodies flowing all around him like he already held one key to the city and was on his way to see the mayor to get a second.

"I see 'im," Raygene said. "But where's Reece and E.Y.?"

"I don't know. He came out alone, I didn't see anybody else with 'im."

"And why's he walkin', 'stead'a takin' a cab?"

"Looks like he *wants* to walk. Like he's all happy 'bout somethin'."

At last, Raygene got his opening and jumped out into the street. Eschewing the left turn he needed to make but couldn't, he leapt across several lanes to turn left legally into the Mirage's main driveway, then executed a hasty U-turn there, finally getting the car headed in the desired direction, southbound toward Caesars and the white boy he was rushing to follow.

"I don't like this. It don't make no sense," he said when they had Trip back in view, just past Flamingo Road. "E.Y. should be with 'im, unless . . ."

"Unless what?"

"Unless Trip gave 'im somethin' else to do. Like keep an eye on Reece, or somethin'." He stopped the car abruptly at the curb, pushed Brew's cell phone back at him. "Get out and go back to Caesars, see if you can find one or both of 'em up in there."

"What? And what're *you* gonna do?"

"I'm gonna stay with Trip, what else? Hurry up, dog, I'm holdin' up traffic."

Brew didn't like it, but he knew what Raygene sounded like

when a tank wasn't going to be enough to move him off of something.

"Watch your ass," he said, taking his phone and getting out of the car.

"Right. Same to you."

Raygene sped off, running through a yellow at the entrance to the Monte Carlo to keep his quarry from getting too big a lead on him.

19

PER TRIP'S RENEWED ORDERS, E.Y. had taken Irving Dvorak into the bedroom to bind and gag him before Trip left for the Hard Rock to retrieve Reece's betting slip, so it was just she and the big bodyguard in the main chamber of Dvorak's suite now.

E.Y. had asked his boss if Reece shouldn't be tied up too, and Trip had turned his nose up at the suggestion, said, "What, you tellin' me you can't handle a pregnant bitch all by yourself, she ain't all tied up like a roped calf?"

To which the bodyguard had replied with a sad, wholly unintelligible mumble.

"The lady ain't goin' nowhere, and she ain't gonna try nothin', 'cause if she does, you're gonna go back in that bedroom and cut that ol' faggot's throat, ear to fuckin' ear. Understand?"

The question had been meant for E.Y., but Trip was staring at Reece when he posed it, more concerned that she understood his meaning than his man.

"Don't hurt her 'less you have to," he said. "The ticket ain't where she says it is, I'm gonna have to come back and talk to her again, so I'm gonna need her ass alive.

"You been fuckin' up all week, nigga, and this is your last chance to get somethin' right. Do yourself a favor and don't blow it."

And with that, Trip was gone.

Mathematically, at least, his departure had increased the odds of her survival twofold, yet Reece found little relief in it. Just as Trip had said, there seemed to be nothing she could do to save herself that wouldn't put both her own life and Dvorak's at risk, and getting Dvorak killed, as Trip knew all too well, was something she was loath to do.

And what could she do against a behemoth like E.Y., in any case? Even without the knife he was refusing to put down now, even for a moment, the bodyguard alone was surely more than she could handle, pregnant or otherwise.

Her situation was hopeless, and there wasn't much point in denying it. Nobody but Dick Montecito knew where she was, and he had no clue she was in danger. E.Y. had ordered her to a seat on a couch, a full ten feet from the chair he was occupying, and more distant than that from the dining table and all the items upon it, which included her cell phone and everything in the room she could possibly use as a weapon against him: the knives and forks, her Mace dispenser, even the roll of quarters she might have wanted to weight her fist with, were she crazy enough to try and punch him.

Reece had only one cause for optimism that she could see, and it wasn't much: She had given Trip what he wanted. In a few short minutes, he would enter her room at the Hard Rock and find the small slip of paper he'd gone there to retrieve exactly where she'd told him he would. And then . . . What? What would he do then? Call E.Y. to have her and Dvorak released? Let bygones be bygones, and trust his two hostages to do the same?

Not hardly.

He would do what any smart man would, under the circumstances. He would silence her and Dvorak in the most permanent, infallible way possible, because nothing less would ensure him an opportunity to actually cash the ticket in.

Strangely enough, however, imminent as it appeared, death was not Reece's most immediate concern. Fear was. Because against all her efforts to hold it at bay, fear finally had her by the throat, and the tighter its grip on her became, the more susceptible she was to a stress-induced delivery. A delivery she knew her baby might not survive. Away from an antiseptic hospital room and all its attendant emergency facilities, with no one to help her bring the child into the world but a knife-wielding thug with the IQ of a doormat . . .

No, Reece promised herself. *I can't let it come to that.*

And she said a silent prayer to God in heaven, asking for the strength to be true to her word.

STANLEY WINSTON didn't know what good it would do him to join the party out in Las Vegas, but he was thinking about making the trip nonetheless. After filling his head with a nightmare cast of characters—Raygene, Trip Stiles, *and* Clarice Germaine, all in Vegas together, *holy Christ!*—Aeneas Charles had stopped taking Stanley's calls again, and having just had Raygene accept one was perhaps worse than not hearing from either one of them at all. Stanley's client wouldn't answer most of his questions, and the ones he did, he answered mysteriously, leading the sports agent to wonder how in the hell his presence out in Nevada could possibly make the situation—whatever it really was—any worse.

"I ain't got time for this right now, Stanley," Raygene had said. "And anyway, you're lucky I'm even talkin' to your sorry ass."

"Me? What'd *I* do?"

"Aeneas told me the truth, all right? 'Bout my big 'book deal'?"

"Oh. That. What'd he—"

"He *had* to tell me. I would'a figured it out on my own, sooner or later, don't think I wouldn't've. But he told me now himself 'cause Reecie needs our help, and her and the baby come first, don't nothin' else matter."

"'Help'? What kind of help? Raygene, don't—"

"Don't worry 'bout *me*, Stanley. Worry about Trip. He's the one whose ass is grass now, not me."

"What do you mean? What are you going to do?"

"For the moment, I ain't gonna do nothin'. I'm just watchin' homeboy, that's all."

WATCHING Trip Stiles was all Aeneas *wanted* Raygene to do. Brew had apparently called the writer—"writer," bullshit, Raygene reminded himself, the man was a private cop—right after Raygene left him at Caesars, and Aeneas had in turn called Raygene immediately afterward, giving him specific instructions not to do anything with Trip Stiles but keep an eye on him. Follow him from a distance, try not to get spotted, and report back to Aeneas on the white boy's movements every few minutes or so. Meanwhile, Aeneas and Brew were going to look for Reece or E.Y. at Caesars.

Raygene hadn't been happy about it, being handed a game plan and told to stick to it by a man who was by extension actually working for *him,* but Aeneas's instructions seemed to make too much sense to argue with, so Raygene continued to go along with them, at least until Trip did something to demand he get his ass kicked instead.

Like come downstairs from Reece's room here at the Hard Rock now with a reluctant or, worse, even slightly bruised Reece in tow, for instance. That was all Raygene would need to shift from observation mode to assassination mode in five seconds or less. But Aeneas, upon being told where Trip was, had assured Raygene that Reece wasn't in the building. He'd just come from the Hard Rock himself, he said, and she hadn't been anywhere in evidence.

"But the fact that he's there at all isn't good," Aeneas admitted, referring to Trip. "Especially without E.Y. And you say he went straight to the elevators upon arriving? He didn't look the place over, or stop at the front desk first?"

Raygene told him no, the white boy had just walked in, found the elevators, and disappeared inside the first one to answer his call.

"Then he knew where he was going. He not only knows Reece is staying there, he knows what room she's in." Aeneas's voice was tinged with dread.

"So I better get up there, right?"

"No. Not yet. I was just up to her room a few minutes ago, like I said, and if E.Y. had been in there with her, waiting for Trip to show, I would have heard him."

"But—"

"Relax, Raygene. She isn't there. If Trip left Caesars with the knowledge of where she was staying, then he probably got that info from her, right here. Or he got it from E.Y., who got it from Reece somewhere else. Either way, the best way to find her is to keep doing what we're all doing right now. You stick with Trip, and Brew and I will look for Reece here."

It sounded risky to Raygene, but again, he agreed to follow Aeneas's orders, afraid to do anything that might end up later having disastrous consequences for Reece and/or their baby.

Now, if he could just get Stanley to clear his goddamn cell phone line . . .

"Raygene, please," his agent begged him. "Talks with the Cowboys have been going swimmingly, we could have a deal for you to consider by the end of the week. But if you do anything crazy out there . . ."

"Ain't nobody gonna do nothin' crazy, Stanley. This is Gene the Dream you're talkin' to, remember? If somebody gets whacked out here, it ain't gonna be me, so chill, all right?"

AND THEN Raygene had hung up. Not even throwing a "good-bye" in at the end to cushion the blow.

If somebody gets whacked out here, it ain't gonna be me, he'd said.

Whacked!

Would that perhaps move the Cowboys to reevaluate their burgeoning interest in Raygene? Stanley wondered. His getting mixed up in something down in Las Vegas that involved somebody getting "whacked"? Regardless of who was the "whacker" and who was the "whackee," wouldn't such an incident be likely to have some kind of diminishing effect upon

Gene the Dream's prospects for a new deal, from the Cowboys or anyone else? Or was Stanley simply making a bigger deal out of the word "whacked" than was really necessary?

When he did a silent inventory, even a very brief one, it always came out the same: Stanley Winston had everything to live for. He had a lovely wife, two beautiful kids, a thriving career in a field he still had passion for, and more money in the bank than many of his multimillionaire clients.

So why, he asked himself now, did he continue to have moments like this one, in which he wanted to run a hot bath, slit his wrists, and *whack himself*?

"OH GOD, NO," Reece said.

E.Y. almost hadn't heard her. But then he looked away from the magazine he'd been flipping through, checking himself, and saw that the lady's face was scrunched up with what appeared to be pain and terror, the fingers of both hands clawing deep into the fabric of the pillows on either side of her.

"Please, God, *please* . . . !"

"What's wrong? Shut the fuck up!" E.Y. said, only half-heartedly.

Reece ignored him, starting into the deep-breathing exercises she'd been practicing for weeks now: "*Whooooo-whooooo-whooooo . . .*"

"What the hell're you doin'?" E.Y. asked.

Reece finally looked over at him, still sucking air, tears shining in her eyes. "My water just broke," she said.

"What?" He glanced at the couch, saw something wet and dark staining the cushion beneath her. "What you mean, your—"

But Reece cut him off with a scream, high-pitched and hor-
rifying, that tailed off into: "*Ohhhhhaahhhhhgoddamnit, no!
Not now! Please not . . .*" She tried to stand, but only got
halfway up, struck by another apparent spasm. "Aw, fuck!"
She lost her balance and rolled forward, clearing a fruit bowl
and a miniature bronze of Michelangelo's *David* off the coffee
table in front of her on her way down to the floor, where she
lay on her back like a beached whale and grew momentarily
still.

E.Y. finally jumped to his feet, panic setting in rapidly now.
"Knock that shit off! You scream like that again, I'll tie and
gag your ass, all right? I mean it!"

But Reece was doing that heavy breathing thing again,
whooooo-whooooo-whooooo, eyes fixed straight at the ceiling above her, tears now streaming freely down both sides of
her face. Had Trip's man been standing on the street outside
the hotel, twenty-eight floors below, she could not have seemed
more oblivious to his presence.

"Look, if this is a trick—" E.Y. started to say, only to be
drowned out once again by a second bloodcurdling howl of
anguish that removed any remaining doubt in his mind: Reece
was having her baby. Right here, right now.

And there was nothing he could do to stop her, short of
killing her.

TRIP FOUND the Caesars Palace betting slip exactly where
Reece Germaine had said he would: curled up inside the open
roll of toilet paper in the bathroom. He wondered if he ever
would have thought to look for it there if she hadn't bitched
up and told him where she'd hidden it, and he had to admit

that he probably wasn't that smart. Hell if Raygene's lady friend wasn't a player after his own heart.

At first, the ticket didn't look right to him. It was too goddamn simple. It was a three-inch square of salmon-colored paper stock, bearing a Caesars Palace watermark on both sides, but there was next to nothing printed on it. Just the basic details of the bet—$25,000 on the Arizona Cardinals to win Super Bowl XXXVIII at 50–1—plus the date and time the bet was placed. That was about it. The ticket said absolutely nothing about the person who had bought it. Was that even possible?

Then Trip gave the matter a little thought and realized, yeah, this was probably what these things looked like all right, because who gave a shit about the identity of the wagerer until he or she was trying to cash the ticket in? Incoming money didn't need a name on it, but outgoing, well, that was the cheddar the casinos had to account for, from the first penny to the last.

Trip slipped the ticket into his wallet and started out of the room, anxious to rejoin his man E.Y. at Caesars Palace before his bodyguard could find yet another way to fuck him up again. But halfway to the door, Trip changed his mind and decided to call E.Y. instead. Why spend any more time at the scene of an impending double homicide than was absolutely necessary when he could just give his boy the order to kill Germaine and Irving Dvorak remotely?

He sat down on Reece's hotel bed, propped the pillows up behind him to get good and comfortable, reached in his back pocket for his cell phone . . . and it wasn't there. Shit, where had he left it? He tried to remember the last time he'd used it, came to the conclusion it had been sometime the day before.

So the phone was probably back in his room at the Bellagio, he'd just forgotten in all his excitement to jack Germaine to bring it along this morning.

Trip put a hand out for the landline phone on the bedside table beside him, thinking he'd call E.Y. on that, but then it struck him that that option wasn't available to him, either: He didn't know E.Y.'s cell number by heart, he always used auto-dial to call homeboy. He could try calling Dvorak's room at Caesars instead, hope that E.Y. would pick up . . . but he knew the nigga wouldn't, because that would be stupid, and it would be just like E.Y.'s dumb ass to choose this moment *not* to be stupid for once.

"Shit," Trip said. He had to go back to Caesars.

But maybe not right away.

Because he had the ticket now, right? And Reece's bed felt so damn good . . . He hadn't slept a wink last night, why shouldn't he be able to kick it here for a few minutes, just to catch his breath? E.Y. was a bust as a bodyguard, it was true, he'd made that perfectly clear to Trip this weekend. But how could even his sorry ass, armed with a knife, fail to watch an unarmed pregnant woman and a hog-tied old fag without letting either or both get away from him?

Hell, Trip decided, he couldn't. No way.

He took the betting slip out of his wallet, began to examine it again with a dreamy, lustful eye. One-point-two-five million dollars, he thought. What a fucking stroke of luck, the Raiders' Kenny Edwards breaking his wrist like that.

Ten seconds later, Trip had dozed off.

20

"NOTHING?" AENEAS ASKED.

"Nothing," Brew answered. "Either she ain't here, or she's upstairs somewhere."

Aeneas nodded, grimly accepting the unacceptable. He and Raygene's bodyguard had just hooked back up after scouring Caesars Palace individually for almost thirty minutes, and still, neither of them had come across Reece or Trip's man E.Y. Which proved absolutely nothing, except that Reece was going to be impossible to find, if Aeneas and Brew even cared to keep trying to look for her. Going door to door to check every room in the 2,400-plus-unit hotel, or moving their search to all of Las Vegas beyond, either way, their chances of tracking Reece down now, in anything close to a timely manner, were going to be virtually nil.

"What do you wanna do?" Brew asked.

Aeneas said he didn't know, and that was the truth. He wasn't a man who had much use for second-guessing, but now he had to at least entertain the thought that he may have made a serious mistake, not letting Raygene follow Trip up to Reece's room at the Hard Rock. Because if she *had* been there instead of here when the white boy arrived, and Trip had gone up there with the specific intention of killing her . . .

"Dog, that's your phone," Brew said, snapping Aeneas out of his reverie.

Certain it was just Raygene again, looking for another update, the P.I. hit the instrument's call button and threw out a brusque, "Yeah?"

But it wasn't Raygene. In fact, it wasn't anybody Aeneas had ever spoken to before.

"Aeneas Charles?"

"That's right. Who—"

The man told him, using the twenty-five-words-or-less method for the sake of complete discretion. "A friend down in Florida says you've got some information for me."

Shit, Aeneas thought, *not now.*

He stepped away with the phone to put some distance between himself and Brew, and lowered his voice to complete the call in semiprivacy. Raygene's bodyguard wasn't sure, and he barely cared enough to be curious, but it seemed to him that Aeneas was negotiating with the caller for an extension in time of some sort, which he ultimately received.

"Who was that?" Brew asked when the P.I. rejoined him.

"If we're lucky, the answer to all our problems. Or at least, to one of the larger ones."

Brew was about to ask him to elaborate, until he saw that the man's mind had already drifted off again.

Aeneas scanned the gaming floor at Caesars as he thought things through once more, testing and retesting his logic for flaws. *Reece gets a call at the Stratosphere that, as near as he can make out, has come from a potential buyer for her betting slip. She leaves for parts unknown, and less than an hour later, Raygene and Brew spy Trip exiting Caesars alone, on foot, walking, Brew says, like a man who'd just jettisoned his last care in the world. He goes straight to the Hard Rock and—barring some incredible coincidence—straight up to Reece's room. Which can only mean he's suddenly learned that she's staying there. How? Almost certainly because Reece has given him that information, or his boy E.Y., something she would not have done willingly in either case.*

So the phone call that had drawn Reece away from the Stratosphere had to have been the bait in a trap of some kind. The question was, where had that trap been sprung? Out at the Hard Rock, or here at Caesars?

If it had been at the Hard Rock, then E.Y. would have been the one who did the springing. He held her up in her room, called Trip to let him know where they were, then waited for the white boy to join them from Caesars. All very possible, except . . . E.Y. was a total fuckup, and Trip knew it. His boy had been letting him down since they'd stepped off the plane at the airport on Friday. There was no way in hell Trip would *run* over to the Hard Rock from Caesars, let alone walk, with E.Y. standing guard over Reece alone. Trip would take a taxi from Caesars, and tell the driver to step on it.

"They hemmed her up here," Aeneas said, finally breaking the silence he himself had initiated.

"What?"

"Trip and E.Y. They got Reece over here with a phone call, ostensibly from a buyer for her betting slip, then they grabbed her. Only, they had help."

"I'm not followin' you."

"She seemed to know who the caller was. And she wasn't surprised that he had her number. So it wasn't Trip or E.Y. on the phone. They had somebody else make the call for them."

"Who?"

"I don't know. But I think I know who to ask."

"**COME ON,** Trip, goddamnit, answer the phone!" E.Y. said. But he was still talking into a telephone that had no one on the other end of the line to hear him.

"Shit!" The big man tossed the phone aside, showing no regard for where it landed. Fucking Trip. He'd left E.Y. here with a pregnant hostage without saying shit about what he should do if the baby came! Like E.Y. was supposed to *know* what to do without being told, because this kind of thing happened to him every goddamn day.

And the Germaine woman's baby *was* coming, hell yes. E.Y. had told her three times now that he'd take the knife he still had in his hand and slit her fucking throat if she didn't stop trying to bullshit him and shut up, and still she lay curled up in a fetal position on the floor, moaning and cursing, and every now and then, crying out like he'd *already* cut her. She didn't seem to care *what* E.Y. said or did, so great was her discomfort and rage.

But he couldn't let her go on like this. That much E.Y. *did* know. Another scream like the last one, and somebody somewhere was going to call the front desk, and the next thing E.Y. knew, he'd have security crawling all over his ass.

"Aarrrrgghhhhhhhshit!"

There girlfriend went again, fists balled tight with the pain, eyes scrunched closed, trying with little success to hold the cry down deep in her throat to avoid pissing him off.

"You've got to get me a doctor. Please!" she said, fighting for every breath, when the contraction seemed to let up.

"Fuck that! You . . . you're on your *own*."

"No! I can't . . . I can't do this al—" But she couldn't finish the sentence, had to break once more into that crazy breathing exercise she kept doing, *whooooo-whooooo-whooooo . . .*

E.Y. was as lost as a blind man in a blizzard. What the fuck was he supposed to do? Stand here and watch the woman drop a baby on the floor at his feet? Tie her up and gag her, which even he had enough brains to know would almost guarantee the baby's death, if not the baby's and hers both? Or should he just kill her now and get the fuck out, let Trip clean up this mess all by himself?

E.Y. glanced around for the phone, having decided to try calling Trip one more fucking time . . .

"Help me," Reece said.

He turned back toward her, distracted. "What?"

She was looking right at him now, all the previous spitfire in her eyes displaced by pitiful desperation. "I need you to help me. Please." She paused. "Just tell me if you can see the baby's head."

"*What?*"

Still on her back, she'd begun struggling out of the panties she was wearing under her skirt, kicking and pushing them off like a toddler who'd only learned how to undress herself the day before.

"I need to know how dilated I am! Just look and tell me if you can see its head, *please!*"

She brought her knees up and opened her legs, waiting. E.Y. opened his mouth to protest, but she'd already stopped listening to him, *whooooo-whooooo-whoooooing* more emphatically than ever now.

Goddamn Trip's fucking ass! he thought.

FROM THE beginning, it had been Aeneas's suspicion that the person who'd called Reece at the Stratosphere was somebody associated with a casino sports book. He'd seen enough of the lady to know she liked to think ahead, so it wasn't hard to envision her asking around, finding out who in Vegas might be interested in buying her wagering ticket prior to tomorrow's game, and for how much. And who else would she have asked but the sports books, starting with Caesars first, since this was where the ticket had originally been purchased.

But no one at any of the sports books Aeneas had either visited or called earlier had admitted speaking to her today, though a few had confessed to knowing her. Including the man at Caesars. Aeneas had spoken to Dick Montecito by phone, and all Montecito would say was that nobody of Reece's description even sounded familiar to him.

As he continued to assert now, at least initially.

"Sorry, pal. But even if I had seen your friend in here the last couple of days"—he waved his hand at the standing-room-only crowd choking the teeming sports book area under his purview—"as you can see, I'd have a hell'uva time remembering it. It's Super Bowl weekend, right?"

Which was his way of asking, *What are you, asshole, blind?*

"We wouldn't have bothered coming in here in person, to

ask you a question you've already answered over the phone, if we weren't concerned that the lady might be in some danger," Aeneas said. Unable to determine yet whether Montecito was bullshitting him or simply blowing him off.

"Danger? Naw, she isn't in any danger." The Caesars employee dismissed the very idea with a grin and a shrug.

"Excuse me?"

Montecito recognized his error immediately, but there was nothing he could do about it now but attempt to gloss over it. "I mean, why would she be in any danger? If she's somewhere here at Caesars, she couldn't have possibly picked a safer place to hang. This is one of the safest hotel/casinos in the world, my friends."

He grinned, waited to see if either Aeneas or Brew was buying it.

"Look, Mr. Montecito," the P.I. said dryly. "You're a busy man, and the privacy and security of your guests comes first with you. I get it. But it's like this. If you know where Ms. Germaine is, and something happens to her because you dicked us around, I'm going to hold you personally responsible. Which is my non-actionable way of saying I'm going to come back here and stick both my feet in your ass until I'm standing on your face."

"Me too," Brew said, humorless as a totem.

Montecito's conflict was almost palpable. Should he call security and risk the pair's wrath later, or tell them the truth and expose himself as the condescending, self-important company wag he was?

"All right, fellas, take it easy," he said eventually. "Your girl's upstairs with a treasured guest of the hotel. But I can assure you she's in no danger whatsoever." He turned on the high-beam smile again to reinforce the absolute of this truth. "I'd bet my left nut on *that*."

"**PLEASE,**" Reece begged E.Y. again. "All I'm asking you to do is *look*!"

She pulled her legs open wider still, trying to make the view of her body's most private regions as accessible to him as possible.

"No," E.Y. said, barely able to hear his anemic reply himself.

"You don't have to *do* anything! Just look and tell me what you see!"

E.Y. meant to say no again. He didn't *want* to look and see if her baby's head was visible down there. He was a professional bodyguard, not a goddamn doctor! And yet . . .

The idea held a certain, undeniable fascination for him. Seeing something he'd never seen before, not even on TV, and was never likely to ever see again. He'd always wondered what the big deal was, watching a baby come into the world, live and in person. Blood and slime and goo all over the fucking place. Some of the fathers of his acquaintance who'd done it talked about the experience like it was supernatural or something. He didn't believe that shit for a minute, but . . . If he was ever going to know how much of that was real and how much was bullshit, this was his chance to find out. Maybe even his only chance.

Before E.Y. knew it, he was standing at Reece's feet, the steak knife still in his right hand, inching his head down like the cage on a cherry picker to peer into the mysterious space between the prone woman's yawning legs.

"Can you see its head?" she asked, with what sounded like equal part dread and excitement.

Practically on his knees now, E.Y. gazed in toward his target, focused and then refocused his eyes to be sure he was seeing right.

"No," he said, clearly disappointed.

And then Reece lurched up on one elbow and brought the little Michelangelo's *David* she'd been so careful to keep within reach across the top of his skull, and E.Y.'s view of the room did a wild counterclockwise spin before crashing hard to black.

"Well, I can see *yours*," she said, pushing herself to her feet.

She was tempted to stand over the big man, just to record for posterity the sight of perhaps her greatest triumph over a fool. But she didn't dare take the time. She did, however, step quickly over to the couch, reach behind one of the cushions to remove the empty wineglass she'd hidden there after creating her phony amniotic fluid spill. She felt bad enough about damaging such a lovely couch, and she didn't want the crystal wineglass on her conscience too, should somebody break it before it could be discovered.

Had E.Y. only looked up from his magazine to see her take the glass off the coffee table between them, or simply noticed its absence when she went into her "pregnant lady in labor" act, he'd probably still be watching over her now, finally pushed into binding and gagging her up like a smarter man would have in the first place. But E.Y. wasn't a smarter man, as everybody in Vegas but Trip Stiles seemed to know, and that had been Reece's ultimate salvation.

Or at least, it had been so far. She still had to get out of the suite before the big man came around again, and she had to take Irving Dvorak with her.

She hurried into the bedroom, found the poor bastard trussed up on the bed, alive but unconscious. He was bleeding profusely from the knife wound in his right buttock, but beyond that, he seemed to be okay. She'd brought another knife from the dining table in with her to release him, and the first thing he wanted to do when she cut his gag off and brought him around was talk, but she hushed him up quickly, finished untying him, then told him in no uncertain terms to follow her out and move his ass. Only he didn't have the strength; she was going to have to help him.

E.Y. was already up on all fours, trying to shake the cobwebs off, when they crab-walked back into the suite's front room. The steak knife was filling his right hand again, but Reece's right hand was empty; her knife was back in the bedroom, where she'd set it down to help Dvorak to his feet.

"Shit!" she said.

DICK MONTECITO talked the entire twenty-eight floors up to Irving Dvorak's room, painting the elevator's walls and ceiling with assurances about his good friend Dvorak's impeccable reputation, and Reece's utter safety in his care. Aeneas and Brew just let him speak, not even feigning interest. Both men thinking ahead, imagining all the terrible things that could be awaiting them if their worst fears about Dvorak and Reece were correct, and they were arriving too late now to save either one of them.

The elevator finally stopped on twenty-eight, and the first thing the three men saw when they stepped out into the hall was Reece, twenty yards away, all but dragging a man only Montecito knew was Dvorak toward them, E.Y. in hot pursuit. Reece was screaming for help at the top of her lungs, and E.Y. was holding what looked like a large steak knife in his right hand, his face zebra-striped with blood.

"Jesus!" Montecito said.

Brew reached Reece and Dvorak first, but only just as E.Y. did. Blinking blood out of his eyes and still not fully conscious, Trip's man grabbed Reece from behind and spun her around, poised to plunge the knife into her as she cried out. But Brew pinned his raised arm to the wall with one hand, and jabbed the nose of E.Y.'s own nine into his left temple with the other. Making a statue out of the larger man instantly.

"Drop the knife, dog," Brew said.

Reece scrambled away to join Aeneas, taking Dvorak with her, and the two bodyguards were suddenly alone, caught in a fragment of time like insects in amber. And just like that, Brew realized where he was. Finally, inevitably, this was the moment of truth, the kill-or-be-killed situation he'd been anticipating for over a week now, knowing its conclusion would mark him as either a redeemable man of God, or a servant of the devil who was doomed forever.

"Drop the knife, dog," he said again, and for the last time.

But E.Y. just continued to maddog him, glaring deep into his eyes for some indication of what to do. Comply with the order, or ignore it? It only took Trip's man a split second to have his answer, and for Brew to recognize the meaning of the change it brought to the other man's blood-streaked face.

E.Y. jerked his knife hand free from Brew's grip and swung his body around to cut him, the gun at his head no longer deserving of a second thought. Brew moved to defend himself without it, already certain that he would die trying . . . then suddenly saw Aeneas appear out of nowhere to physically restrain E.Y. from behind.

"Hit him!" Aeneas barked, when he grew tired of waiting.

Brew put the gun in his left hand to free his right and did as he'd been told, throwing a punch at E.Y.'s face that required no follow-up. Trip's bodyguard went limp in Aeneas's arms, lost his grip on the knife, and the P.I. released him to race the weapon down to the floor. The smaller dead weight won.

"I couldn't shoot 'im," Brew said, peering down on the unconscious giant, trying to make sense of it.

"So I noticed. But don't sound so broken up about it." Aeneas eased the nine out of his hand. "The killer instinct's a little overrated, as qualities of the species go."

TRIP WAS out for more than forty minutes, and when he awoke and saw the time on the nightstand clock, he cursed himself like a bitch. He hadn't meant to fall asleep. It was one thing to trust E.Y. for five minutes on his own, and something else altogether to give him damn near an hour to play with. That shit was flirting with disaster.

He gave the hotel phone another quick glance as he leapt off the bed, and once more chose not to use it. It was too late to do things remotely now. He had to get his ass over to Caesars and direct the executions of Reece Germaine and Irving Dvorak personally.

After that, he and E.Y. could have a nice, leisurely dinner somewhere and talk about where they should go to watch the game tomorrow.

. . .

MEANWHILE, down in the Hard Rock's carport, a tiny little man in the back of a rented limo fumed behind the car's black glass, impatience churning up his insides like rodent's teeth. He was waiting for a phone call, and that wasn't his style. He was no bigger than the average six-year-old, bought most of his clothes right off the rack in the children's section at Sears, but back home, people waited for *his* call, not the other way around. Sitting here doing nothing, on the receiving end of another man's instructions, was as counter to the way he normally did business as black was to white.

But he had information that this was the place to be, if he wanted to finally scratch the fucking itch that had been driving him nuts for more than a week now, so here he sat. Propped up in the backseat of the stretch limo on the booster seat he always traveled with, watching the suckers flow in and out of the Hard Rock from a vantage point over 1,500 miles distant from the comfort of his own bed.

He checked his watch, saw that he'd been here now for almost an hour.

"This is bullshit," the dwarf said to the other, normal-sized man sitting across from him, just as his cell phone finally rang.

AENEAS HAD wanted to call Raygene before Raygene could call him, but in all the excitement following Reece's rescue at Caesars, he didn't make it.

"You guys find Reecie yet?" Raygene asked.

"Yeah, she's right here. She's a little shaken up, and the

paramedics are giving her a thorough going-over, but she and the baby are fine."

In fact, Reece was just now returning to Aeneas's side, ready to hang on his every word. Along with Brew, they were down in the anteroom of Dick Montecito's office, trying to help the frazzled sports book manager make sense out of the bizarre kidnapping that had just occurred in his hotel. Reece had left the paramedics to attend to Irving Dvorak in the next room, and Montecito and hotel security were holding E.Y. for the Las Vegas P.D. elsewhere in the building.

"All right, good, good. Where was she?" Raygene asked.

"Exactly where we thought she was. In a room with E.Y. upstairs, waiting for Trip to come back. We'll fill you in on all the details later, but right now I need to know about Trip. He still upstairs?"

"Yeah. Unless there's some other— Yo, hold up! Here's the asshole now, comin' off the elevator. Punk-ass mother—"

"All right, Raygene, I want you to listen to me very carefully: Let him go," Aeneas said. "Don't follow him anymore, and don't approach him."

"Say what?"

"I mean it. Let him go. Everything's under control."

Raygene didn't know what that meant, "everything's under control," and he told Aeneas he didn't really give a shit. Trip had been asking for an old-school ass whupping for five days now, and Raygene was finally tired of depriving him of it. But Aeneas was adamant.

"Just trust me, Raygene, all right? *Let the man go,* and get over here to Caesars as fast as you can. Peace."

Aeneas hung up and put his phone away as Reece watched him, no less confused by what she'd just heard than Raygene.

"What the hell was that? 'Let him go'?"

"Relax. I know what I'm doing."

"Good for you. Now how about telling *me* what you're doing."

He smiled, amused for some unknown reason by the distressed look on her face. "What? You afraid Trip will get away with your betting slip?"

"Of course! What do you—"

But his laughter moved her to silence.

FIFTEEN SECONDS after Aeneas hung up on him, Raygene decided to renege on his promise to leave Trip alone. Stanley Winston's private investigator had been right about almost everything so far—he and Brew finding Reece safe and sound seemed evidence enough of that—so it was hard for Raygene to go against his wishes now. But he'd just been told that Trip had indeed been holding Reece against her will, just as they had feared, with the intention of doing God only knew what to her and the baby—*Raygene's baby!*—later, and that was it. End of the road for the white boy. It was time for Raygene to settle up with his old Riviera Beach homie, once and for all, damn the consequences.

He watched Trip make his way across the Hard Rock's gaming floor from the elevator, seemingly on his way to the lobby, and started to follow.

But then a big man with a salt-and-pepper ponytail, stuffed into the widest blue suit Raygene had ever seen, came out of nowhere to cut Trip off, and Raygene held back, eased up behind the cover of a change booth to wait and see what was going down.

Trip didn't seem to know the man at first; he looked ready to shove the guy out of his way and keep going. But then the man put a gentle hand on Trip's left arm and whispered something into his ear, two or three words at most, and Trip's whole demeanor changed. Raygene couldn't see his face, but he could see the shift in Trip's posture clear as day; it had gone from O.G. hard to respectful compliance in a heartbeat. Not afraid, exactly, but committed to cooperating, which for Trip was akin to prostrating himself.

The big guy with the ponytail began to lead Trip off, in the direction of the lobby and the hotel entry doors beyond, and Trip went along with him like a dog on a leash. By the time they reached their ultimate destination—a menacing black stretch limo taking up two spaces out in the carport—Trip had regained most of his bad boy swagger, the initial shock of this sudden change in his plans having apparently worn off.

The big man opened the car's back door for Trip, deposited him inside, and closed the door behind him, then got behind the limo's wheel and drove it smoothly away, all as Raygene watched from a distance, slack-jawed.

What the hell had he just seen happen?

NOT UNEXPECTEDLY, Trip was stunned to find a dwarf among the two men waiting for him in the back of the limo, and was unable to keep the fact from being glaringly obvious to them both.

"That's right, Mr. Stiles. I'm a dwarf," the Memphis drug dealer named Pierce said. "Ironic, isn't it?"

Trip looked over at the bald, stone-faced giant seated across from them, seeking clues as to how best to answer the question.

"Ironic? Naw, naw. It's just—"

"It's all right to be surprised. Everyone is, at first. But then they get to know me a little, and they forget all about how 'small' I am."

Trip stopped smiling, having no trouble following the dealer's meaning. "Getting to know" Pierce, according to his reputation, was often the painful prelude to winding up dead.

"How'd you know where to find me?" Trip asked.

"You'd like a little conversation before we get down to business, I see." Pierce shrugged, a grotesque doll with adult features crowded together on a little boy's head. "Fine. A man named Aeneas Charles told me I could find you here. Do you know Mr. Charles?"

"I know 'im," Trip said, making a mental note to kill Aeneas later. "But how'd *he* know—"

"Enough. Let's talk about my money. Do you have it, yes or no? Four hundred and fifty thousand dollars, Mr. Stiles, I'm tired, and I want to go home."

"I've got it. With interest. Only . . ."

"Only *what*?"

"Only, it ain't in cash. Here."

He fished Reece's betting slip gingerly from his wallet, gesturing as he did so to make sure both Pierce and his friend understood he wasn't trying anything crazy.

Pierce took the ticket from Trip's hand, examined it with great indifference. "What the hell is this?"

"Right now, it's about eight, maybe nine hundred grand. But tomorrow, after the game, it's prob'ly gonna be worth more'n that. One-point-two-five million, to be exact."

Pierce glanced over at his associate, who produced a semiautomatic pistol from within his jacket and held it flat against his lap, acting with all the nonchalance of a passenger on a train preparing his ticket for the conductor.

"What the fuck are you talking about?" Pierce demanded, finally betraying some impatience.

"It's a Caesars Palace bettin' slip, dog, just like it says." Having lost some of the edge on his confidence, Trip pointed at the print on the ticket. "Twenty-five G's at fifty-to-one on the Cardinals to win the Super Bowl tomorrow. Twenty-five G's at fifty-to-one is . . ."

"One and a quarter million, yes, yes, of course. I know how to fucking multiply, asshole."

Pierce looked the betting slip over again, this time with greater attention to detail. He passed it over to his friend, asked, "What do you think?"

The bald man studied the ticket at length, registering its every aspect: size, color, texture. Even, it seemed to Trip at one point, its weight. Finally, he handed it back over to his employer.

"It's a fake," he said dryly.

"*What?*" Trip cried. "Bullshit!"

"The Caesars watermark should be raised on both sides. That one's flat. Feel it yourself. It's a fake," the big man said again.

Pierce tried it, rubbing his own stubby fingers across the ticket's smooth surfaces, then flipped it back at Trip's face, satisfied that his man spoke the truth.

"Hold up," Trip said, bitching up large now and not giving a damn, because this was as close as he'd ever come to actually dying and *fuck!*, now that he was here, incredibly, the shit scared the living hell out of him. "If this ain't the real ticket . . ."

"Shoot him if he says another word," Pierce told the man with the gun. "But don't *kill* him."

Trip shut up, requiring no further encouragement to do so. It was over; the most he could hope for now was that Pierce would whack him quick, in too great a hurry to get back home to Memphis to bother with an extended torture session. Trip looked out the car window, feeling his bladder threatening to empty itself without his consent, and saw that they were already well off the Strip, moving ever deeper into the vast Nevada desert south of the main highway. The last thing he wanted to do at this moment was give Reece Germaine her props. But there was no way of getting around it.

Raygene's pregnant bitch had played Trip Stiles yet again.

21

"SO HOW DID YOU KNOW?" Reece asked.

Aeneas grinned. "You're joking, right?"

"No, I'm not joking. How the hell did you *know*?"

They were all having dinner at the Bellagio's Le Cirque restaurant early Saturday night: Reece and Aeneas, Raygene and Brew. The Le Cirque was the finest eatery the Bellagio had to offer, so the price of libations alone made it less crowded than it was elsewhere tonight. Still, the house was packed, if not stifling, and their table was regularly surrounded by people moving to and fro, many of them fans of Raygene's who came by to gush over his greatness and beg for an autograph.

"You had a couple of receipts in your bag when you dropped it last night," Aeneas said. "One for some color copies you made here in Vegas yesterday, and another for a FedEx shipment you apparently sent out shortly thereafter. When exactly will you be getting the real ticket back, by the way?"

Reece gave him a look intended to sting. Now she was sorry

she'd insisted on knowing. "You saw everything else, smart-ass. How did you manage to miss that?"

Aeneas shrugged. "I only had a few seconds to work with, and I was doing my best to be discreet."

She gave him the look again, said, "I requested a Monday morning delivery. It's guaranteed to arrive at the Hard Rock before noon."

"You mailed it to *yourself*?" Raygene asked, finally getting it.

"Smart," Brew said, nodding his head.

"I'm sorry, Raygene," Reece said. "I was thinking about you at the time, not Trip. I had a feeling you might come after the ticket after our little argument back in L.A., and I didn't want it on me if you did."

Raygene shrugged, feeling no pain. "Don't sweat it, Reecie. I been treatin' you badly from day one, you did the right thing."

"For everybody except Trip, anyway," Aeneas said.

"You're sure he's gone for good?" Reece asked, still not completely convinced. "He's not still out here somewhere, waiting to kill us all?"

"I can't be entirely sure, of course. But I'd say the odds of him being permanently out of the picture are astronomically in our favor. From what I understand, his friend Pierce doesn't have much patience for people who try to punk him, and if Trip tried to give him that fake ticket . . ."

"Damn," Raygene said. "I still can't believe how you guys set the boy up. Both of you." He had spoken with obvious admiration, but with a small sense of loss, as well. Once upon a time, Trip Stiles *had* been his best 'boy, after all. "You callin' Pierce out here after his ass," he said to Aeneas, "and then *you*"—he turned to Reece—"hidin' that phony ticket up in-

268   RAY SHANNON

side a roll of toilet paper so he'd think it was real . . . That was wack, y'all. You people need to be workin' for the FBI or somethin'."

He was even more euphoric than they could have imagined. His friends thought Trip Stiles was dead, and the Las Vegas Police Department thought he had simply taken flight, but all of them believed the white boy being gone meant nothing more to Raygene than a secret past remaining secret. Raygene, however, knew the ramifications of Trip's disappearance ran far deeper than that. Because if Trip was really dead, E.Y. was the only one left alive who could implicate Raygene in the murder of Luis Ortiz in Dallas Tuesday night—a murder Raygene still had no idea had been faked for his benefit—and E.Y. wasn't likely to out Raygene anytime soon. Already facing a host of felony charges related to Reece's and Irving Dvorak's kidnapping, Trip's bodyguard would be loath to tell the authorities or anyone else about yet another crime to which he'd been connected, however peripherally.

Aeneas turned his attention back to Reece, openly assessing her appearance. "How are you doing? Still okay?"

"I'm fine. Worn down to a nub, but fine."

"And the baby?"

"Kicking and stomping with all the usual disregard for its mother. So everything's fine there too. Stop fussing over me, please."

But she was only telling him half the truth, and he knew it. It had been a long and stressful day, and her grand performance of a woman delivering her baby under extreme duress up in Irving Dvorak's room had been closer to reality than she had let on with anyone, even the paramedics who had looked her over afterward and encouraged her, unsuccessfully, to spend the night in a hospital for observation. At one point, the Braxton Hicks contractions had been coming in full force, thirty seconds long and only five minutes apart. Had she waited any longer to fake labor, she felt certain now that her act eventually would have been supplanted by the real thing, with no one but Trip's man E.Y. around to bear witness, let alone call for help if she needed it.

Even four hours later, it was a terrifying thought.

"If you won't see the ticket again until Monday," Aeneas said, "your options for a pre-game sale would seem to be out the window. To receive any return on it at all, looks like you're stuck counting on the Cards to come through for you now."

"Not necessarily. I've still got one good pre-game offer on the table, even without the ticket."

"Yeah? From who?"

"Dick Montecito at Caesars, who else? He's offered me seven-fifty not to cash the ticket in should the Cardinals win tomorrow, and I've got right up until game time to take him up on it."

"Smart man," Raygene said. "Better to lose seven hundred and fifty grand than a million and a quarter. 'Cause I still say, the Raiders ain't got a prayer of winnin' that game tomorrow with Cal Schroeder at quarterback, that ol' dog should'a retired four years ago."

"You're probably right. But Montecito feels genuinely terrible about what happened to Reece at the Palace, so it could be he's not just being smart," Aeneas said. "Maybe he's simply being a nice guy who's trying to make amends."

Reece cut him a skewed glance. "You don't really believe that?"

Aeneas laughed. "Hell no."

"I've got a question," Brew said. "If you keep the ticket and the Cardinals do win tomorrow, how're you gonna explain where you got the money from? The twenty-five G's Ray gave you to place the bet in the first place, I mean?"

"We've got that all figured out," Reece said. "We're just going to say it was a gift. Raygene gave me the money, all right, but with no strings attached. The decision to use it to bankroll a Super Bowl bet was mine, and mine alone."

"Ain't nobody around to say any different," Raygene added. "Why not?"

Just then, three more of the baller's admirers, all female and attractive, sidled up to the table to introduce themselves. Raygene welcomed them warmly and, with the charm and generosity he'd been demonstrating to others all night, signed personalized autographs for each.

When they were alone again, Aeneas asked Reece if she thought it would help stem the flow of groupies if she got up and sat down next to Raygene, a "pregnant girlfriend" warning sign for all other would-be interlopers to see.

"It wouldn't make a damn bit of difference," Reece answered, shaking her head. She turned to Brew. "Would it?"

"Nope," Brew said. "Sure wouldn't. This man draws women like a horse draws flies."

And everybody had to laugh.

LATE THAT night, after everyone had gone their separate ways, and Aeneas had seen Reece safely to a new room at the Hard Rock that Trip Stiles, if he were still alive, couldn't open with his stolen cardkey, one of Raygene's more gorgeous fans showed up at the P.I.'s door. She was a blue-eyed, raven-haired knockout in a black silk dress, as aerodynamic as a bullet and twice as hard, and he recognized her immediately as one of the visitors to their table at Le Cirque earlier in the evening.

"Oh," she said, looking surprised to see Aeneas standing there. "I thought—"

"You were looking for Raygene's room. Right. He's one door down, in sixteen-twenty-four. I don't think he's in yet, though."

"This isn't sixteen-twenty-four?" She looked at the number on his door, saw that it was 1622. "Oh, Jesus, I'm sorry." She brought a hand to her mouth, embarrassed. "I hope I didn't wake you?"

"It's only ten o'clock. I've got a ways to go before bedtime."

"Maybe you remember me? I came by your table at Le Cirque tonight to say hello?"

"I remember. Your name's Lenore."

"That's right. You *do* remember." The recognition made her giggle. "And you are . . . ?"

"Aeneas Charles. It's a pleasure." He shook her hand, and a silence neither of them seemed to know what to do with suddenly imposed itself upon them.

"Well," she said finally, "sorry again for disturbing you. Have a nice night."

He told her he'd try to do that, and she shimmied off down the hall. Five minutes later, though, she was back.

"You were right. He isn't in," she said when Aeneas answered her knock the second time. "But he gave me his number to call in case we got crossed up. I don't suppose . . . ?"

"You want to use my phone to call him? Sure, come on in."

He let her into the room and closed the door behind her, watching the fine muscles move under her dress as she walked.

He figured her for a dancer or a personal fitness trainer, maybe even both.

He pointed to the phone on the desk and told her to help herself.

Raygene's lady friend picked up the receiver and opened her little black handbag, turning away from him slightly to sift through its contents. "I've got that number in here some-where," she said.

Then she spun back around and showed him the gun, a blue metal nine-millimeter with a stubby snout. "Carmen Oliveras says to say hello, ass—"

But that was all of the intended epitaph she was able to get out before a giant figure leapt out of the dark bathroom on her right to disarm her.

"Who the hell's Carmen Oliveras?" Raygene asked Aeneas, tossing him the gun.

"An old friend from Newark. It's a long story," Aeneas said. He looked at the woman who called herself "Lenore" and gestured with her gun. "Do I have to actually point this at you, or do you think you can behave until security gets here?"

The dark beauty looked Raygene up and down, measuring her chances against both him and the gun, then smiled. "Looks like I may as well behave."

"Make the call, will you, Raygene?" Aeneas asked, coming around his would-be assassin to take the other man's place be-tween her and the door. Raygene eased the phone's receiver out of her hand and punched in the number for security.

"You knew I was coming," the lady said.

Aeneas shrugged. "We had a vague idea you might drop in on one of us. We just didn't know who until you knocked."

"But he was already in here when I came in. How—"

"Adjoining suites." Aeneas nodded toward the unmarked door on his left. "If you had come to his door first instead of mine . . ."

"You'd have been waiting in *his* bathroom. Sure." She smiled again, a good sport in the face of a crushing defeat. "Mind telling me *how* you knew I was coming? For my memoirs?"

"I think we should let Raygene answer that question. He was the one who figured it out, not me."

Raygene wrapped up his call to security and hung up the phone.

"She wants to know how we got on to her," Aeneas said.

Raygene beamed and held a small ball of white paper up in front of the lady's face. "You fucked up, Lenore. Recognize this?"

"No. Sorry. And please—call me Lenny."

Raygene unfurled the paper knot and carefully flattened it out in his palm, revealing a Le Cirque bar napkin bearing a brief message and his signature in blue ink. "I sign autographs like this for pretty women like you a hundred times a day, 'Lenny,'" he said. "But tonight was the first time I *ever* saw a girl toss hers in the trash just two minutes after I gave it to her."

LESS THAN three hours later, while working her customary late shift at the Hard Rock, Carmen Oliveras was taken in for questioning by the Las Vegas P.D. without incident. Her old flame Lenore "Lenny" Echols hadn't uttered a word to this point to corroborate Aeneas's and Raygene's claim that Oliveras had been behind her attempt on Aeneas's life, but the detectives investigating the case had to admit that nothing else made sense, Echols having no motive to kill Aeneas otherwise.

Aeneas went along for the ride when they picked his old friend up, curious. He knew that a cop's "betrayal" by his or her partner left deeper scars behind than most, but he was still having a difficult time believing Oliveras could hold such an immense grudge against him after all these years. Aside from telling the truth at her Review Board hearing, he had never mistreated her in any way. He didn't care what her sexual preference was, and always wondered why she bristled so at anyone who questioned it; none of that had any bearing on what kind of cop she was. But in retrospect, perhaps that had been his great mistake: leading her to expect his unqualified loyalty by leaving all the woman-bashing and lesbo jokes to the Neanderthals who were their fellow officers. She had counted on Aeneas alone to have her back when no one else would, and he had failed her.

And yes, even five years later, she still remembered the slight. When they slapped the cuffs on her and she saw him standing there, her undying hatred for him was impossible to miss.

"I'm sorry, Carmen," he said as they led her away.

Expecting no response from her, and receiving none.

MUCH TO Dick Montecito's chagrin, Reece ultimately decided to decline his $750,000 offer and hold onto her Super Bowl betting slip. Raygene thought she was crazy, and Aeneas openly wondered if she wasn't trying to ride a good luck streak further than common sense should have allowed, but her mind was made up by noon on Sunday, and she wasn't going to change it. Only Brew fully agreed with her decision; even with the game well under way, he would look up from the copy of the New Testament he'd been stealing glances at all day to nod encouragement at her, and say things like, "Don't worry 'bout it, Ms. Germaine, it's gonna be okay."

But Reece *was* worried, because the entire world had either lied to her about Cal Schroeder, or the Oakland quarterback had saved the game of his life for this occasion. The man was simply phenomenal. He moved like a pack mule in the pocket, and walked to and from the sidelines as if he were wading through mud, but his passes were crisp and accurate, and the Raiders around him seemed to be playing far over their heads in response to his spectacular show of leadership. All day long, the old veteran had the Arizona Cardinals off balance and reeling, no doubt scratching their heads along with everyone else over the Lazarus-like miracle of his performance.

Midway through the fourth quarter, Oakland was up by the incredible score of 30 to 21, and the crowd watching the game at Caesars sports book, where Reece and her entire party were guests of the house, was buzzing with both excitement and dread, resigned to the inevitability of a stunning Raiders upset. Even Montecito could smell Cardinal blood in the water; the hangdog look he'd worn on his face at kickoff time was gone now, and he was even coming by every few minutes or so to ask if Reece or her friends needed anything, anything at all, his dedication to customer service suddenly revived by the prospect of his beloved casino dodging a $1.25 million bullet.

And then, without warning, less than seven minutes shy of

the greatest gridiron victory he would ever live to orchestrate, reality hit Cal Shroeder with a thud. An interception on one Oakland possession, followed by a fumble on the next, and Shroeder had put Arizona right back in the game, trailing the Raiders only 30 to 28 with under a minute to play, and with possession of the ball.

With all of Las Vegas and the American football-watching world holding its collective breath, the final Arizona drive stalled at the Oakland 45 with only nine seconds left on the clock. A second-year kicker out of Oregon State named Jarrett Anderson stepped onto the field for the Cardinals to attempt a forty-five-yard field goal that, if good, would win the NFL championship for them, and a million and a quarter dollars for Reece Germaine. In hushed tones more befitting a golf telecast, the ABC colorman anxiously pointed out that Anderson had already missed a thirty-six-yarder earlier in the day, and that forty-seven yards was his career best, college and pro.

Oakland called its last two time-outs in an effort to shake the little kicker's concentration, then had no recourse but to let him do his thing and hope for the best.

The clock was restarted, the ball was snapped, and the hold was picture-perfect. Jarrett Anderson put his right foot into the kick and Reece said, "Oh, God, no . . ."

And this time, she wasn't acting.

BUT IT was false labor.

The child Reece Germaine eventually delivered at University Medical Center in Las Vegas was actually born two days later, a healthy and exuberant eight-pound six-ounce boy. He had Reece's eyes and her burnt-sienna skin coloring, but everything else about him belonged to Raygene, who cried real tears the moment he saw him. Afterward, from the moment they cut the baby's umbilical cord, Reece was so exhausted, she wasn't sure she could ever allow them to discharge her from the hospital. She'd been through hell and back over the last seven days, and amazingly, six hours in heavy labor had been the least of it.

Still, it was hard to complain. Aeneas was acting like he might like to remain in her life as well as the baby's for a while, and Raygene was showing signs of maturity he'd never demonstrated before. So it seemed she might have more moral support, and romance, as a single mother than she had ever dared anticipate.

And the baby? Well, her heart did a total meltdown every time she touched him, and the staff in the hospital nursery practically came to blows over the right to attend to his every need. Which was something Raygene's son was probably going to have to get used to, Reece knew, because heirs to great fortunes were almost always catered to more than others, and this young man was *loaded*. His father was due to sign a new four-year, $12.8 million contract with the Dallas Cowboys, and as a result of the recently concluded Super Bowl XXXVIII, his mother was a very wealthy woman in her own right.

Reece named him Jarrett, of course.

Raygene didn't like it, but that was tough.

	DATE DUE		

Bms